THE WAR NERD

ILIAD

ISBN: 9781627310505

10 9 8 7 6 5 4 3 2 1

Published by
Feral House
1240 W Sims Way #124
Port Townsend WA 98368

Design by Jacob Covey
Cover Art by C.M. Kosemen

THE WAR NERD

ILIAD

MODERN PROSE TRANSLATION
OF HOMER'S ILIAD BY

JOHN DOLAN

FERAL HOUSE . PORT TOWNSEND, WA

Three people helped make this:

———————

Jan Frel, who came up with the idea;
Katherine Dolan, who read it first;
and my mother, who taught me to read
and know proper behavior with
a child's version of *The Iliad*.

TABLE OF CONTENTS

TABLE OF CONTENTS

INTRODUCTION

I DIDN'T WRITE THIS STORY. I'm just delivering it. Every now and then it has to be repackaged and delivered. It comes from way back, from the gods. You'll meet them in here. They're not the gods you might be expecting, though. These are more like The Sopranos.

You may have heard of this story as something called *The Iliad*, found only on undergraduate syllabi. But this story was never meant as a textbook. This is a campfire story, the greatest of all tall tales. It moves easily from tone to tone—from raw slapstick comedy, to ultraviolence that makes *Clockwork Orange* seem like a panto for Eton lads, to hard-earned pathos that will moisten your mucous membranes whether you like it or not.

I've called it *Rage* because that was its name back when people listened to it around the hearth. My job as delivery guy is to give you this wonderful story as close to its raw, funny, weepy, haunted original as I can.

To do that, I've ditched the poetic meter. I'm delivering it to you in prose, because prose is what our culture reads. (Trust me, I started out as a poet and learned this the hard way.) What was the last book-length poem you read? Such things might get published occasionally, but they don't get read.

In our language, poetic effects work best in paragraphs. Besides, this was always more a story than a poem. Virgil, gods curse him, wrote poetry; Homer wrote a story.

I think it works. Read on and decide for yourself.

THE WAR NERD

ILIAD

1

TWO KINGS, ONE ARMY

THE CAPTIVE GIRL IS WAITING TO HEAR if she's going back home. She watches her old father, the priest, limp down the beach toward her master's tent.

Her father's carrying a bag and a wreath. The wreath is a flag of truce from his god. She's trying not to think about it. She needs to forget her old life. Back then she was from a good family; she'd never even been out of the family compound without a slave to guard her. Until the day the Greeks ran up from the sea.

Her town was on the coast, allied with Troy. But the Trojans weren't around on the day the Greeks swarmed off their long ships. There was nobody around who could call himself a warrior. Fishermen and traders, mostly. The Greeks splashed ashore at a run, not saying a word. They killed all the men without a sound. And even the little boys, to prevent future vengeance. Easier that way. They caught her favorite brother, still learning to talk. She remembers him, spitted on a spear, wriggling in the air. When the first Greek ship hit the beach, she had three brothers; an hour later, no brothers at all.

She lost a husband too that day, but you can always get another husband. Where will you get more brothers? They didn't kill her father. He's a priest, and not just any little god's priest. He belongs to Apollo. The Greeks fear Apollo. He loves her country, the east coast of the Aegean. But you can never count on a god. Apollo, her father's lord and master, did not exert himself to stop the Greeks that day. He must have been watching, but he did not lift one godly finger. Apollo prefers not to get involved.

He's watching now, as his priest limps toward the Greek camp at Troy. Apollo is an old god, though a young man. He's from the East, and he doesn't like Greeks. Loud, pushy, new people. Worse yet, they're favorites of his little sister Athena, a new god.

Apollo prefers the old ways; he goes way back, to the dawn, the glow in the east. He speaks without words, with music in a good mood, with the glare of sunlight, and in his rougher moods, with his bow. He loves to teach lessons with the bow. He's planning a great lesson for these Greeks.

Apollo sees how the priest's visit will end: Agamemnon, the Greek commander, will shame him, make the old man cry. Which will give Apollo all the pretext he needs to punish these Greeks. Apollo feels a vague pity for his pawns, the girl and her father. They're loyal enough, good eastern folk. But people are to be used.

Once Agamemnon has talked loudly to them, as Greeks always do—no respect, no manners—Apollo will have a free hand. No god can kill without a nod from the Olympians, the whole squabbling family.

He'll have it now. He remembers the day the Greeks stormed ashore and insulted his priest. He was there, in low orbit, zeroing in, as the Greeks enjoyed themselves; they didn't lose a single man, burned everything they didn't kill, and took everything they didn't burn.

Apollo was floating in the sunlight, hoping they'd kill his priest, the girl's father, and free his bow-hand for revenge. But the Greeks knew better than to kill Apollo's priest. They settled for killing his sons, then kicking the old man around, telling him all the things they'd do to his wife and his daughters. Then they left him crying in the dust.

Apollo remembers that day very well. It is like a happy song in his heart, because now it will all be avenged. All these things work out, in the long run ... for the gods. He remembers leaning into the wind that day, keening with the simple blood joy of a falcon, watching the Greeks run through the alleys of the town. He knew it was all to his advantage.

The girl can't see that, of course. There are always casualties. Apollo turns his falcon eye to her for a moment, as she watches her father approach Agamemnon's tent. Her sorrow interests him, as a musician. What happened to her interests him, as a tactician. Otherwise—just another weeping woman.

She catches Apollo's thought—god thoughts are contagious, even when not meant to be—and remembers her father sprawled in the dust, with a bloody face, the Greek warriors laughing as they tied her and the other decent-looking girls and women in a coffle and set them down on display on the shore. The Greek chiefs strolled along, checking a set of teeth here, feeling a buttock there, before they took their pick. She went first, to the commander, Agamemnon. Even now, the name makes her gag. But then she blanks it all out again.

When Agamemnon wants her, he grabs her arm and throws her down. He seems to hate her, but then he hates everyone, even his own people.

She feels shame for her father. He's a fool to come here. He has no idea what the Greeks are like. Why is he coming? They should have killed the whole family, but Greeks are too cruel for that.

He'll beg Agamemnon to let him take her home. But Agamemnon will never let her go. Her father is a kindly old man, and Agamemnon will enjoy making him beg, hearing him weep. Agamemnon has always been cruel, but he's worse now, with the war going nowhere.

Nine years they've been camped on this miserable beach, and the walls of Troy are intact. The Trojans still jeer from the walls, throwing anything they have at the Greeks, anything from pig shit to spears. The Greeks are always running short—water, firewood, wheat. The tents are full of sand and fleas; half the best men are dead; and there's nothing to show for it, not one Trojan earring, not one Trojan woman to sell.

And it's all Agamemnon's fault. It's his war, him and his family. Everyone knows they're cursed. He knows it too, and takes it out on everyone.

A slave man runs into the tent to tell Agamemnon a stranger is coming.

She hears Agamemnon buckling up inside the tent. She knows all those sounds of dressing and undressing, and goes to hide behind the tent so she won't see her father. So he won't see her. She can hear the old man's ragged breathing. He's been limping across the dunes, and his knees are bad. She hears him take a breath, begin speaking in that pompous voice he uses for formal orations. It makes her eyes moist to remember it, and her breath catches as she hears him chant:

"O noble Greeks! Noble Achaeans! And most noble son of Atreus, Agamemnon, king of kings!"

No answer. She can imagine the sneer on Agamemnon's face.

The old man goes on: "I wish you success in your enterprise! May you sack Troy! May its riches become your property, its people your slaves, its cattle your sacrifices!"

Silence again. She knows her father, poor old man—how he loves these courtesies! But he's come to the wrong place, he's flattering the wrong man. Agamemnon will be enjoying himself now, sneering, waiting for more.

Her poor old father goes on: "I will offer prayers to Apollo that you take Priam's city, but I beg you, take this offering ..."

She hears metal clink; it must be the gold the family buried in the corner. She winces; that little handful will only infuriate Agamemnon. The old man goes on, oblivious:

"And return my daughter to me in return for this ransom! I ask this in the name of the god I serve, Apollo, son of Zeus, lord of all!"

She hears some approving grunts from the soldiers. The Greeks are afraid of Apollo; they don't like the idea of offending his holy man. Bad luck.

But Agamemnon laughs: "Waddle back home, old bed-wetter! And take your wreath with you!" She gasps. It's one thing to insult her father, but to insult his master, Apollo, is asking for death. There's muttering; the Greeks don't like the way Agamemnon's acting.

Someone in the crowd yells, "Take the gold!"

Another voice: "What's the point? Why make the god angry?" Someone else yells, "Let her go home!"

Another, a squeaky voice, the comedian of the crowd: "You've already had her a hundred times, Agamemnon; that tent's not as thick as you think!"

They all have a laugh. This is Greek tact, a way of letting the boss know what he should do while showing him proper respect.

It would probably work on anyone but Agamemnon. He can't stop himself, won't stop until he makes the old man cry.

Agamemnon makes a spitting noise and sneers, "Look at the worthless trinkets you bring me!" Metal clinks again. "Worthless trash—just like you, old man!"

Now she hears her father's breathy, choked weeping. She tries to bury her face in the goat-hair of the tent. He should never have come. They should both have died that day. If only the Greeks would kill them both, together, father and daughter.

But Agamemnon is not kind enough for that. He wants to draw this out. He imitates the old man's weeping noises. No one laughs; they don't like this. It's bad luck. But Agamemnon doesn't care. He's breathing heavily, like he does when he's excited.

"You want to know what will happen to your daughter, old fool? I'll tell you: She'll live and die as my slave, my property. She'll scrub floors all day, and when it's night, I'll take her to my couch and bend her over, bend her any way I please! While she's young, that is. After I've used her for a few years, she'll be too old and ugly to be worth having, and then she'll carry out the shit-jars every morning and sleep with the pigs, and when she's old she'll die one day and be dragged off to where we bury the livestock."

The old man is weeping more loudly now. Worse than she imagined, and she knew it would be bad.

Agamemnon, though, is happy. Relieved, relaxed. Almost the way he is after he finishes with her.

Agamemnon sneers at the old man, "You want to cry? You want something to cry about, drooler? Dog-face? If you don't get out of my sight right now, I'll show you what it is to cry! So GO!"

She hears a shuffle, an old man's stumbling walk, fading away.

Agamemnon shouts after him, "That's right, waddle off!"

The soldiers sigh, get up to leave. No use arguing with Agamemnon when he's like this.

The feeble old priest stumbles off, over the dunes. He has been shamed, but he has a weapon of his own. He can call on his master, Apollo. He has credit with the god; he's spent whole decades burning meat and fat on Apollo's altar, sending up the nice steak smell the gods like, just so he'll have a weapon to deploy in a moment like this.

He limps down into a hollow in the dunes and falls to his knees. He breathes more slowly and deeply; the sniffling stops. He calls to the sky, in a younger voice: "Apollo! You heard all that as well as I, Lord; you saw what the Greek king did to your priest. I am nothing, but for the sake of all the fat meat I've sent smoking up to you, for the sake of your own pride, punish them! Kill them, Lord Apollo of the bright bow! Make them beg me to take my daughter back!"

This is music to Apollo, floating, riding the breeze from the sea. Besides, he likes the old man. Many a fine strip of fat has this priest laid over marrow-thick femurs, for Apollo to sniff. And the human is humble, unlike those pushy Greeks. And what he asks is what Apollo has been itching to do anyway. That always helps.

Apollo hates the Greeks. He's been flexing his bow, waiting to be provoked ... and now Agamemnon has given him the perfect excuse to send some poisoned arrows at the Greek campfires on the shore.

Apollo laughs, glittering like sun on the waves: Thank you, Agamemnon, you are my favorite Greek!

Apollo is as good at drawing out the pain as Agamemnon himself, so he doesn't kill the Greeks immediately. That sort of quick, easy death is something only an amateur would do. Apollo wants to have some fun with Agamemnon, just the way Agamemnon likes to have his fun with the slave girl. And he wants to make it last.

So he starts killing everyone in the Greek camp—but just to increase the terror and draw out the agony, he starts low: the animals.

First the mules, tied up near the beached boats.

Apollo sends his virus arrows fizzing and sizzling down through the mules' thick hides, easily as a needle through flax. The mules' eyes cross, their muzzles foam, they kick and squeal and topple over. By the time the slaves wake at dawn, the Greeks' mules are lying as stiff as fallen trees, their legs splayed out at every angle.

Then it's the dogs. If there's one thing these little kings love more than their mules, it's their dogs. Friends on the hunt, the one contribution they deign to make to feeding their people. Friends at the feast, toss 'em a hunk of bone and gristle before passing out drunk at the table. Friends in battle, providing a little comic relief by biting the corpses their masters have just made, lapping up the enemy's pooling blood. Oh, they love their dogs.

So Apollo sends his fizzing arrows festering with tiny malevolent life into the dogs. And the hounds howl and twitch and die there on the beach, ending lineages longer and purer than their masters'.

By this time, the smarter Greeks can see the trend. Mules, then dogs ... not hard to figure out who's next.

And sure enough, the men begin to die. Apollo starts from the bottom again, killing commoners first. He loves this game. He even deigns to coalesce, become visible, for a fraction of a second just above his chosen targets. A few look up and see him as the envenomed dart dissolves in their flesh. Their expressions are hilarious.

Soon, the unburied bodies are swelling up and bursting with a terrible smell all over the camp. The Greeks can only sit in their tents, feeling for sores or bumps, some sign they'll be next to be cremated.

Where's the loot? Where's the rape spree Agamemnon and his stupid cuckold brother Menelaos promised? They're going to die out here, or if they're lucky, go home poorer than they came.

For nine straight days Apollo practices his archery, picking victims at random like they all had bull's-eyes on the top of their heads.

He moves up the chain of command as the days pass, killing mid-level men, then nobles. What really amuses the god is the rich Greeks' notion that they can hide from his arrows in their tents. His divine arrows slip through the goat's-hair weave of the tents as smoothly as a shrimp through a fish net, without a sound. The Greek cowering under his sheep hide feels something like a flea bite, a pinprick ... and a day later, his corpse greets his slaves, covered in puke and shit and piss, cold as yesterday's roast.

For nine long days, the arrows fall from the sky. Greeks are dying so fast that all the slaves are busy collecting driftwood along the beach for the funeral pyres. Nobody knows who'll be next. And they can just about hear Apollo's chuckle.

Everybody knows whose fault it is: Agamemnon, showing off as usual. A bad king, everybody knows it. But nobody wants to say it out loud, because Agamemnon isn't just mean, he's also got a long memory and never forgets a grudge.

What they need is a certified expert to say what they all know. Enter the shaman, Kalkys. A scientist who can look at the intestines of a dying goat as they spool out into the dust then figure out what note the gods are writing in gut-cursive.

They drag Kalkys along to an emergency assembly. Kalkys is terrified. He knows Agamemnon's nasty reputation. And now that he's staring into Agamemnon's mean little eyes, and he can see Agamemnon thinking how easy it'll be to have this pedant's throat slit.

But they won't let him go before he says what everyone knows. If he talks, Agamemnon will kill him; if he doesn't, the other men will.

So Kalkys turns to the one man everyone fears, Akilles. He turns to Akilles and stutters: "Listen, before I say a word, I want you to swear, Akilles, right here in front of everybody—I want you to swear you'll protect me."

Akilles is half-god. Thetis, a sea goddess, is his mother. A real goddess: lives in the depths, never dies, parties with the Sky Gods on their mountaintop.

You can tell when someone has a god in the family tree. They're bigger, better-looking, cleaner somehow. And Akilles got all the genetic luck his goddess mom could provide. He's twice as big as anyone else, standing like a redwood in a row of brush. He kills where he pleases, with anything that comes to hand. Sword, spear, his bare hands.

Yet, he's never happy. His name means grief. Because the one thing he didn't get from his mother, kind of a major omission, was immortality. Everybody knows Akilles is doomed to die young. He knows it himself, mostly because EVERYBODY KEEPS REMINDING HIM OF IT. So there's something impatient, offended, and gloomy about Akilles. Killing is all he's good at, and what good does it do him? He could kill the whole army if he felt like it, but it wouldn't add a day to his life.

It's a sad story, and it follows Akilles around. As soon as he's safely out of sight, somebody's sure to whisper, "See his heel? That's where he's going to get it. His mother dipped him in the Styx when he was a baby but she held him by the heel and it never went under the water. Nothing can touch him ... except at the heel. That's where he's gonna get it."

They don't say it to Akilles' face, obviously. They just grovel and hunch when he passes by, then stare after him, quietly enjoying the sight of his heel, taking a coward's revenge for their fear of him.

It would sour anyone's temper. Akilles is not a bad man, under the circumstances. He doesn't kill people just for fun, as a rule. Lets most of the Trojans he takes on raids pay a ransom and go home, or at worst sells them into slavery. He's moody, touchy, very young ... but not mean at heart like Agamemnon.

So now Akilles stares at poor old Kalkys, sees the little dweeb's fear, and takes pity on him. Besides, Akilles hates Agamemnon—it's mutual—and he knows the shaman is about to blame Agamemnon. He doesn't want to miss that. So it pleases Akilles to offer Kalkys his protection. Noblesse oblige.

Akilles holds up a shovel-sized hand and says grimly: "I swear to you, Kalkys, in front of everyone, that I'll protect you, no matter who you tell us is causing this plague—even if it turns out to be Agamemnon himself, here."

Which it will, of course. Which everybody already knows. But they have to hear it officially.

Kalkys, reassured, takes a nervous gulp and blurts: "The real reason that Apollo's shooting us down is that Agamemnon insulted his priest! The old man came to ask for his daughter Chryseis back. He asked nice and politely, in the name of the god, which he's entitled to do as a priest! Brought the proper ransom, and a wreath!"

All the men grunt and nod. They knew it!

Kalkys feels their approval and goes on, more loudly and accusingly: "But Agamemnon purposely insulted him! Threatened him! Laughed at the poor old man! Wouldn't give his daughter back even though he asked politely!"

Everyone nods and tells each other, "I told you that was it! That damn Agamemnon! Gonna get us all killed!"

Kalkys concludes, "So we have to give her back! To her father, the priest! Or Apollo will kill all of us! And not ask any ransom for her or anything!"

More nodding and grunting from the crowd. They knew it'd come to this.

Kalkys pushes his luck now, brave like nerds are when the crowd's egging them on: "And we have to send a sacrifice with her! Treasure, and gold, and calves and sheep, ones with no spots or scars! Perfect specimens, the kind Apollo likes!"

More grunts and nods. Kalkys is drunk on public approval now, delighted with his own courage—and then he turns and sees Agamemnon and sits down very suddenly.

Agamemnon stands up, with the hate pouring from him like heat from a rock on a hearth. The crowd goes quiet. It's odd, how they fear Agamemnon. He isn't all that tough in battle. And he's nowhere near as big as Akilles, or as strong as Ajax, or clever like Odysseus. Doesn't even fight in the front rank most of the time. But he is hands down the meanest man in the army, maybe the world. He never forgives, never forgets the tiniest slight to himself or his precious relatives.

Him and his relatives! That's what this whole army is doing here, avenging Agamemnon's useless brother Menelaos, who married a woman way too beautiful for him—half goddess, in fact—and got dumped for a younger, hotter man. Who happened to be a Trojan prince.

That's why they've all been camping out here for nine slow, deadly years: Defending the nonexistent honor of Agamemnon's blank of a brother, the fool Menelaos, Menelaos the cuckold.

And now Kalkys has blurted out the one thing they're all thinking: It's Agamemnon's fault we're here! It's his fault we're dying under the magic virus arrows! And we didn't even get any booty out of it!

Agamemnon stands, sneering, letting the crowd vent a while, then drags out the silence so they can feel his hate. That's where Agamemnon really shines—the best hater in a world where hate is much respected.

When he's made them all flinch away from his stare, he turns to poor old Kalkys: "You, Mister Science! You just love giving bad news, don't you? You little coward, egghead. Did those entrails you claim to interpret ever once, even once, tell you anything good about me? Did those dead goat guts of yours ever tell, even one time, that I, your king, had made a good decision? No! No, because you only want to tell me what I've done wrong! Because you're a cowardly little whiner!!"

Kalkys groans and hides in the crowd.

Then Agamemnon turns on the rest of them. He may be a bad king and a bad man, but he's not afraid of anybody, especially the mob of killers squatting around him. He gives the circle of dirty, smoky faces a long hard look and says slow and quiet: "All right, then. Have it your way. We'll give the girl back. Take a ship, get a good crew, fill it full of goats and calves, and send it to the old man, along with his daughter, even though she's my rightful property."

They relax. Maybe Agamemnon will be reasonable for once.

Then he goes on: "But I'll tell you one thing: I'm not letting you cheat me. That girl's worth a lot! Beautiful! And smart too, good singer, embroiderer, as good quality as my own wife!"

He stops for a second, wishing he could kill every man in the circle with a word. But he can't. He has to bargain with these treacherous bastards, his troops. So he waits a second for the grumbles to bubble down, then goes on:

"So if you're going to take her away, then you're going to give me another one just as good."

The men are muttering, "Where're we going to get a girl like that? No plunder till we take Troy!"

Akilles, looking for a way to provoke Agamemnon, says in a syrupy, fake-reasonable tone,

"O noble, kingly Agamemnon ... noble and, let's face it, kind of greedy ... noble and greedy Agamemnon, please, can't you think of the cause for a moment? We're all in this together, O noble king! One for all? All for one? Don't worry, we'll give you all the Trojan girls you want, once we've taken the city! Be patient, dear greedy old pal, Agamemnon!"

It's not difficult to drive Agamemnon into a rage, and Akilles is better at it than anyone. He's playing Agamemnon like a rage-harp.

For a moment, Akilles is treated to the sight of Agamemnon's ruddy, flat face turning purple with rage. But Agamemnon suddenly smiles; he's thought of the perfect solution.

Agamemnon answers quietly, calmly, "All right, then ..."

Uh-oh! It's very bad news when Agamemnon talks calmly. He's thought of something mean to do. A mean king is worse than all the demons ever invented.

"All right, Akilles. I'll send back my slave girl. But you're not as smart as you think, big man. Because I've thought of proper compensation. And it doesn't have to wait for us to take Troy. No, I want my replacement girl right now ... from you, my boy. Yes, that's right! In return for giving Chryseis back, I'm taking your favorite girl, Bryseis."

Akilles is stunned. He's just a boy, really, didn't think of this. And he actually likes his captive girl. Everyone knows he's soft that way, sentimental about people.

Agamemnon goes on: "Yes, that's right, O mighty warrior, you're going to find out that I'm in charge here. I'm going to send my people to your tent and grab your prize girl by the arm and drag her to my bed, and there's not a thing you can do but watch me."

Agamemnon finishes, mockingly, "Come on now, Akilles, think of the common good! Isn't that what you told me, 'Think of the cause'?"

Akilles roars, "You dirty little thief!"

Akilles' voice, at full power, shakes the dust. The men cower, some holding their ears, as he goes on in a voice bigger than any mere human's: "What am I doing here, fighting for your useless brother Menelaos?"

Akilles' first rage subsides, but he goes on, still furious: "Why should I die for your Atreus clan, when everyone knows the whole bunch is accursed? And why am I killing Trojans? They never hurt me or mine, but I've been slaughtering them just so your cuckold brother can get his wife back!"

Agamemnon just sneers. The insults are nothing new. He knows what they think of him. What matters is that he has the power to take the girl—and most of all, he can see how much it's hurting Akilles.

Akilles chokes back a sob, clenches his huge fists, and groans, "Well then, I quit. You won't see me fighting for your worthless kin again! I'll stay in my quarters. You can go and fight the Trojans without me!"

The thought of losing Akilles horrifies the fighters. Just having him on your side makes the enemy start thinking about throwing down their shields and hiding in a gully.

But Agamemnon doesn't care about the war at the moment. He's possessed by hatred, and all that matters to him is seeing Akilles suffer.

So Agamemnon shrugs, "Go ahead, quit! Take your spear and go sulk. We have plenty of warriors. You need to realize something, Akilles my boy: the gods made you a perfect warrior, but those were just gifts handed out at birth. You didn't earn them. You need to learn a little humility. So I'm taking your girl. I'm in command here, and you're nothing."

This is too much. Akilles has killed so many men who were stronger, braver, quicker than Agamemnon. To kill him now would be as easy as swiping off a thistle's head with a stick.

They all know what's going to happen. No one can stop it. Akilles stands up and grabs the hilt of his sword. Every man in that room considers Agamemnon already dead.

And then everything stops. Akilles is alone, in a different light, hard, metallic. There's a figure standing in front of him, twice human size. A woman? Seemingly. She carries a spear. Somehow she has made everything stop, so that only she and Akilles are still alive and awake.

Akilles knows a goddess when he sees one. And this is one of the great goddesses, not a minor deity like his mother. This is Athena, Zeus' daughter, so strong she chewed her way out of Zeus' skull to be born. Smarter than any shaman, stronger than any warrior, and more powerful than any god except her father—and even Father Zeus prefers not to upset her.

She pushes Akilles' sword back in its scabbard and says, "Not now."

It's a voice like a chorus of a thousand voices, most of them women. You obey this voice; it's not even possible to imagine disobeying it.

Akilles drops his head, still fuming, "Did you hear what he said, Goddess?"

She repeats, "Not now, Akilles. Be patient. My mother and I love you, and we swear you'll be rewarded later, but you can't kill Agamemnon. We need him to lead the army."

Akilles feels like crying. He's very young, and he isn't going to live very long. All he has is this ability to kill anyone who crosses him, and now they're taking that away?

The goddess consoles him in that vast thousand-voice chorus: "You can curse him, little cousin, to your heart's content, but you must not kill him; he holds the Greeks together."

Akilles can't look at her anymore; it's like looking at the sun. Compared to this goddess, his goddess-mother is like a campfire at noon, a tiny flame lost in a vast light.

He sighs, chokes back a sob: "I have to obey you, Goddess, you and your mother, but ..."—he brightens up a little—"you said I can curse him all I want?"

Athena nods, a huge nod like the world tilting, and somehow the nod absorbs her. She vanishes up into the dark and glaring world of the gods, all black and gold.

Akilles is back in the crowded room, staring at Agamemnon, who still has that unbearable smirk. Akilles starts his curse with Agamemnon's face: "Hey, Atreus-son, did you know you have a face like a hound?" Akilles pulls his jowls down to look like a saggy old dog, and the chuckles increase. "And the heart of a frightened deer to go with it?" He mimes a deer's bounding gait with his fingers, and the chuckles become open laughter.

The barons have been waiting a long time for someone to say all this to Agamemnon. Akilles plays to the crowd, asking: "When did this worthless excuse for a king ever fight in the front rank in open battle? Hands up if you've ever seen him go out at night on a raid. I knew it! Never! You all know as well as I do he's a coward! He stays in his tent drinking wine, and then he pisses it out as vinegar through his filthy mouth!"

The giggles die away. This is too far. One or the other has to die now.

The barons are watching, wondering which side to take. That's the key to being what these people called a "king," a local chieftain with a long genealogy and a few dozen spears following you: knowing when to jump ship, change sides. Someone's going to die now, and they're trying to figure out which one it's going to be.

Then Nestor, the oldest baron in the whole assembly, stands up. Everyone knows what he's going to say. He's the voice of dull old reason. He's the human fire extinguisher. Boring, and that's his secret weapon. In a world where everyone is big, crazy, and armed, it helps to have a boring, feeble, longwinded old man around to keep the tribe from slaughtering itself.

Nestor starts with the "aid and comfort to the enemy" argument: "O, Akilles, and you, King Agamemnon, how happy the Trojans would be to see you quarreling!" Then he preaches peace, which is his job—to ramble till everyone's bored enough to calm down: "I knew your fathers, both of you, and I tell you, young Akilles, you shouldn't put yourself up against our proper king, Agamemnon! Have some respect, now!" Akilles whines, "Did you hear what he said to me, Father Nestor?"

Nestor nods, turns to Agamemnon, "Yes, yes, you have a point, my boy! Agamemnon, you are older than Akilles here and you should be restrained, not offend him needlessly, because he's our best warrior."

They both start yelling, the same old he said/he said—but at least no swords will be drawn.

Akilles gets sick of this pointless yelling and stands up to leave. On his way out, he curses Agamemnon and the army one last time: "You can have the girl, but I swear you won't see me in battle again. I'll watch you all die, sipping wine in my tent, and believe me, the day'll come when you beg me to come back!"

Akilles stomps out—everyone giving him a nice, wide berth—and goes back to his own compound, just in time to see a couple of Agamemnon's terrified slave men pulling the girl Briseis away. She's crying and she looks toward him for help. He can't do a thing.

But there is one card Akilles can play. It's handy sometimes to have a goddess for a mother, even a little goddess like Thetis. He goes to the beach to call her. She spends most of her time out there in the Mediterranean, about fifty fathoms down, but she can be on the spot very quickly when her only son needs her. They have a connection; when he cries she can hear it, no matter how deep in the sea she is. And Akilles cries a lot. The greatest who ever lived, and doomed, doomed, doomed.

He weeps for a second by the sea, head in his hands, hearing only the little waves ... and then the wave sound stops, all sounds stop. She's here. Thetis is only a little god, so she can't bend space-time like Athena does, but she makes a warm bubble of foam with only herself and her dead, doomed son inside. He's crying like a big baby, as she's seen him do so many times before.

He whimpers, as he has so many times, "Why'd you have me, mother?"

There's no answer. That's just how it is. They both know that.

She lets him weep and complain a while longer.

He mutters, "I'm going to die, everybody's always telling me I'm going to die soon, and that's supposed to be all right because I'm the greatest man alive, while I live. But what's the point, when Agamemnon—who I could tear apart with one hand—gets to take my favorite slave girl away?"

She strokes him with a hand like the waves.

He repeats, holding out one huge hand, "Seriously, I could kill him with my off hand, my left. Easily."

She strokes his head as he calms down. Finally he tells her what hurts: "They came to my tent and just dragged her out! Two of them, you could see they were scared to death, but I didn't hurt them, mother—you know I'm not a bully, I don't kill slaves—I didn't hurt them, I let them take her ... she was crying, she didn't want to go ... she really liked me ... they took her anyway ..."

They're both weeping now, in their bubble. It is a deep grief and shame to the whole lineage, this episode. He can hear something else in the sound-bubble around her now, a furious hissing. She is angry on his behalf.

Thetis does not speak. She doesn't need to. He knows she'll go to Zeus, the Godfather, and get a promise from him. Revenge. That's the only reward this world can offer: seeing some of your enemies die horribly. She'll see to it. They have a connection; he understands, and stops crying. He wouldn't like to be seen like this.

The bubble vanishes; his mother is gone. Akilles is back on the same old Trojan beach, where Agamemnon rules. He can see right down the beach to the big, black goat-hair tent where Agamemnon sits and drinks, where they've taken his favorite slave girl to be used by the man he hates most in the world.

But Thetis is already on her way to the overworld, to lobby for her doomed son. She flies straight to Zeus' throne and clasps the Godfather's knees with both hands before he can ward her off.

This is the approved suppliant gesture, a very serious matter. Not even the father of the gods can refuse a woman who has taken his knees in her hands.

Zeus grumbles—the thunder—and writhes—the lightning—and finally screams, "All right! I'll do it!"

And Thetis subsides, her foam-bubble ebbing from the patriarch's knees, flowing back into the sea.

Now her son will be avenged. Now they'll see, and die. Many.

2

STICK TO WAR;
LOVE IS TOO DANGEROUS

NOW ZEUS HAS TO KILL even more of the Greeks. His first thought, a painful, wincing one: "Hera's not going to like this." His wife and sister Hera always knows what he's up to, and she's soft on the Greeks. She's permanently mad at him anyway, because he's just an old horndog pretending to be in command when he can't even command his own penis.

These people were very down on lust. That's one of the ways they weren't like us. We love lust. They didn't. It was too dangerous, and it gave women too much power. So lust is a bad thing in this story. To these people, a real man doesn't get led around by his dick. And if he does, he's not a man at all. A stud, to their way of thinking, is a sissy. And above all, a sissy/stud is dangerous, capable of wiping out an entire city.

The man who started this whole war was a stud, a Trojan prince named Paris, fitting for a man with the sexual ego of Pepé Le Pew. The only reason he didn't drive a Porsche or wear Ray-Bans was because the infrastructure wasn't there yet. He'd have defected to Malibu in a second if the airport had been ready. And this princeling, Paris, had the chance to judge a beauty contest of three female gods. And that's what got Troy besieged.

It was all a plot by the goddess Hate. She is a great and ancient goddess around the shores of the Mediterranean, then and now. Read the news if you doubt it.

What set her off was that she got left off the guest list for an important wedding, the nuptials of Akilles' parents, Thetis and a mortal king named Peleus.

You know how hate and weddings go together. So naturally Hate was offended. She brooded a long, long time; Hate always comes up with the best plans. She went down to her stinking cellars, where the groaning never stopped, the chains always clanked, and the fumes would have made a buzzard faint.

She smelted and hammered and filed, and at last she had a perfect gift: an apple, pure gold, inscribed in sweet cursive, "For the most beautiful." A Hell weapon. She drops it among the dancers at Thetis' wedding feast, who are too drunk to wonder why a golden apple has rolled onto the dance floor. Meanwhile, Hate oozes back to her lab like the shadow of a tarantula, giggling to herself.

As soon as they see it rolling across the floor, flashing, all the goddesses at the party want that apple. They've been eyeing that handsome Trojan prince, Paris. One of them comes up with a flirty drunk plan, a beauty contest among the top three goddesses: Hera, wife and mother, relentless virtue incarnate; Athena, her fierce, brilliant daughter, master of war, cunning, strategy; and Afroditi, sweet girl-god of love. The contest, they decided, would be judged— giggle-giggle—by, oh, let's say, by that handsome Trojan prince, Paris.

No sane man would have accepted that job. Paris did. And if a smart man had been forced to choose one of the three, he'd have gone with Hera, Zeus' battle-ax, the Godmother; and if not her, then Athena, the androgyne brainiac/ warrior, a terror as an enemy, but the best ally a man could have.

So what does Paris, with his idiot studliness, go and do? He actually picks a winner based on looks and gives the prize to Afroditi, ditz-goddess of love and distraction, useless in a world of arranged clan marriages and endless war. And that's why Troy will die soon, and everyone in it will die or be enslaved. Love kills.

The three goddesses tried to bribe him, of course—this is Greece, after all. And the first two, the big two, offered bribes that still make you drool. Hera told Paris he could be king of the entire world if he just gave her the damn apple. She was pretty drunk, but she'd have gone through with it. He wasn't interested. He turned her down, the idiot! Then Athena took him aside and made him an offer no real prince would have refused: her powers, her advice, her friendship for life, in war and peace. A man named Alexander took that deal, many centuries later, and did well with it. There are cities named after him everywhere.

But Paris, the idiot, the stupid stud animal, shrugs and goes to the last and least of the goddesses, the giggly airhead Afroditi. She swings her hair back, slides her fingers down his arm, and whispers that he can have the most beautiful woman in the world if he picks her.

Which is stupid. This isn't California, this is a world of hunger and war, where you can have each and every woman in any city you own. With Hera's help, Paris could've had every city in the world, so by definition all the women would be his; with Athena's fearsome expertise, he could have taken any city that held a woman worth having. Who needs love when you've got the world at spear-point?

He's too vain to see it. He wants to have the world's most beautiful woman fall in love with him, a sappy story. A fool's story.

So he picks Afroditi. The two greater goddesses shawl themselves in darkness and vow hate for Paris and his people forever. Afroditi takes her apple, giggles, and gives him a thank-you kiss.

Oh, she kept her word to give him the most beautiful woman in the world. Which was the worst thing she could have done to Paris' poor Trojan clan.

Afroditi wafted over to Sparta and blew powdered ecstasy into the nostrils of the queen, Helen, most gorgeous woman alive. Next morning she's gone, eloped with Paris.

Disaster. See, Helen was married at the time ... and not to just any fool. No, to a fool named Menelaos, who happened to be Agamemnon's brother. And this is not a world of no-fault divorce. No-fault murder, yes; no-fault divorce, never.

Next thing you know, Paris and Helen have skedaddled, with Afroditi's trancey dazed perfumes enclosing them in a frail bubble that pops inside the walls of Troy.

And they've been hiding in their doomed Trojan love-nest for nine long years, plenty of time to repent at leisure. This is what love gets you. Love will get your kin killed.

Agamemnon's family, the house of Atreus ... they're the best haters in the world. So before Paris and Helen had wafted over the Aegean to their Trojan boudoir, Agamemnon had started making war, gathering all the clans, every man in Greece who could hold a spear. He promised them loot, he called in favors from five generations back, he threatened to visit their towns in a non-friendly manner if they hesitated.

And soon he and his shamed gelding of a brother had the biggest army Greece ever produced. Those are their ships, lined up along the beach near Troy nine years later, rotting. Many of the warriors who came over looking for loot or women are dead, but the rest are never leaving, not while Agamemnon's pure hate still lives.

The Greeks have worked very hard for the last nine years to make sure the country around Troy will never be habitable again. They've killed the best men and boys in the city, chopped down every olive tree within twenty miles, made a point of shitting and pissing on every sacred shrine in the countryside, polluted the wells with dead donkeys and dogs, killed the men and raped the women of every village allied with Troy, and eaten all the livestock up and down the coast.

And sooner or later, the Greeks will get lucky and breach the walls. The Greeks only have to be lucky once; they outnumber the Trojans by three to one, so as soon as they breach the walls, it's all over. They can wait. Sooner or later, the Trojans will make a mistake, and they'll all die, and their sons too. Even Hektor, Paris' much better brother, the Trojan champion, the one man on Earth who could go three rounds with Akilles. Well, two rounds maybe.

The Trojans are doomed, and they know it. They'll lie unburied on the dust fields outside the walls, to be gnawed by dogs. Their wives and daughters won't die, but they'll wish they had, as they're sold at auction, passed from one bloody hand to another in trade for a few coins or some livestock.

Now you see why real men don't do love. It's too dangerous. Real men stick to killing and war. Because it's safer.

3

MORALE

GAMEMNON IS SLEEPING. He drinks a lot of wine, and spends most of his days sleeping it off. Tonight is no different, though a new girl is lying next to him—Briseis, the girl he grabbed from Akilles. She is reacting to her first night with the king of kings by weeping softly while Agamemnon snores. He is so different from her last master, Akilles. Belonging to Akilles had been a shock, then something else, and finally something she would never have described as pleasant, not out loud. She saw so clearly what Akilles himself would never see: He was just a good boy, in the body of Death itself. He himself never noticed his moments of decency, would have been shamed if he had; but she noticed them.

Whereas Agamemnon ... ugh. All the other girls say Agamemnon killed his own daughter. She never believed it till this night. Now she knows for certain it's true. She wishes Akilles had killed her rather than let her go to this man. If Akilles had cared for her at all, he would have killed her. She hates him now, though not as much as she hates, with every heartbeat, the mound of hairy back rising and falling beside her. It goes without saying that she hates Agamemnon more than anyone in the world.

Zeus isn't very fond of Agamemnon either, and he's watching the two of them, watching with his eyes closed as he sits on his great rock throne. He has a promise to keep, the one he made to Thetis, the minor but lovely, so very lovely, sea goddess. He promised to kill some Greeks to please her. To avenge her son. That's what it is to be godfather, one favor after another, calling them in or handing them out, keeping a rough body count for future calling-in purposes.

The deal ... yes, he remembers now, breathing as slowly as the tectonic plates: He is going to kill a lot of Greeks to please Thetis, to show them they need her precious son.

Well, why not? Akilles is a good boy, half-god; they all went to his mother's wedding. Besides, everyone knows—the poor boy is not long for this world. A shame, because he's one of the few mortal/god hybrids who bred true to the God side of the family. Zeus can think of certain full gods like Ares, so-called "God of War," who aren't half the god-material Akilles is. But Ares is a full-blood, and Akilles a half-breed, so Ares will live forever as a cowardly murderer, and Akilles is going to die, die, die. Zeus has it all down, the time, the place, the weapon, and it just can't be helped. You have to have rules.

But in the meantime, it'll be a pleasure, killing some of the Greeks who've offended Thetis' brave son. Hardly even counts as a favor; more like fun. Just to see Agamemnon squirm. The Gods don't like Agamemnon any more than Briseis does. Nobody likes him. The camp dogs don't like him, run away when they see him.

So Zeus chuckles deeply, on the Richter scale, and decides to start with Agamemnon. Yes, let it start inside that fool's skull. Let's infect that little wet world and let it spread until half the Greeks are dead.

Zeus calls. Without words, it comes: A Bad Dream. It floats in mid-air before the Godfather, revolving, every point on its green sphere pulsing with tendrils eager to make a connection with you, with anyone, to infect you with terrors and lies you never even imagined, sights from Pluto's horror-world under the earth that you can never un-see, once they've been squirted into your sleeping brain. One of the gods' favorite weapons; the gods have N-space warehouses full of these things, whispering and vibrating in endless rows, waiting to be sent on a mission.

The dream's tendrils reach out lovingly toward Zeus, but he's immune.

He invented these things. His eyes are still closed, but he is instructing the dream. A nanosecond to load, and it hums lovingly, ready to obey. He opens his eyes and says, "Go."

Briseis has turned on her side now, away from Agamemnon, as far as the couch will allow. She sees a green flare through her eyelids and ignores it. She's seen enough.

The Dream is humming a high keen as it probes Agamemnon, a wonderful subject—such self-love, such malice, such power and stupidity! The Dream keens its thanks to Zeus for this mission, and injects its lies.

Agamemnon dreams that Nestor is shaking him awake, shouting, "Listen, Agamemnon, my king! O noble one, your time has come at last! I come directly from the throne of Zeus with a message!"

The Bad Dream giggles to itself at this point; after all, isn't that the truth, in a way? Didn't Zeus, father of them all, send it to Agamemnon with this message? As so often the Bad Dream sighs that it can never reveal the funny side of its endlessly interesting job. Ah well!

For a second, it turns Nestor's head in the dream into itself, a green pulsing sphere with jellyfish tendrils licking out toward any mental activity it senses. Agamemnon starts to wake in terror. The Bad Dream is ashamed—unprofessional!—and sends Agamemnon waves of comfort and vanity, his favorite food.

The sleeper relaxes again, and the Bad Dream, in character as the stolid, honest old baron Nestor, intones: "Hear me, Agamemnon Atreus-son! The Gods have united behind us, Hera has persuaded Zeus to take our side, all the clans are with us, and Troy will fall as soon as we advance! March on the city! Now!!"

Agamemnon murmurs, sighs, and smiles in his sleep. The Bad Dream caresses his pocked face one more time, this time for its own pleasure, and vanishes.

Agamemnon wakes, feeling odd. "Pleased," or "happy," one of those words people use. Strange, but never mind. He has work to do. The girl, the new one—what's her name? Something with a B ... she seems to be gone already. Strange, the way they always seem to wake early and go off. Chores, primping, who knows? He has an army to assemble.

Then, in a pure Agamemnon moment, he has himself a better idea. Agamemnon is always getting a better idea, and may the gods help anyone on his side when that happens.

He thinks, "Why attack Troy? That's too simple! Too obvious!" Like all truly stupid people, Agamemnon hates the obvious.

"No," he thinks, "I'll test my army! I'll see who's really loyal enough to me. I've already got Zeus' word, through his dream, that we'll take Troy as soon as we advance. So why let disloyal bastards share in the booty? I'll call an assembly—I'll act all mopey, tell them it's hopeless, we've tried for nine long years and it's not working, blah blah blah ... perfect! O god, I'm so smart I scare myself sometimes! The cowards and shirkers and traitors, who've always hated me—they'll flee! So only the loyal ones will march into Troy with me! I won't have to share the booty and the slave girls with any of them!"

He slaps his thigh at the brilliance of his plan. Then he realizes there's yet another bonus, the sweetest of all: "Akilles will have to watch us trooping back to the ships so loaded down with loot we can barely sing a hymn of gratitude! It'll kill 'im, seeing us like that! Beautiful!"

Zeus, not guessing quite how stupid Agamemnon can be, is waiting for the dream to take effect, for the Greek armies to march from the beach to the walls of Troy as the dream commanded. Instead, he zeroes in on the Greek camp to find Agamemnon has called ... an assembly? Why an assembly? Zeus is disgusted. He says to his "cupbearer," Ganymede, his boy, "Look at this idiot! He's so stupid you can't even trip him up properly! Some of these mortals are so slug-stupid you can't even warp their brains with a tailor-made false dream! I send him a dream that he should march on Troy, and the moron calls a meeting! What is he even think—" At this point Zeus decides to find out what's going on; he blinks his eyes shut, looks at what's in Agamemnon's mind, then opens them and says, "Oooooo, I can't even ... that is the STUPIDEST plan I've ever ..." He turns to Ganymede, who is kneeling now before his throne, as so often before, pushes the boy's head away and says, "No, not now, I have to ... can you believe it? This idiot Agamemnon has actually tried to improve on the carefully sabotaged plan I gave him. Some people you can't even sabotage; they're just too stupid. Apollo was right; just kill the idiots, but if I did that, Hera—you know her ..." The boy nods, with feeling. He knows Hera all right.

Agamemnon is in fine form. He has all the barons filing into his tent. He has center stage and a cunning plan; he's in heaven.

He walks up and down, excited, talking in a stage whisper:

"My noble friends, this will be the first of two meetings I've planned today. This one, you can see, is just us, the noble-born, the kings. After it's finished I'll have a big outdoor show for the spear-carriers. See, something big has happened. I had a dream last night, straight from Olympos, from Zeus Himself! He came to me in the form of Nestor—" pointing to the old fool, who blushes proudly— "... and we all know why that was: because we all trust Nestor, everybody loves Nestor! Sign of trust, reliability, and so on. So the dream is a definite valid prophecy. And in this dream, Nestor, I mean Zeus in the form of Nestor, told me this ..." Dramatic pause. "Friends, we will take Troy first time out! No opposition. All the gods are with us. We'll roll into the city like a boulder through a herd of goats."

The nobles cheer, beginning to believe. But Agamemnon holds his hand up to quiet them, goes on: "Wait, there's more! When I woke up, I thought, 'Why let all the traitors and the liars and the cowards, and you know very well this horde is full of them ... why let them in on the loot and the glory?' So here's my plan: after this meeting I call a second outdoor assembly for the commoners and tell them, 'Woe is me, soldiers! It's no use! These Trojans have called up all of the mainland of Asia, hordes of alien freaks! We'll never beat them all! Let's go home, boys, home to the wives and the kiddies!'"

He stops to let the beauty of the plan sink in. There's a deep silence from the barons. Are they hearing him correctly? He's going to tell the men they're doomed? Agamemnon sees the puzzled frowns and thinks, for the thousandth time, that his genius is wasted on these lunkheads. He'll have to explain his cunning plan to them. He begins, "See? The weaklings and traitors and cowards, they'll all run for boats and set sail, and we'll be left to stroll into Troy on our own! Ha! And Akilles won't get so much as an old Trojan widow to scrub his floors! It's perfect!"

No one seems to want to be the first to jump up and shout for joy at the brilliance of the plan, but Nestor, childishly pleased at being the star of Agamemnon's dream, stands up and addresses the barons: "My lords, you have heard our leader's plan. Now, if anyone else had told us such a thing, we would have said he was simply a madman ... but, ah, Agamemnon is first among us, the very liver of our army, so, ah, we must respect what he gives us."

A dark voice from the assembly says, "Nonsense! Agamemnon is like a bad liver; all he gives is bile!" The barons laugh at this, but Agamemnon stands up to see who dared to say that.

Ah, it's Odysseus. He should have known. Insolent as ever.

Odysseus stares back, unafraid. If Agamemnon is the liver of the army, and Akilles the spear arm, then Odysseus is the brain. He has bright red hair, and the face of a fox with blood on its muzzle. He's also a head shorter than Agamemnon, two heads shorter than Akilles. It makes him permanently offended. It's bad enough being the smartest man in the room, but to be the shortest as well makes Odysseus more than ready to match wits, fists, or spears with anyone, god or mortal. And short as he is, Odysseus' shoulders are as wide as a giant's, and his hands are as fast as a snake's strike.

So Agamemnon lets the insult go, and gestures the meeting to an end.

Now the heralds go among the nobodies, the spear carriers. These men have no names, no lineage. They're just "the men from this place," or "the men from that town." They live and die in groups, led by a lord, a man who has a name and knows his ancestors five generations back.

At first they're puzzled that Agamemnon has invited them to an assembly. They don't usually get asked what they think, especially by Agamemnon. He's not a friend of the common soldier. They've been starved, frozen, rained on, shot with arrows, hit with rocks, slashed with swords, skewered by spears, and pocked with disease for nine long years and Agamemnon never seemed to care. Now he wants to consult them? It's strange. What could he say that would mean anything to them, except, "Men, we're going home!" And it goes without saying that he'd never say that.

Agamemnon stands up and says, "Men, we're going home!"

All hell breaks loose. The soldiers are shouting with joy; some weeping, the rest are running at top speed for their flea-infested little huts to grab what they can and be the first on board when the ships are ready to go. In two minutes, no one is standing near Agamemnon except old Nestor, who looks like a puzzled, well-meaning old sheep, and Odysseus, who looks even more disgusted with Agamemnon than usual.

Agamemnon turns to them and says, "Wait, it wasn't supposed to go like that."

Nestor, stroking his white beard, says, "Mmmm, yes ... indeed, Atreus-son, I thought not."

Agamemnon: "They didn't let me finish!"

Odysseus stares at the two of them, mutters, "Stupid goats! Stupid bearded goats!" and stomps off, too disgusted to talk anymore.

Odysseus has had enough of these idiots. He knows most men are not as bright as he is, and he tries to be patient. Sometimes he even enjoys dealing with these noble, two-legged beasts. But there are times when he'd like to see them all eaten by a pack of dogs.

There's nothing he can do to stop the catastrophe. The men will swarm onto the ships, all rotted after nine years beached, row out to the sea, sink and drown. The Trojans will loot the camps, slaughter any laggards, and laugh at the Greeks, as they flip corpses looking for metal.

Then something comes over Odysseus, something huge. He is in a god-shadow; Athena is beside him. He has met gods before, and he knows the vertigo that comes when one of the greater gods stands beside you, as if a planet were leaning over your shoulder.

She speaks, starting in mid-conversation because she can read minds: "Yes, they're stupid, they deserve to drown; but still, Odysseus, you have to stop them."

He alone among mortals has the strength of mind to refuse the gravitational pull of that huge thing beside him. Resisting, he says, "Why? Why should I help them?" She says simply. "My Greeks must win."

He's a stubborn man. He grits his teeth, forces a question: "Why? Why must they win?"

She likes his strong, stubborn will, warms to him. If only he had a longer life span than a mosquito ... But her job is to stop this, so she repeats, leaning a fraction more of her strength on him: "This time, my stubborn little Red-Beard, the Greeks must win."

She ruffles his beard with a hand three times the size of his, whispering: "Not for their sake, nor their children, nor grandchildren ..."

"I don't understand you."

Her shawl brushes his face, the cold dark of stars and the grim slice of the geological strata blanking the sunlight: "See? You live only a moment, you see only a little."

He's frozen, feeling the cold of deep time. She goes on, "But we're alike in one way, Red-Beard. We both have to deal with fools. You with stupid men, and I with stupid gods. Now go, stop the fools from ruining my plans."

She's gone, the lurch of earthly gravity returning.

Odysseus stands stunned for a moment. Then he runs back to fix things. Agamemnon is still explaining to Nestor how his cunning plan was supposed to work.

Odysseus has no time to be gentle. He rips Agamemnon's scepter out of his hand and runs down to the ships. The scepter has a nice heft. Before it became a badge of office it was a mace, and a good one. Odysseus likes the feel of it. It feels as eager for this as he is.

But he needs something with a little more heft to persuade the common soldiers. Some of those lunkheads are giants. Spotting a nice driftwood tree-branch, he grabs it without breaking stride.

When he sees a chieftain wavering or making for the ships, he waves the scepter in his face and says, "Get your men in ranks, by the king's order!" They are trained to obey the man who holds that sacred mace.

When he runs into common soldiers lugging their loot to a ship, he's more direct. He hits the biggest guy on the back of the head with the tree branch, lays him out and roars at the rest, "Get back to your chieftain, peasants, or you're dead!" Nobles and commoners obey without much quarreling. An angry Odysseus is not a pleasant sight, and something of the goddess trails after him, a cold, grim authority.

Soon the troops are straggling back to the assembly point, where Agamemnon and Nestor are still standing around like ducks that have been hit on the head.

Odysseus herds the last stragglers in. He sees that Thersites the radical, the jailhouse lawyer, is orating at Agamemnon, who's too stunned to react. Thersites is the ugliest man in the army, some kind of spinal case. A commoner too, and he's picked up a little ideology somewhere. He talks in a high, whiny voice, and he's on his usual theme: The Unfairness of It All. "You there, Agamemnon, 'the king' as you high-and-mighty like to call yourselves, how come you get all the pretty slave girls, and we get the dregs? Why should your lot guzzle tender meat every day, whereas the ordinary soldier gets bread and a little oil? And how come ..."

Odysseus wastes no time arguing about justice. He employs an older and more puissant rhetoric, hitting Thersites in the face with the tree branch. Thersites' teeth spray out of his mouth and he flies through the air, landing on his back, out cold. Odysseus turns to the crowd, growling: "Any more democrats? Good. Now ..." he turns to Agamemnon, shoves the scepter back in his hand, and whispers roughly, "You, O great king, great idiot—stop trying to be clever, because you never will be. Your job is to lead the army; just do your job, for once in your life!"

Agamemnon is still too confused to react. Odysseus turns back to the crowd, leads them in a martial cheer, then leans into Agamemnon's ear again and hisses, "Call for a sacrifice! Tell them to get ready to march on Troy!"

Agamemnon obeys, shouting: "Let every man polish his armor, whet his sword-edge, and eat a good breakfast! Feed the horses on your best grain, for today we shall take Troy!"

Men are fickle, as plastic as wax. An hour ago, they all wanted to sail home. Now, after a few whacks from Odysseus, they want to burn Troy to the ground. After all, once they've done that, they can go home—a lot richer.

Agamemnon finishes: "While you prepare for battle, my priests and I will make sacrifice, that the gods may favor us in battle!"

The troops are screaming and whooping, ready to storm Olympos itself. They don't know what's going on and don't care. All they know is that one way or another, this miserable nine-year stalemate looks set to break. Any ending is better than another year of eating windblown sand and scooping rainwater out of a rat-hole with your shield.

Finally, some fighting! The kings and nobles are sitting in a circle, waiting for the sacrifice. A slave leads the young bull to the center of the circle. It's a beauty. Five years old. Not a mark, not a bruise or freckle on it. Blinking calmly, not a clue what's about to happen to it. Still got balls, hasn't been gelded.

Agamemnon lets them all appreciate it for a while, then waves to the chopper, a big man with a bronze axe. The bull blinks at him: More grain? It's been pampered all its life, till now. One chop to the back of the neck, and it wobbles; another, better, right through the spine, and it falls.

Slaves sop up the blood, mix it with barley for instant sausage. More slaves swarm the carcass, and in a minute it's arranged, bones and meat, in two piles.

The priests put two femurs oozing with marrow on a driftwood pyre. Then they take two nice fat steaks and put them on top of the femurs. This is what gods like to sniff. They light the driftwood, and the sacred smell of steak rises to the Overworld.

Everyone waits for a sign of acceptance from Zeus. They know he hasn't been pleased with them lately. But this is prime beef they're offering, good rich marrow. Most people don't taste meat once a year. The oily smoke curls up to the blank blue sky.

Nothing. Zeus is not shy; he'd show it if he was pleased. Nothing. Not a bird, or a breath of wind. This is a definite No from the Father.

The priests whisper to each other nervously. Their leader shuffles over to Agamemnon, shrugs. He doesn't need any more scientists to tell him what it means.

It means they're going to charge out to fight the Trojans, and they're going to lose. To die.

Can't be stopped now, no matter how grim the auguries are. Agamemnon has whipsawed the men too much already. He has to go through with the attack.

He calls to his messengers, "Get the men together at the ships. We advance immediately."

The trick now is to get the men marching before rumors of the failed sacrifice start circulating. They don't have a clue, the commoners. They're all eager for the fight, bashing spearheads and swords together, roaring. Every second more stragglers come in at a trot, contingents from the boondocks. Those country boys are always a little slow but good once the fighting starts.

But all the chieftains, who saw Zeus refuse their sacrifice, know something the soldiers don't: It's going to be a bad day for Greeks, a good day for crows.

The chariots are in place now, lined up on the beach, the little horses stamping nervously. You can throw a spear from a chariot; that's the idea. Or shoot a bow. You have a driver, a slave usually, to keep the two-wheeler from crashing into a wadi, while you focus on finding a target. Occasionally it works; mostly they overturn or an axle breaks. If the ground is at all uneven, you can't use them at all. But they're expensive, a mark of status; they don't have to work very well.

Agamemnon's contingent is the biggest, richest, best armed. A hundred ships it took to ferry them across the Aegean. The other chieftains brought thirty ships, or twenty, or ten; some are standing with nothing but a few cousins around them. All of them twitching and yelling, eager to get the battle started.

Zeus has no time for these Greeks, not today. He wants to talk to the Trojans. He sends Morning to warn Troy. She finds old Priam, King of Troy, and comes up to him in the form of one of his sons. But as soon as the weak old man breaks into a toothless grin, she lances him with her glare, showing her god side.

"Old man, you're wasting time. The Greeks are coming, more than any mortal army has ever faced."

He moans; it's too much for him at his age.

She turns down the glare and speaks more softly, "You have your allies here, tribes so strange none of you Trojans can talk to them. Send your sons to their chief, and have each tribe's chief arrange his people. Only if you bring all the tribes together, all the freaks and monsters of Asia, can you face this united Greek host."

Priam nods, sends a slave for his sons, who scatter among the wild men who have swarmed in to hold off the invaders. Hill tribes, mountain tribes, desert raiders; tribes who eat dogs, others who eat scorpions. Some eat people, or so the rumors say. There are tribes who worship the lion, the snake, the stinging fly; tribes who jabber in tongues like birds twittering or howl like wolves howling or geckoes chuffing. There are tribes who keep their language secret, don't speak at all, just watch the Trojans and arrange their fighters with hand gestures. Tribes who veil their faces and others who wear hyena skins, lizard pelts, flax robes. Some fight with bows, curved or straight; some with spears too long to lift alone; others with stabbing spears so short they're more like knives with long handles. Some slash with swords, in every shape from sickle to scimitar.

The Trojans need every one of these inland mutants. Alone, they're outnumbered by the Greeks ten to one. With all their allies, they have about a third as many men, barely enough to defend with. And only as long as their alliances hold. Some of the Trojans' outlandish allies might decide to leave because the moon rose the wrong way, or a sparrow spoke rudely to their chief. It's a fragile alliance, and when it fails, the men of Troy are dead, the women of Troy are sold as slaves. No quarter asked or given.

The Trojans have no one who can match Akilles. Their best man is Hektor, Priam's favorite son. The old man has many sons, but most of them are disappointments. Not Hektor. He is, if anything, too good a man. A good father. A good husband. A good son. A good warrior, too ... But, only "good." All that matters now is war, and in that, Hektor's no match for Akilles. If they ever go one-on-one, everyone knows how it will end.

For now, the Trojans and their allies are united. They deploy on a hill outside town as the Greeks march toward them.

There's a ritual to this, a proper way to start the day's fight. The armies don't run at each other immediately; that would be uncivilized. First, there must be single combat, a quaint old custom from the days before men learned to make barley. Back in those days, warriors were scarce resources. You spent them one at a time. When one band met another, the best man from one band stepped out and so did his opposite number, and everyone else stood and watched to see who killed who.

It was a good way to keep from wasting a whole generation in one battle. A warrior costs so much to raise.

But these days towns are growing, warriors are cheap, and these single combats are really just an opening act. Whoever wins, Trojans and Greeks will end up attacking each other, and men will die in hundreds. Still, the ritual must be followed. It's a matter of pride: Our best can kill your best.

The Greek horde marches up to the hill where the Trojans wait. Silence. Amateurs yell; real warriors advance in total silence. Freaks 'em out much better.

The Greeks come within bowshot of the hill. Now it is time for Troy to offer a champion. So out steps ... Paris himself, the selfish stud who started this whole mess by stealing Helen. He's a good enough fighter, as they go. He's no Akilles, but who is? Paris has killed his man more than once. Good with a bow, adequate with spear and shield. No coward; you can't say he's afraid of battle. He's a selfish man, and this whole mess is his fault, but he's no coward. He's a king's son, after all; they love to kill, those princes.

The Trojans are happy to see him step up like this. With luck, Paris will die today and the Greeks will be appeased. Once Helen has been widowed, they can just ship her home, hand her over. She might cry, but she's just as much to blame as Paris and if Troy can get rid of both in one day, maybe the city won't be wiped out.

Or maybe Paris will win today, kill the Greek champion, whoever that turns out to be.

Paris stands out there alone, waiting for a Greek to step out.

The Greek shields open, and out steps ... Menelaos.

Menelaos, Helen's rightful husband. The man Paris wronged. Agamemnon's brother. King of Sparta.

Now that Paris sees who's facing him, he sags. He can't fight Menelaos! Every god will lend strength to the wronged husband's spear, and to blind Paris, weaken his thrusts, dissolve his shield.

He didn't know this was going to be moral. He breaks and runs for shelter towards the Trojan shields.

Suddenly Menelaos is standing out there by himself.

A huge laugh goes up from the Greek army. No one has ever run away from a single combat before it even started. After breaking your spear or being wounded, maybe—though even then, most nobles would much rather die than be shamed in front of everybody. But running away before the fight even starts? That's never happened before.

Agamemnon laughs with the rest, wondering if maybe the auguries were just wrong. Damn scientists, acting like they know everything—all bluff! It's going to be a great day for the Greeks!

Odysseus knows better. This is a sideshow. They're going to lose badly today. He has to be ready to hold the army together when that happens.

Akilles, far off in his tent, hears the cheering and shrugs. He knows his mother hasn't let him down. He sips wine and waits, wishing ill to his former comrades.

Paris, slapped into dignity by the Greeks' roaring laugh, slows down as he approaches the Trojan shields. He wants to make this look like he's simply calling time, to consult with his brothers. Hektor steps out to meet him, in a rage. After all the disasters Paris has already brought down on the family, he has to shame them too? Hektor is a good man, and he hasn't scolded Paris for bringing ruin on the city. After all, Paris is a prince; he can do as he pleases. But this is too much. Nine years of pent rage spew up out of Hektor's lips as he grabs Paris and hisses at him:

"You miserable pervert! Lecher, you've never cared about anyone but yourself! Always primping in the mirror, flirting with any woman who looked at you, no matter whose property she was! We should have stoned you to death as the law commands when you brought a noble-born man's wife back here. And now you won't face the man you robbed? Go out there and fight Menelaos!"

Paris says, "Yes, I admit all that's true ... but you just don't know. You never met Afroditi, you don't know how good it feels; it's a whole different world. You're always talking about your duties, always doing the right thing; you just don't know ... But you're right, I have to go back out there. But let's use this combat to make a deal with the Greeks. Tell them that if I die today, you give Helen back to them and they go home. That will make up, maybe, for what I did to the family."

Hektor grabs the chance. He has to make a deal fast, before the two armies swarm each other. The Greeks are so excited by Paris' cowardice that they're already throwing sling-stones and firing arrows at the Trojans, and the Trojans are getting angry too, ready to charge downhill at the Greeks. Hektor pushes the Trojans back, using his spear like a staff, then says, "Wait, hold the line! Paris will fight for us." Then he goes out to negotiate with the Greeks.

Hektor walks halfway to the Greek shield wall and calls, "Paris agrees to fight Menelaos, but let us agree that this fight will settle the war. Paris against Menelaos, the two men whose quarrel started all this. Let everyone on both sides put down their weapons, sit on the ground, and watch them fight. Winner takes the woman and all she has; everyone else goes home, and the war is over."

Menelaos has been waiting all this time, standing alone in front of the Greek horde. He's not the fastest thinker among the Greeks, but he likes this idea of fighting the man who stole his wife, with everyone watching. He'll kill that preening pretty-boy, and everyone will see he's not just a punch line. When your claim to fame is being the most famous cuckold in the world, and everyone whispers that it's because you didn't know how to please your wife, life is rather unpleasant. He hears the snickers when he walks past the tents. He's heard the Menelaos jokes: "Helen is complaining the way wives do, 'Look, I don't have a thing to wear!' Menelaos walks behind the screen where she keeps her finery, says, 'What are you talking about, wife? Look, here's a fine gown, and here's another—oh, hello, Paris!—and here's a nice shawl, and another gown ...'"

He's been hearing those jokes in his head in his sleep for nine long years. And now he has Paris right here, with everyone watching. It's a joy that almost makes him sick, for fear someone will take it away. Why can't they just get on with it?

But this negotiation is a serious business, and that means priests and kings. The priests have to drag bulls and sheep to the space between the armies, where the two men will try to kill each other, and kill the animals, and move the meat around in the divinely approved manner.

And the kings have to parade before the two armies. Helen is there, with old Priam and the rest of the Trojan royals. Menelaos sees her, all right. When Paris is dead, and she is his property again, he will have a great deal to say to her. Not now. Now his job is to kill the pretty boy.

But he has to wait forever. The priests take their time, the smoke rises to heaven, the soldiers point to Helen and Priam, telling the same cuckold jokes Menelaos has been hearing for nine years. It will never stop. Maybe it would be better if Paris kills him. Maybe then it would stop. But no, from what Menelaos has heard about the afterlife, it's even worse than this one, about like being on a becalmed ship in the dark, forever. Not much to look forward to.

Finally, the preliminaries are over. Priam and Helen return to Troy. Hektor handles the toss to see who gets to throw the first spear, because they all trust Hektor.

Paris wins the toss. He steps back, makes his run, throws. The spear hits Menelaos' shield and scores a long tear in it without sticking.

Now it's Menelaos' turn. He's sick with eagerness, praying hard to Zeus: "Father, God, Zeus, please, please, listen to me for once: The man I'm aiming at, he was a guest in my house! A guest! If anything means anything, a man's house, his wife—I may not be as smart or handsome as some people but the man was my guest! Give me his worthless life!"

Paris is waiting, hunched low. Menelaos throws. It's a good throw, right through the shield, through the breastplate. But Paris is a prince; princes practice fighting all day, from the cradle. Paris knows what to do. He flips his torso as Menelaos' spear screeches through his shield, as the shield slows it down and gives him time to dodge. He's not hurt, though he has to throw away his shield.

Menelaos can't believe it. A perfect throw! Nine years he's dreamed of this chance, and now that he's done it, the gods have denied him. He was born to be humiliated.

He pulls out his sword and lunges. But swords are bad weapons; the metal-workers haven't really got it figured out yet, the tech support isn't there yet. When you hit someone on the helmet, the sword usually ...

Menelaos' sword hits Paris on the helmet, and shatters.

That's it. That's the moment Menelaos' last faith in god and man explodes into rage: "Damn every one of you, gods and people, and you, Zeus, especially! You're supposed to protect a man like me who keeps the rules and makes the sacrifices and does what he's supposed to do, and now, I wait nine years and you warp my throw and then the sword breaks like a stick?"

The only things Menelaos trusts now are his own two hands. He reaches out and grabs Paris, who's wobbly from the whack on the helmet—grabs him by the helmet and starts dragging him back toward the Greek line. The Greeks are cheering hard now, all the cuckold jokes forgotten. "Yeah! Bring him! Drag him like a calf, Menelaos!" Menelaos finally feels something besides shame. This is joy! To hear the cheers of the army, and know that for once, someone else is the butt of the joke. Paris, the big stud—he has to be the punch line now, as he's dragged by the helmet, woozy, helpless! A few more steps and Menelaos will have him safe inside the Greek shields, and then the Trojans will have to beg to get their stud back alive. Or Menelaos will make him die slowly, screaming, to make up for all those jokes.

But Paris has a friend, a goddess: Afroditi, the sweet cheat. She wafts down to the battlefield, snips the strap of Paris' helmet with her nail scissors so it comes off in Menelaos' hand, and takes Paris up with her, vanishes him. If there's one thing she's good at, it's hiding men, and she hides her favorite stud now, so that right there, in broad sunlight, with two whole armies watching, Paris is gone. It's ridiculous! It's impossible! Suddenly Menelaos is holding an empty helmet—he's the punch line again, the fool, the cuckold.

Helen saw it all, from the city wall. Her stud lover Paris, dragged through the dust by her ex-husband, Menelaos. All the maids were giggling at her, just loud enough for her to hear. She gave up everything for Paris, and he's a loser. Had to be rescued by that immortal slut, Afroditi.

So when Afroditi suddenly appears to Helen, disguised as an old nurse,

Helen isn't in the mood for more God antics. Afroditi, putting on an obviously fake old-crone voice, tugs at Helen's robe: "Come to your chamber, my lady! Paris is waiting for you there, clean and eager! You'd never think he's just been in a fight! He's more like a young man at a dance!"

Helen shrugs off the Goddess' hand: "Oh, stop this nonsense! I know it's you, Afroditi; your illusions are getting sloppy. And I'm not going to that coward's bed. Oh, I should have stayed in Sparta, with Menelaos! He's the better man, even if he isn't exactly exciting! You took me up in your love-bubble with Paris and dropped me here, far from home. If you like Paris so much, you bed him, you can have him! Be his wife, be his slave-girl better yet, but I'm not going anywhere!"

Afroditi is angry, and lets the disguise slip away. She looms before Helen, a very dangerous bitch-giantess: "Little hussy, you'll regret it if you disobey me. I told you: Go to Paris, now."

Helen goes, still sulking. She sits in the bedroom facing Paris, but she won't look at him. Afroditi has arranged for sweet perfumes to suffuse the room, it's so warm in there that clothes suddenly seem like a bad invention, and there's a pulsing music coming from everywhere. Helen's not impressed with these tricks, though. Not today.

Paris is lolling on the bed, sure of himself as ever. Like he hasn't just shamed himself, shamed her, losing in front of everyone and being rescued by Afroditi. Just lying there, grinning at her, ready for love. Well, it's not going to be that easy for him this time.

She starts, "I thought you were so good with your hands. Isn't that what you always said, how good with your hands you are? With your sword? If your precious Afroditi hadn't scooped you up and saved you, you'd be dead out there. My poor Menelaos is a better man than you!"

Paris grimaces, "Woman, don't start with me. It's been a rough day. Menelaos had Athena with him, and she loves war, she's born for it, freak that she is. There was nothing I could do, fighting both your damned ex and the goddess at once. Look, darling, there'll be another day; I still have gods who like me."

He grins and leans toward her: "And you like me too, don't you?" She doesn't answer, just huffs. Which is good enough for him. He pulls her toward him, and she goes—grumbling, but she goes. And they go at it.

4

AGAMEMNON

OUT ON THE BATTLEFIELD, no one knows what to do. Paris has vanished, Menelaos is standing there holding an empty helmet. Agamemnon tries to bluff it out, stomping out halfway to the Trojan line waving his arms and yelling, "You all saw it! My brother Menelaos is the winner! Give us back the woman, Helen, and we demand a ransom, too—but we'll settle that later. The point is, we win!"

The Greeks all cheer. The Trojans aren't sure what to do. There's a lot of milling around behind their shields. Paris lost the fight, but where's his body? Until they see his corpse, they're not conceding. Zeus is watching it all, feeling bad. His wife Hera and her all-too-precocious daughter Athena! This is all their doing, because they hate the Trojans so much. Zeus likes the Trojans. Good pious people, always laid out some good fat meat for his sacrifices. But those two, mother and daughter, they just won't rest till Troy is wiped out. He has another gulp of nectar and grumbles:

"Why can't we just let Menelaos take his wife back? Then Troy won't have to be wiped out. What did the Trojans ever do to you, anyway?"

Hera glares at him: "Do you know how hard I've worked, holding all these quarrelsome Greeks together for nine long years? I'm not wasting all that effort."

Zeus is almost weeping now, drunk and maudlin: "I like Troy! They've always been good, loyal worshippers of mine. What if I took it into my head to destroy one of your favorite towns, how would you feel?"

Hera doesn't hesitate: "My three favorite towns are Sparta, Argos, and Mycenae. You can destroy all of them, anytime you want, and I won't say a word. But in return, let me have my way with Troy."

Zeus is beaten. She called his bluff. She sees it and pushes her advantage: "So why not settle things right now? Send Athena, to trick the Trojans into shooting first, breaking the truce."

Zeus has another gulp and grimaces. Athena ... that girl, or whatever she is ... she scares him sometimes. Just look at her, looming over her mother, that damned owl on her shoulder staring at him ... his head still hurts where she chewed her way out to get born. Not worth it, opposing Athena.

So he nods, "Go down there then, girl. Talk your way into some Trojan's head. You're good at that." And he has another gulp of wine.

Athena smiles, nods to her mother, and vanishes.

She comes to Earth clothed in fire this time. No sneaking about it. She wants everyone to know that one of the greatest gods has come, roaring down onto the dust plain like a blazing comet, a shaft of fire that disappears as it touches the ground.

Every man on the field knows something will happen now. Nobody knows what.

Athena turns herself to Pandarus, a Trojan ally from the back country. A hick, but a fine sniper, all hand-eye coordination, born with a bow in his hand like so many of these back-country Easterners. She has no trouble getting into his mind, what there is of it, whispering, "Listen, archer, don't you see Menelaos standing out there in the open? What a target! You know who'd be grateful if you put an arrow right in his belly? Apollo, the patron of all bowmen. He'd reward you well if you took Menelaos out right now. And so would Priam and the Trojans. Do it! Do it now!"

Pandarus gulps once or twice—he's one of those gawky kids, all Adam's apple—and nods. He calls his hick friends to form a shield around him so no one will see him draw his bow. That bow is a thing of beauty, two huge ibex horns joined with sinew, strung with a thin strip of hide. He fits the arrow and pulls the bow back and back, into a circle, then a flattened oval, till you'd think it would fall apart, and then lets go.

Menelaos is standing out there between the two shield walls in a rage. Perfect target. But Athena is watching over him. She tracks the arrow in slow motion as it pushes through the air toward Menelaos. To her, there are eons of time between the moment it left the bowstring and the moment it slides through Menelaos' linen shirt.

She guides it, slows it, sends it lovingly through Menelaos' shirt near the belly. She enjoys this part a little too much, perhaps, every layer unfolded in a slow tease. She lets the arrowhead penetrate the belt buckle, then sends it burrowing through the second layer of leather Menelaos wears around his waist, and then gently scratches his skin with it, like a playful cat—just the point, not the barb, enough to draw a little blood.

And then she's gone, back up to the Overworld to watch. Menelaos doesn't even know he's hit yet. He stands there between the two armies, bleeding like a woman, the red streaming down his legs.

Menelaos feels the wound, looks down, sees the blood. He sits, then lies down. Agamemnon, still orating at the Trojans, hears the Greeks' cries, turns around, and sees his brother lying there with an arrow in his belly.

Agamemnon runs over to Menelaos, howling like a child: "O dear brother, I've been the death of you!"

Agamemnon is shrieking: "I've ruined us all! This was my war and I've lost it all, and now you're going to die! Oh, my poor Menelaos! We'll bury you out here in the dust fields and some damn Trojan kids will play on your grave and laugh and say, 'Agamemnon's brother is buried here' ..."

Menelaos isn't listening to his brother. He's feeling the wound, and soon realizes the arrow barely broke the skin. The barb didn't go in, that's the main thing. No barb, no problem. It's just blood, and a man has blood to spare. Agamemnon is still holding him, howling: "... You'll lie forever here in the middle of nowhere! They'll say, 'He died in Asia, back when the Greeks wasted their strength trying to take Troy and then sailed away, a failure!' That's how I'll be remembered, as a failure! 'Agamemnon, the Big Failure,' that's what they'll call me!"

Menelaos lifts himself up on one elbow, growls: "Shut up! You're scaring the army! It's not deep, it's nothing! Stop talking!"

Agamemnon turns and screams, "Somebody get the surgeon! The one who got those magic herbs from the Centaurs!" Machaon, a hereditary healer, runs up and kneels by Menelaos. "It's just a scratch," he says, disgusted with Agamemnon's dramatics. He yanks the arrow out with one quick pull. "That's all; he'll be fine. I can apply some magic ointment to take away the pain ..."

Agamemnon is still ranting: "Yes, yes! The ointment! My poor brother!"

The first time in nine years of battle, Agamemnon's blood is really up. He's watched thousands of Greeks die, but now that his own kin is wounded, it's suddenly real to him. He stomps around, yelling: "Ready to attack! The Gods will be with us! They'll never back cheaters like those Trojans!"

He runs up to Ideomenus, lord of the Cretans, and yells, "Look at you all, waiting around! You're always the first in line when I pass the wine around at my feasts, Ideomenus, but look at you now, too scared to attack!"

Ideomenus is used to Agamemnon's nonsense. He just shrugs, tells Agamemnon, "Go motivate somebody else. We're ready to move when the army does. We can't do anything till then."

Agamemnon is already gone, running down the line looking for someone else to shriek at. He finds old Nestor getting his chariots in a line. Nestor's giving a speech, as usual, reminding the drivers to keep a straight line, "... Yes, that's how we won battles in the old days, boys, all in a good straight line!"

Agamemnon runs up and hugs the old bag of bones till Nestor's thin shoulders ache, and yells, "Oh Nestor, wise old advisor! If only your body matched your mind!"

Nestor wriggles out of the bear-hug and mumbles: "Oh, I may not be as young as I was, but ..."

Agamemnon has already run off to bother Odysseus and his men. They're ready; they've been ready for a half-hour, waiting for the call to advance. But Agamemnon just sees them standing still and launches into a rant: "Odysseus! I should've known! Cunning as usual, waiting for everyone else to go first, let someone else absorb the Trojans' spears! You're quick enough when I pass around the wine at a banquet, aren't you, but now ..." Odysseus has had enough of Agamemnon for one day, and shoves him off: "What are you talking about? We're ready to move with the army. Go bother someone else!"

Agamemnon slaps him on the back and yells, "Yes! That's the spirit! I'm just inspiring you, Odysseus! Motivating you!" And he runs further down the line, while Odysseus grinds his teeth.

Agamemnon runs to Diomedes, standing in his chariot, waiting for the order to charge. Agamemnon starts in again, "What are you waiting for? Oh, you're not your father's equal, Diomedes! He'd be charging the Trojans already!"

Diomedes' young cousin starts to object, but Diomedes pushes him back until Agamemnon has run off down the line. Then he tells his cousin, "Never mind; let him rant. At least he's acting like a king for once. Maybe it'll help."

Now the Greeks advance in total silence, no sound but the clang of their armor. They're one people, one language, the whole host moving like a huge beast. Athena inspires them; they breathe her spirit as they move, and she's silent as a chess champion looking at the board.

The Trojans are waiting, but not in silence. Their allies are barbarians from all over the East, and the orders are flying in a dozen weird languages. It sounds like an aviary on their side of the line, as all the different contingents chatter in their languages, one like crows, another like sparrows, a third like screaming hawks. The only god on their side now is Ares, the filthy spirit of slaughter, decay, and burned cities.

Ares has brought a friend with him: Fear, who turns the stomachs of the Trojans, wobbles their knees, squeezes sweat out on their foreheads. They don't want this fight.

The Greek horde runs at them in silence.

There's a moment when the two shield walls face each other, near enough to see each others' faces. They know each other by now. They've been facing off for nine long years. They stare at the enemy, seeing who they'll have to face. Then with a rush, the Greeks slam against the Trojan shields.

That's when the noise starts. The slap of ox-hide shields, the clang of bronze on bronze, and the screams that follow. You can tell the kind of wound from the different screams.

For now, the Trojans' big shields are holding. A few of their men are down, but as long as the shield wall holds, the Greeks can't do much damage. The Greeks need someone to charge, break that wall. Antilokas tries first. He runs at the Trojan shields and slams his spear right into the forehead of Ekepolas, who's holding his shield a little low. Antilokas' spear point goes through the thin metal of the helmet (metal is expensive, and bronze is heavy, so helmets are thin), then through skin, skull, brain. The world goes dark for Ekepolas.

Once you've killed a man, your next move is to grab the body, strip the metal off it.

Antilokas' friend Elfenar makes a grab for Ekepolas' corpse. But when you bend down to grab an enemy's body, your side is wide open to a spear-thrust. And sure enough, Agnar, a Trojan, sees his chance, shoves his spear right into Elfenar's side.

Now there are two bodies to fight over, and it's a swarm of spearheads, shields banging against each other, and screaming. Ajax, the biggest Greek on the field, sees an opening and slams his spear right through the right nipple of young Antemyon, a boy from the mountains. The spear-point slides easily through Antemyon's shirt, through his body, and out the other side.

Lukas, one of Odysseus' men, hoping for a quick profit, stoops to grab the Trojan's body—and gets a spear right in the balls. Lukas goes down screaming. It's dangerous, trying to grab these corpses. Leaves you wide open every time.

Odysseus groans, seeing his man go down in agony. It's been a long, miserable day for him. First he had to deal with Agamemnon's idiotic scheme, then be scolded as a slacker, and now he sees one of his vassals writhing in the dust. He's had enough.

Odysseus steps out from the shield wall, spear held loose, sidearm, looking for a target. The Trojans scatter, nobody wanting to be an easy target. Odysseus sees a worthy target at last: Demokoan, one of Priam's bastard sons. Not as good as killing a legitimate Trojan prince, but better than wasting his spear on a commoner. He throws.

Demokoan never knows what hit him. The spear punches through the thin metal of his helmet, right through his left temple, plows through his brains, with enough energy left to punch through the other side. It's one of the all-time great throws, and the Greeks roar with delight. They grab all the dead bodies, all that precious armor, as the Trojans back away, badly rattled.

Apollo has been watching, and he is not pleased. His pushy sister Athena is animating her Greeks, as usual. Apollo is not as human-friendly as his little sister; he doesn't like dealing with these creatures, but he can't let the Greeks win so easily. Grudgingly, he radiates. A brave warmth suffuses the shaky Trojan host. Suddenly, each one of them can see spaces between the Greeks' helmets and shields, gaps where a spear would go nicely. How sweet it would be to stick a spear point through that gap! It's suddenly obvious to every Trojan fighter that they can win, that these Greeks are not so big. Athena feels her brother's energy infusing the Trojans, and doubles her efforts among the Greeks. The two armies stare each other down for a few seconds, and then both charge at once. The deaths come so fast now that it's hard to keep track. Pyeraws, Imraws' son, a Trojan ally from the wild hills, picks up a stone and throws it at Dyorez. It hits the Greek in the ankle, and you can hear the bones crunch. Dyorez goes down screaming, and Pyeraws jumps on him like a big cat, jamming his spear into Dyorez's belly, slashing it around so the Greek's guts come rolling out onto the dust. The Trojans cheer. But Pyeraws is bent over, a perfect target. Thoyas spears him in the chest, holds the spear in place to keep Pyeraws upright, and calmly takes out his sword, opening up Pyeraws' belly so the guts pour out while Pyeraws is still upright. That was a great kill, and the Greeks cheer. But Thoyas can't get the barbarian's armor, because Pyeraws' comrades, their hair all in tufts the way barbarians wear it, cluster around their chief as the Greeks try to strip the body.

And now everyone is stabbing, screaming, bleeding, making deals with any god who'll listen, praying to kill someone without being killed.

5

GODS

ATHENA NEEDS A HERO to lead the Greeks. Akilles is sulking in his tent, so she picks Diomedes, the second-best man they've got. She lights him up like a torch, suffusing every cell in his body with her relentless will. His spear leaves a wake of light like a ship moving through the night sea, his shield flashes like a sun.

He kills anyone he chooses. First a rich Trojan in his fancy chariot goes down, with Diomedes' spear right through his chest. The Trojan's brother, who was driving for him, jumps down and runs off as the Greeks hoot at him.

Now Athena flies over to Ares, the only god who's helping the Trojans today, to talk him out of the fight. She despises Ares, god of massacre and rape, but he's so stupid she can make him do anything. So she puts on a worried look and says, "Ares, I've heard that Zeus, our father, is angry at us for meddling in human fights. I think we'd better get out of here."

Ares turns from watching the battle, staring at her for a long time with his huge, brutal face, trying to think. Finally he nods, afraid of his father's anger, and his strength leaves the Trojans. In an instant, every man in the

Trojan force feels as if the blood has drained out of his body. All they feel is fear. They turn to run, their chariots wheeling back toward the city in a cloud of dust.

That's a fatal move. As long as you're facing front with a shield up, your eye on the enemy, friends beside you, you're fairly safe. When you turn and run, you're a target. Fleeing men are easy kills.

Even Agamemnon gets a kill, his spear slamming into a chariot-driver's back. His brother Menelaos, healed by the magic herbs, lets fly and brings down another running Trojan. It's a good day for the Atreus-sons.

The most gratifying kill so far is Fereklas, the Trojan shipwright who made the boat that took Paris to Sparta—and took him home to Troy with Menelaos' rightful wife on his arm. All the Greeks want him dead.

Fereklas dies trying to run away. A Greek spear hits him right on the ass, bites deep into the bladder, and he falls on his knees, screaming like a rabbit, thrashing in the dust in a fountain of his own blood and piss.

Pedeaus, a high-born Trojan bastard, gets a spear in the back of the neck as he tries to run. The spear goes up through his palate, smashes out through his teeth. Pedeaus dies with the taste of bronze in his mouth.

Khipsenar, a priest of the river that flows past Troy, has his hand lopped off and dies staring at it, lying on the ground as his life squirts out in pulses from his wrist.

And still Diomedes sweeps the field, with Athena's actinic light around him. The Trojans can't match his spear; they need to use the bow, the favorite weapon of the East.

Pandarus, the archer who shot Menelaos, takes out his ibex-horn bow and aims for the center-of-mass in that glob of killing light that is Diomedes. Takes aim, holds for a second, allows for forward motion, lets go.

The arrow speeds toward Diomedes, hits him in the meat of the shoulder, sticks. Diomedes can hardly believe it; this is his day! He can't be hurt!

He calls his cousins to pull the arrow out, and the blood comes with it in a gush. He's furious, and screams to Athena: "Daughter of Zeus, let me find the coward Trojan who shot me from far away! Give me strength to slam my spear right through him!"

Athena is there, the flat, sizzling god-world smell. In a second, Diomedes is healed, and she holds him in her world for an unmeasurable moment, whispering to him, "You're healed, Diomedes, and I've given you something else: Today you'll be able to see the gods. Soon you'll see my little sister Afroditi. She'll come down to the battlefield to rescue her son Aeneas. Now listen carefully: You can't kill her, but you can hurt her. I want you to hurt her, Diomedes."

She flips worlds, and Diomedes is back on the dust plain—healed, furious, fuming with Athena's will. He sweeps the field again, a joy to watch. First the spear: a Trojan gets it right in the nipple, goes down. Then the sword, a beautiful sweep of his goddess-lit arm down into a Trojan's collarbone, so the whole haunch of shoulder comes off and dangles like a pork leg at a butcher's stall.

Next he chases down two Trojans, the two sons of a famous fortune-teller. People say these two inherited their father's talent and can read dreams, but their last vision was of Diomedes' flaring shield, the spearhead, and the dust. They didn't predict that one!

Diomedes runs head-on at a chariot with two of Priam's sons in it. One man against three horses? It's madness. He should end up dead under their hooves. But somehow he's through the horses, jumping onto the car, killing the two Trojan princes and throwing their bodies to his followers, roaring, "Strip their armor and I'll drive the horses back to our line!"

And all in less time than it takes to tell it.

The bow is still the Trojans' only chance against Diomedes. So Aeneas, who's half-Trojan and half god, finds Pandarus and yells, "Pandarus, what's wrong with you? You can't even hit Diomedes well enough to bring him down!"

Pandarus, a talkative boy, whines, "I swear, Aeneas, it's this bow. If only I had my chariot, my spear! But I didn't want to bring my horses with me, because these Trojans are city people, they don't know a thing about care and feeding, and I love my horses."

Aeneas yells, "Never mind all that! We need you to stop Diomedes!"

But Pandarus is on a talking jag. "So I thought I'd just bring my bow, leave the chariot and the horses at home, but this stupid bow of mine, I think there's something wrong with it. I can't shoot straight with it; first I wing Menelaos and he's already healed, which was bad enough but there's Diomedes, I hit him and he didn't even seem to feel it. I don't know what's wrong ..."

Aeneas tries to shout some sense into him: "Be quiet!"

But Pandarus can't stop: "I'd like to take this bow here and throw it on a nice hot fire! The thing just won't shoot straight! If I had my spear, now, and my horses ..." Aeneas shouts him down: "Fine! You can use a spear! We'll take my chariot! I'll drive! We need to kill Diomedes before he wipes out our whole army! In fact, I'm not sure it's him. He's so strong today, I wonder if it's some god pretending to be Diomedes."

Pandarus has a marksman's eye, and says, "No, it's Diomedes all right; I can tell. But he's got god-light flickering around him. I think you should drive, Aeneas, because they're your horses, and you know how horses are; they don't like to have a stranger holding the reins."

Aeneas cuts him off: "Fine, I'll drive; take the spear. I'm going to drive straight at Diomedes. This time throw hard, and hit him somewhere fatal!"

Diomedes' men see them coming and tell him, "That's Aeneas and Pandarus coming at us, lord. Aeneas is half-god and Pandarus is a good shot. Let's get out of here while we can!"

Diomedes laughs. "I don't run from anyone. I'm going to kill them and take their horses. Aeneas is half-god, true, but his mother is Afroditi. She's nothing to be afraid of. I've got Athena firing my blood today."

Aeneas has wheeled the chariot into throwing range. Pandarus leans out and throws hard into the middle of Diomedes' shield.

It's a perfect throw, but the spear spends all its momentum punching through the shield. There's just a little scratch on Diomedes' breastplate.

But Pandarus thinks he's killed Diomedes. He leans out of the chariot to gloat: "Ha! You survived my arrow, but not my spear! Got you right in the liver!"

Diomedes yells back, "The shield stopped it, fool! Now the dogs will lap your blood!"

Diomedes throws fast, straight at Pandarus' foolish face leaning out of the car. The spearhead crunches into Pandarus' cheekbone and smashes his teeth into white slivers scattered through the red chaos of what used to be his mouth.

As he dies, Pandarus sees the horses rear up, horrified at the smell of his blood. He always loved horses so much, and now they're deserting him as his life pours out from the ruin of his face.

Aeneas sees the boy tumble out of the chariot and stops the team, stakes them to the spot, jumps out to protect Pandarus' body. His duty is to hold off Diomedes' men, keep them from stealing the corpse.

Diomedes' followers come at a run, then stop short, seeing Aeneas ready to fight. They circle like hunting dogs, taunting Aeneas, pointing to his friend's mangled corpse.

None of them want to close with Aeneas. He's half-god, and he looks dangerous, crouching over Pandarus' bloody body like a big cat. They back off to wait for their chief.

Diomedes trots up and decides not to bother with a spear-fight. He picks up a boulder, so big that three of us weaklings today couldn't lift it. Diomedes picks it up with one hand and throws it as easily as a boy tossing a rock at a stray dog.

The boulder hits Aeneas with the speed of a meteor, right in the groin. He goes down in agony, writhing in the dust, too brave to cry out.

Diomedes' men rush in whooping, ready to drive their spears into Aeneas.

But Afroditi, seeing her son about to be killed, flies howling with grief down to the battlefield. She throws her god-body over her son, grasps him tight and begins lifting him from the dirt and pain of our world to the overworld. Diomedes looks on, astonished. He just smashed Aeneas' hip with a boulder the size of a bull's head, yet now Aeneas is wound up in some sort of glittering dust cloud, and the whole swirl is rising to the sky.

Diomedes gets a glimpse of Afroditi, there in the swirl. And he remembers his orders from Athena: She wants him to wound Afroditi. It's a dangerous move, raising a weapon against a god, but when you have to choose between offending Athena or her soft, sweet little sister ... well, that's an easy one: make sure you do what Athena wants. That's where Paris went wrong, pleasing Afroditi instead of Athena.

So Diomedes stares into the glittering cloud, waiting for a chance to give Afroditi a light wound. There! Her soft, white hand, flashing for a moment in the swirl—and Diomedes stabs up into the cloud with his spear.

He hears a huge, world-breaking scream. A scream like every girl who ever had to endure being sold to the wrong man, every daughter raped when her town was taken, every woman who died in childbirth, all screaming at once.

The cloud vanishes. Aeneas is falling back to earth now, easy prey for Diomedes.

Apollo, who's been watching the whole inept affair, grimaces in annoyance, but acts. He catches Aeneas and hides him in darkness, like a squid's ink-cloud in mid-air.

Afroditi flees upward. She's lost interest in her son, the war—everything except her throbbing, dripping wrist. Oh, the pain! Goddesses don't know much about pain, so this is a new horror for soft, sweet Afroditi, getting hurt like a mere mortal. Diomedes' spear-point grazed her wrist, and the cut is oozing golden ichor.

The gods don't bleed red blood like we do. Their veins run with the golden essence of the nectar they drink, so when they're wounded it's golden liquid that flows out, sweet and glittering like late-summer sunlight. And of all the gods, Afroditi's ichor is the sweetest, stronger than any wine. Just the scent of it, a few drops, will make a man dizzy.

Diomedes inhales that delicious taint of ichor, fading as Afroditi flies off. He's drunk with pride, and shouts out at Afroditi, "Now you know not to get mixed up in warfare! That's a man's job! Stick to love affairs!"

Afroditi flies to her half-brother Ares. She needs help now, even from a filthy beast like Ares: "Brother! Lend me your chariot! I'm hurt! I'm hurt by a mortal!"

Ares laughs at her: "Nyaaah! Stupid woman, let herself get cut by a little human!" After gloating a while, he tosses her the reins of his chariot, a fancy, unpleasant thing—all covered with gold but stinking of old blood.

Afroditi steps in, holding the reins with one hand and moaning, "Ow! Ow! My wrist!" as she flies up to the overworld.

Afroditi runs to her mother Dione and falls on her knees, crying, "Look, mother! Look what a mere human did to me!" Her mother wipes away the ichor, and tries to comfort her daughter as discreetly as she can; Hera and Athena are watching. They both hate Dione, a lesser wife. So Dione strokes her daughter's bleeding wrist; one touch of her mother's hand and Afroditi's fine, clear skin is perfect again, the pain gone. But she's still in shock; men never behave so rudely with her. She's still weeping, and her mother tries to comfort her, whispering, "Hush, child. We gods have to put up with worse than this. I've told you a thousand times, humans are nothing but trouble! Hush now, you'll forget all about it soon ..."

Athena announces as loudly and rudely as she can: "Oh, look over there, father Zeus! Do you see? The slut-goddess seems to have hurt her poor little hand somehow! Perhaps she was trying to make some Greek wives go with Trojan men, and cut her wrist on one of the women's brooch-pins as she tried to drag her off to Troy! The poor little slut is bleeding!"

Zeus chuckles. "Afroditi, you know better than to play war, a sweet girl like you! Leave all that to the tough ones, Ares and Athena. You stick to love affairs."

Down in the dust of Earth, Diomedes is still trying to finish off Aeneas. He knows Aeneas is somewhere in front of him, but Apollo is shielding him, blurring Diomedes' view. So Diomedes stabs blindly at the ink-cloud in front of him. Three times he tries to jab his spear through the murk, but the fourth time, Apollo, tired of this stupid game, says one huge word: "Stop." The command penetrates every cell of Diomedes' body, dousing his rage instantly. He backs away, not afraid but not foolish enough to oppose Apollo directly.

Apollo takes Aeneas, still writhing in pain, to Pergamus, the hill where the gods are watching the fight. Apollo calls his sister Artemis, who slinks over in a strange half-crouch and passes her hands over Aeneas, whispering alien words.

Apollo makes a dummy of Aeneas and throws it onto the field, for the Greeks and Trojans to fight over, then takes his seat next to Ares and lets his big, stupid brother feel his glare for a few moments. Ares understands; Apollo is angry that Ares, fooled by Athena, has stopped helping the Trojans. Ares, realizing he's been duped by that clever girl yet again, sighs and jumps several miles, down to the Trojan lines.

He knows what he has to do: Get Hektor, Troy's best fighter, back in the battle. So Ares stands behind Hektor, focusing the wrath of the Trojans on him. Every man in the Trojan horde suddenly wonders at the same moment, "Where's Hektor? He's supposed to be our best man, and he's hanging back!"

Sarpedon, the King of the Lycians, runs up to Hektor in a rage, shouting, "What are you doing, hanging back, Hektor? You're losing your people! You expect us Lycians to fight for you, when you won't fight for your own city? Aeneas is down, your best man, and you still let us foreigners do your fighting for you! Either you fight now, or you lose your allies, your town, everything!"

Hektor is shamed. He takes up his spear and runs toward the Greeks, Ares with him, a stink of blood, a smeared shadow. Where Ares passes, the Trojans find themselves thinking of slitting someone's throat, how easy it would be. Or how sweet it would be to jam a spear right through some Greek's liver, take his expensive armor and sell it for a nice profit. How easy, how pleasant, to kill and kill and kill.

The Trojans are transformed. They form up in a tight shield wall and charge like a storm wave. Ares darkens the air around them, so the Greeks can't aim at them. They come on like a bank of clouds from the sea, unstoppable. And Hektor is everywhere now, killing where he pleases. He's killing by pairs, not wasting time on one man at a time. He yanks both driver and spearman out of a chariot, killing them before they hit the ground. Team by team, chariot by chariot, Hektor sweeps forward, and the Greeks pull back.

Diomedes still has Athena's gift: He can see gods today. He sees Ares' bloody hands moving under Hektor's, slashing faster than mortals can make out.

Diomedes yells: "Back! Hektor's got a god behind him! Pull back, but keep your shields up, face front!"

The Greeks don't need to be told twice. Hektor's a dangerous fighter even without divine help. With a god behind him, he's death walking. So the Greeks, stumbling backward over the blood and corpses, draw close, shield to shield, and give Hektor plenty of room.

Aeneas, lying on Pergamus, stares up at Apollo's fierce sister Artemis as she heals his wounds. She is no friend of men, and works on Aeneas with a lynx's snarl on her face. But as she hiss-whispers over him, Aeneas feels his smashed hip-bone fusing as easily as a pot on the wheel. The pain—was there pain? He feels no pain at all, no injury. The lynx-face stares coldly at him, making sure he's fully healed, then hisses something to her brother and vanishes.

Apollo strides over to Aeneas, gestures—and Aeneas is standing up. Apollo reaches out, takes Aeneas around the waist in one hand and throws him all the way to the battlefield. Aeneas lands softly on his feet, unhurt, in the middle of the Trojan shield wall as it rolls over the Greeks. His comrades can't believe Aeneas is with them again; they all thought he was dead. They cheer even louder to have him back with them, as they stab the fleeing Greeks.

Aeneas celebrates his return by killing two Greeks, twins, vassals of Agamemnon's family, the Atreus-sons. These twins were born together and now they die together at the point of Aeneas' spear.

This enrages Tlepolemus, one of Herakles' sons. Tlepolemus is the tallest of the Greeks, a fine man, not afraid of anyone. He calls out Sarpedon, who's leading the Lycian wing of the Trojan force.

Everyone stops to watch. This will be good. Both men have god-blood, Zeus-blood. Herakles was Zeus' son, so Tlepolemus is Zeus' grandson. Sarpedon is Zeus' son. So it's two of Zeus' bastards facing off.

It's an easy bet, if you know the bloodlines. Always bet on a god's son against a mere grandson.

Tlepolemus starts by loud-talking Sarpedon, never a good idea: "Sarpedon, what are you doing here? You're no Trojan! Why are you fighting for these people? You Lycians are better at drinking wine and playing with concubines than fighting. I don't think you're Zeus' son at all. You don't look it, you fop! My father was Herakles; just look at me! I bred true, not like you!"

Sarpedon smiles, says quietly: "Do you see this spear, Tlepolemus? You'll be seeing it close up very soon. Say hello to Hades when he welcomes you to his kingdom."

They throw at the same time. Sarpedon's throw is perfect, right through the Adam's apple. Tlepolemus falls dead.

But Tlepolemus' throw wasn't bad either, though he died too soon to see the result. His spear got Sarpedon on the meat of the thigh, and scraped along the femur. Sarpedon screams; the pain is unbelievable, bronze ripping along bone. His followers are stunned; they didn't think Zeus' son could be hurt. They finally pick Sarpedon up and start carrying him out of the fight, too bewildered to pull the spear out of his thigh first. So Sarpedon, already in agony, feels the spear scrape every rock along the path.

Odysseus saw Tlepolemus die, and like all short men, his reverence for the very tall is scandalized. He wants to avenge the giant Tlepolemus, so he charges, his men behind him, down on the rabble of Lycian fighters left behind now that Sarpedon, their champion, has been carried out of the battle. Odysseus kills four, six, eight of the Lycians. They're as easy to kill as lambs, now that Sarpedon's gone.

Hektor hears that Sarpedon's been hurt and runs over to him. They've laid him on the ground, spear still in his thigh. Sarpedon lifts himself up on an elbow and groans, "Hektor, please, don't let me die in Greek hands. I know I won't live through this war, the diviners told me that before I left home, but at least let me die inside the walls, not out here in the dust."

Hektor nods and runs at the Greeks, killing at will.

It's been the longest, bloodiest day anyone can remember. By now, both sides are exhausted, weary of killing. The two shield walls face each other, panting, uncertain. If they had an excuse, they'd all go home.

Hera is watching, and this emergent pacifism disgusts her. She fumes, "Look at them, standing around like reeds in a marsh! Useless men! Useless mortals! Athena, you and I need to get down there and take Ares out of the fight!"

Athena nods, and because she wishes it, her chariot is instantly present, ready. She takes the spear, and Hera grabs the reins. They make one quick stop to get Zeus' permission before descending to the dust plain.

Hera pulls up at Zeus' throne, scolding, "Aren't you ashamed, letting Ares, that filthy war pimp, kill so many fine Greeks?"

Zeus shrugs. It's war, it's a messy business. What does she expect?

Hera gets to the point: "Will you let my daughter—our daughter—go down there and punish Ares, or not?"

Zeus has another gulp of nectar and nods. It's not worth getting in a fight with these two, not to protect a swine like Ares. He answers, "Yes, let Athena take care of him; she's been beating him up since they were kids!"

Hera flicks the reins and the chariot arcs down to earth, thundering across the wide sky. As they enter the thick, warm air of the human world, the chariot falls away unneeded; the two goddesses fall toward Troy on their own.

Hera floats over the Greeks, and her voice goes right to the pit of every man's stomach: "Greeks, can't you fight on your own? Or do you only act brave when you have Akilles in front of you? Look at you, backed against the beach, up against the bows of the ships!" The Greeks, shamed by this giant woman's voice, sigh and face the Trojans, ready to level their spears again.

Athena falls toward Diomedes. She pretends to be a mere human, but she doesn't pretend very hard. She gave Diomedes the gift of seeing gods through any disguise; he knows who she is.

He's tired. Athena, playing the old retainer, grumbles: "It's a shame, you know ... I knew your father, Diomedes. Yes, he was only a short fellow, but he could fight. He would never slack off like this. Ah well, it's a shame ..."

Diomedes is angry. She's not satisfied, after all the killing he's done for Athena today? He shouts: "Goddess, I've done exactly what you told me to do. You said, 'Wound Afroditi' and I jabbed her, got her in the wrist. But you also told me, 'If the other gods appear, back off.' Well, Ares is here; you know that yourself! So I ordered my men to withdraw. Tell me what I did wrong!"

Athena laughs hoarsely and shows her true self, changing from a small human into a huge, lank shape, all hand and arm. She picks up Diomedes' chariot driver with one hand and tosses him far away, roaring in a jolly voice, "I'll drive!"

The same huge hand lifts Diomedes into the chariot. The axles creak with the weight of goddess and hero.

The chariot is already moving, faster than horses can run, as she roars happily, "Diomedes, I only spoke harshly just now to put heart in you. You don't need to back away from Ares, that blood-licking jackal! All of us gods despise him. I want you to hurt him today, worse than you hurt my sister. I'm going to give you a perfect shot at him."

They're driving straight at Ares, who's hunched over a dead Greek warrior doing what he does best: robbing the dead, tossing the body for valuables. Diomedes can see Ares' true face. It's worse than he imagined—the rotting skull of a jackal, covered with a halo of flies.

Ares sees Diomedes coming at him and grins. Athena has hidden herself from Ares' sight, so the big fool sees only a suicidal human taking him on in single combat. This will be a fine kill! Leaping up like a carrion fly, Ares falls on Diomedes' chariot, his blood-smeared spear already in flight, right at Diomedes' heart.

It's a perfect throw. But Athena, with a flick of her mind, deflects Ares' spear, sails it high over Diomedes.

Now it's Diomedes' turn. It's a decent throw, but without Athena's help, it would never have hurt Ares. He is a big god, and it takes a lot to hurt him. But Athena's huge arm grabs Diomedes' spear out of the air and sends it burrowing through Ares' armor, right into the groin. That's her little joke, the groin. She digs the spear-point in, squirms it around a little to increase the pain, the mangle-factor, and pulls it out, puts it back in Diomedes' hand.

Ares falls, clasping his groin like a shy slave on the auction block. And then the pain hits him. Gods are not used to pain; they don't like it. Ares screams.

The scream is so terrible that every man on the field freezes. Many of them go down, curled up with their hands over their ears, trying to keep the sound out. The others, the brave ones who stood there and took it, will never be quite the same. The sound is something they'll remember till they're old, and it will come back to them at the wrongest times, watching their favorite sons grow up, lying in bed after a warm day. They'll lie there, hearing Ares' scream again, and their wives will look at them and not even want to ask what they're remembering. If they try to explain, they'll say something like, "Remember that stray dog that got its belly ripped by our hounds? Or that time that bald slave caught a rat, and thought it'd be funny if he squeezed it to death in front of us? Remember? That rat, the sound it made—I had to cuff the slave to get him to finish it off, stop the noise. That kind of sound, or maybe the way a rabbit screams, or one time, when we took a village, there was a child ..." and he'll stop, not wanting to tell that story, and she won't ask any more questions.

There's nothing to pity in Ares' scream, because he's the foulest god of all. But his pain is huge, it's the whole world, and somehow it's just so horrible that eventually, as the men listen to its echoes, they start laughing uncontrollably, laughing too hard to fight.

Then they go silent again, because Ares' scream has turned into a black swarming glob, huge as a rain-cloud, that writhes around the god in his pain—and then the black glob roars up to the overworld, and there's silence on the battlefield again.

Ares has gone to demand justice from Zeus. Which Zeus, and the rest of the gods, find very amusing. Ares? Wanting justice? Ares, who presided over every massacre and rape since the beginning of the world, and enjoyed every second of them?

And now he wants justice—justice! After getting stabbed ... by a woman ... his own sister! In the groin! It's a great moment for the whole family—they just can't stop laughing. As Ares approaches, squelching with his hands over his wet, bleeding groin, Zeus draws out the pleasure, pretending not to know what happened: "Well, Ares, what seems to be the problem? And please, don't drip on my fine marble floor."

Ares is furious: "The 'problem' is your crazy daughter, Athena! She's out of her mind! She's got these Greeks stabbing gods now! When did we start allowing that? Little humans pricking us like bulls at a sacrifice? That gender-bent bitch has gone crazy! First she gets poor Afroditi cut on the wrist, and then—I can't believe it—she latches onto her chosen human Diomedes again, swoops him and his chariot up in her slipstream, sends the man roaring straight at me—and cheating, too, because I would've hit him right in the heart with my spear but she went and deflected it—and then she takes his spear, which would never have hit me, grabs it, right in the air, and—well, just look what she did! Look at it!"

And Ares, not even noticing the giggles of the other gods, takes away his hands to show the bloody groin, the deep, twisting wound down where the belly meets the baby-maker. His ichor is dripping onto the glowing floor of Zeus' court, not clear gold like other gods', but running dark, with a bad smell.

Zeus is disgusted. "So you come whining to me? You, throat-slitter? Back-stabber? Baby-killer? I wish you'd never been born. You've got your mother's mean heart, but not her courage. You can't even take the pain you love to dish out. If you were anybody else, you'd be lying under this floor like the Titans, but what can I do? You're my son. So ..."

Zeus claps his hands. "Healer, fix this fool up. I'm sick of listening to him."

The healer bows to Zeus, applies a magic salve, and Ares' wound vanishes along with the pain. Ares sneaks off, just smart enough to get out of his father's sight before the old man loses patience.

6

FAMILY

NOW THAT ARES IS GONE, the Trojans' courage drains away. The Greeks, seeing them waver, attack. Ajax smashes through the Trojan line like a boulder. His spear goes right through the helmet of the biggest Thracian warrior. Darkness was that Thracian's last thought.

With their shield wall broken, the Trojans scatter. Their chariots are wheeling, trying to get away from the Greek spears. It's easy to kill them now. Diomedes jumps up on a chariot driven by a rich Trojan, a man famous for his generous feasts. His hospitality doesn't do him any good today; none of his guests show up to help him, and Diomedes spits him on his spear, throws him out of the chariot, then kills his driver and whips the chariot back to his own men, a fine prize.

All the richest, proudest men in Troy are fleeing now, stirring up so much dust they can't see where they're going. Adrestus, a high-born Trojan, drives over a tussock, breaking his chariot's axle. He goes flying, lands in the dirt, and looks up to see Menelaos standing over him. All Adrestus' pride is gone. He grabs Menelaos' knees with both hands, begging, "Please, take me alive, Menelaos! My father is rich, he'll pay any ransom you ask!"

Menelaos hesitates, but his brother Agamemnon comes running over, screaming, "Kill him! What, are you soft on these Trojans? You, of all people? Remember your wife?"

Menelaos scowls. He can't look weak, not in front of his big brother, but it's very bad luck to kill someone who's put their hands on your knees. He comes up with a neat solution: lifting Adrestus to his feet, he shoves the Trojan toward Agamemnon, who drives his spear into Adrestus' side, then plants his foot on the body to yank it out.

Nestor is riding down the battle-line, shouting to the Greeks, "Don't waste time stripping the dead! Kill them all while they're running!"

The Trojans are routed. This might be the end.

Then Helnas appears beside Hektor and Aeneas. Of all Priam's sons, Helnas is the strangest. He and his twin sister Kassandra can see things before they happen. People are afraid of those two.

Helnas tells Hektor, "The city will fall today unless you rally the men. Diomedes has them all panicked, he's worse than Akilles ever was. You two must stop the rout. Grab every man you see and form them up right here. And when we've got some kind of line restored, Hektor, you go into Troy and get our mother the queen to make a sacrifice, a big one: twelve heifers, stall-bred, without a spot on their hides. And her best dress too. All to Athena, to beg her to let us live a little longer."

Hektor and Aeneas have grown up with little Helnas; they take it for granted that his advice is good. They follow his orders, running up and down the Trojan line, yanking terrified men into place. The Trojans, cuffed and shoved into place, begin to feel their courage coming back. Hektor shouts down the line, "Hold steady now, don't take one step back! I'm going to order a great sacrifice; the gods will help us soon! Just hold on until I come back!"

He heads for the city, with the rim of his shield banging against his knees and neck.

To buy some time for Hektor to get the gods on Troy's side, Glaukos steps out between the two armies and challenges Diomedes to single combat. It's suicide to go up against Diomedes, everyone knows that. Glaukos is condemning himself to certain death.

Diomedes can't believe it. He doesn't even recognize this fellow, and that worries him. What if this is a god, pretending to be a man? He yells to Glaukos, "Whose son are you, sir? I don't know you, and you must be either a god or a madman to fight me. Do you know how many fathers will be burying sons who came against me today? If you're from the overworld, I won't fight you, but if you eat bread like the rest of us, you die."

Glaukos answers, "Diomedes, why ask me my family tree? I am mortal, like you, and we'll both die someday. But perhaps you've heard of my grandfather. His name was Bellerofon, and he was from your part of the world before his exile to Lycia, where I grew up."

Diomedes whoops happily, lifts up his spear and plants it hard, point-first, in the ground. "Bellerofon's grandson? I won't fight you, my friend! My grandfather Oeneus was Bellerofon's friend. He used to tell me stories about your granddad! He said one time they drank and feasted together for twenty days straight! And on the twenty-first day, they were still strong enough to say goodbye to each other standing up! My grandpa gave your granddad a fine belt; your grandpa gave my grandpa a fine golden cup. A beautiful thing! I still have it at home. Listen, Glaukos, let's be friends and to Hell with the war! If you come to Greece, I'll be your host, and if I go to Lycia, I'll be your guest. There are plenty of Trojans I can kill without hurting you, and if you want targets, just look at all these Greeks waiting for your spear! In fact, let's trade armor! I'll wear yours, you wear mine!"

Glaukos is more than happy to make the trade, because he expected to die today. He's getting a new life as well as new armor. And Diomedes, who isn't as sentimental as he seems, is also happy with the deal, because Glaukos' armor is pure gold, worth a hundred cattle—those Lycians are filthy rich!—while Diomedes' is ordinary bronze, worth maybe nine cattle at most. You can't beat a Greek in a trade!

Hektor enters the town, goes to his father's palace. A vast maze, that palace. Fifty rooms for Priam's sons, and another fifty for his daughters. The old man might have had a thousand great-grandchildren, but everyone knows that Troy will fall soon, and then he'll have none. Hektor's heart breaks, looking at the rooms, each one carved lovingly out of hard stone. He runs his fingertips along the cool, familiar stone, thinking, "All this is gone, all of it will burn, peasants will steal the stones for their sheep-fences, and every one of my brave, cheerful brothers will die, all my beautiful sisters will be slaves ..." Hekuba, his old mother, comes out, worried as usual: "Son, why have you left the battle? Do you want some wine?"

He shakes his head. It's terrible to see his mother now, when he's been thinking of what will happen to the family. "No, mother, don't offer me wine while my hands are covered in other men's blood and filth. It would only anger the gods, and they hate us Trojans already. Mother, please get all the women together and send slaves to the butchers to order twelve pure heifers. We have to make a sacrifice to Athena."

She's puzzled: "But Athena loves the Greeks!"

He nods. He knows it better than anyone. He says, "She's too powerful for us; our gods are no help. Apollo won't lift his little finger for us. At least Athena cares about her people. And she's a woman, they say; maybe she'll take pity on you women and children. So go, get the butchers to bring those cattle, and place your finest robe on Athena's altar. We have to offer her all we have, just to let us live a little longer."

She stares at him, befuddled. Can it be this bad?

He shrugs, "It's all we can do. We don't have much time left. Forgive me, mother, but I have to go see Paris now."

Hekuba grimaces at that name. Hektor nods, sharing her bitterness. "Yes, he's the one who's doomed us all. I wish he'd died as a baby! I hope he dies out there today! If I could just see his conceited face sinking into the underworld, I could go to my grave happy!"

And he runs to find Paris.

Hekuba trudges to the wardrobe, takes out her finest dress, her family's pride, carries it to Athena's shrine and lays it on the altar, bribing the goddess to show mercy to Priam's family.

But Athena looks down and sneers. None of the Trojans will be spared, from the infants to the old.

Hektor trots back, taking his leave of his father's house, touching the stones of the wall, treasuring every block. Ten generations worked to finish that stone. All gone, all gone.

Hektor can hardly bear the sight of Paris. It doesn't help that Paris is lolling on the couch with Helen. Paris grins when Hektor steps into the room, covered in sweat and blood, but Helen at least has the decency to blush. She's always liked Hektor—likes him better than Paris, really. She sees how tired he is, smeared with every kind of filth from the battle, and says, "Hektor, dear brother, take a cup of wine, rest a while before you go back to battle."

Hektor shakes his head: "No wine, Helen. You, little brother, how can you sit there while better men are dying for you?"

Paris drawls, "I was just going to put on my armor. Just saying goodbye to my wife—wasn't I, my dear?"

Helen won't answer, or even look at him.

Paris chuckles, "Yes, just saying my goodbyes, but I'll go now."

He jumps up to get his armor. Helen is alone with Hektor. She begins, "Brother Hektor, I wish I'd been abandoned at birth rather than live to be the death of Troy. Paris is worthless, and I'm no better. But have pity on us; take a cup of wine, rest here a moment, don't despise me."

Hektor shakes his head. He likes Helen, but it hurts him to be with the two of them. So many people, everyone he ever loved, will die for these two. He tells her, "I won't, my sister. I can't. I have to see my own wife and my little son. This might be the last time."

There's a long, awkward silence. Paris is rummaging in the storeroom, taking his time. Finally, Hektor stands up to leave, telling Helen, "When your husband is finished primping and preening, tell him to follow me to the battlefield."

Hektor can hardly bear his last errand in the city: seeing his wife Andromakhe, finest of women, and their perfect son, who will never live to be a man.

He stands outside the women's quarters and calls inside. The housekeeper peeks out, veiling her face, and tells him, "Lord, your wife isn't here. She's up on the city wall; the nurse is with her, carrying your son. We heard the Trojans are routed, running back toward the town, so she's gone to try to catch sight of you."

He finds Andromakhe standing on the wall, looking out toward the far dust cloud where men are killing each other. She's been crying. When she sees Hektor—still alive, still alive!—she runs up and takes his hand in sight of everyone. It's bold behavior for a good wife, but these are desperate times.

She begs him, "Thank all the gods you're alive! Please, husband, fight from the wall today! Don't go back onto the plain! You're all I have; the Greeks slaughtered my whole family. Now you're father, mother, brother, and husband to me. Fight from the wall! Put your men there by the fig tree where the wall's weakest. Fight here, where we can be with you to the end!"

Hektor mutters, his eyes tearing up, "Wife, don't you think I want to stay with you? Soon enough you'll be sold into slavery, to spend the rest of a hard life carrying water and firewood for a mistress who beats you, or emptying the slop jars of a Greek master who'll rape you when he's drunk. But when I'm dead, I don't want anyone saying your husband was a coward. My job now is to die well, so at least they'll say, 'Her husband was the bravest of the Trojans.' And you'll weep for me, not be shamed by the mention of my name."

Hektor sighs, "Now let me see my son."

He tries to take his son from the nurse, but the little boy, frightened by the big horsehair crest of Hektor's helmet, starts screaming. Hektor and Andromakhe laugh together for a moment. Then Hektor, taking off his helmet, cuddles the little boy, holds him up to the sky, and calls, "Zeus, let him rule Troy so wisely that they'll say, 'The son was greater than the father!' That's the last thing I'll ever ask of you, Godfather."

But that's another prayer that will never be answered.

Andromakhe is weeping even while she laughs over the little boy's fears. Hektor can't bear it any longer. "Wife, I have to go. I promise, I'll live as long as I can. And when it's time to die, I'll die as bravely as I can. You're the one who'll have the hardest time, living on as a slave, but that's what the gods have decided; I can't do anything about it."

He picks up his helmet and heads for the city gate, while Andromakhe stumbles back to the women's quarters, looking back again and again for one last sight of him.

Paris has finally dressed for battle to his own satisfaction, and he catches up to his big brother outside the gates, running up behind Hektor and slapping him on the back: "I guess I kept you waiting, big brother! Well, a man can't go into battle looking like a peasant, can he?" Paris is laughing as if they were going to a feast.

Hektor stares him down. "Little brother, what can I say that would get through that childish head of yours? You fight well enough when you can be bothered, but you just don't see—or you don't care, I'm not sure which."

He stares at Paris' handsome, empty face and says: "Well, that's how you are. I can't change you, and it's too late anyway. All we can do now is kill some of these Greeks and hope the gods change their minds."

7

DUEL

PARIS AND HEKTOR run to battle together, and without breaking stride, slam into the charging Greeks. In an instant, the two brothers have each killed a man, both big warriors. The Trojans cheer, take heart, and turn to attack.

Athena won't let the Trojans rally. She comes down to help the Greeks yet again. But this time, her brother Apollo, watching from the highest rooftop in Troy, has had enough. He flies to meet her under an oak tree. The two of them talk there, invisible.

Apollo says, "Little half-sister, are you here to cheat again, to tilt every spear and arrow away from your Greeks? I know you and your mother won't be happy until my city is burnt, but why not let the humans fight with their own strength for once?"

Athena shrugs: "What do you suggest?"

Apollo: "Let the two armies sit and watch while Hektor fights any Greek who'll risk single combat."

Athena agrees, and they convey their decision through the mind of the strange Trojan prince, Helnas. He stumbles up to Hektor in a trance and says in a flat alien voice, "Hektor, Prince of Troy, the gods say you should challenge the Greeks to single combat. They also say that you can be sure today is not your death-day."

Hektor is overjoyed. All he's ever wanted was to take the whole weight of Troy on his shoulders. He would gladly face any Greek, even Akilles, to give the city a few more days.

Apollo and Athena, looking forward to the entertainment, turn themselves into vultures. The two carrion birds perch side by side on a high branch, betting with each other on the fight.

Hektor walks out between the two armies, shouts, "Greeks, listen to me! Today, let me fight for all the Trojans. I see all your princes facing me; I'll fight any man of them, right now."

The Greeks are silent. No one wants to fight Hektor. He has the relaxed look of a man who's been told by the gods that this isn't his death-day.

Hektor goes on, "Greeks, if your man kills me, then he can have my armor, but he should give my corpse back to the Trojans so my mother can wash it and wrap it in linen. And if I kill your champion, I promise I'll give his body back so you can bury him under a mound by the shore, and a thousand years from now, sailors going by will say, 'That's where a great hero was killed in single combat by Hektor,' and my name won't be forgotten!"

None of the Greeks like the sound of this. Nobody wants to end up as a monument to Hektor's glory, or have his armor hung as a trophy in a Trojan temple. Even Diomedes, who's been having such a glorious day, keeps his head down.

It's a long silence, long enough to shame the Greeks. At last Menelaos is so angry he jumps up and curses them all, "You pretend warriors! You're just girls in armor! The whole world will laugh at us Greeks if nobody meets Hektor! All right then, I'll fight him myself!" and he stands up, muttering, "It's all in the gods' hands anyway."

Sometimes it seems like Menelaos wants to die. If he goes out there, Hektor will kill him.

Agamemnon grabs his brother, pulls him back down, whispering, "Menelaos, are you crazy? Even Akilles is wary of Hektor! Sit down and be still! Somebody else will volunteer, and I'm telling you, whoever it is, he won't come back alive!"

Menelaos always does what his big brother says. He sits back down. There's another long, embarrassed silence. At last Nestor, stands up, leaning on his stick, and says disgustedly, "The Greeks aren't what they used to be! When I was a young man ..." Nestor launches into one of his long, boastful stories of a kill he made in his youth, winding up with "... and he was so huge, this warrior I killed, that his corpse took up an acre of land! More than an acre! Ah, but that was me, and now not one of you has the guts to face this Trojan!"

The speech has its intended effect. A dozen Greeks stand up, volunteering to fight Hektor. Anything's better than being scolded by that old man any longer.

Nestor grins through his few teeth, amazed at how easy it is to make young men do silly things. "At last, some brave men! Now, only one can fight Hektor, so all of you take a rock, scratch your mark on it, put it in my helmet here—yes, that's good, not much use for anything else at my age, my helmet ... ah, good!"

The whole army is watching, silently hoping Agamemnon's name will fall out so Hektor can kill him.

Old Nestor shakes the helmet, and a rock falls out. He picks it up, reads the mark: "Ajax! Ajax will be our champion!"

Ajax stands up shyly, huge and dim as ever. According to protocol, he has to make a speech before going out to fight. He does his clumsy best: "My friends, don't worry, I'll kill Hektor, I'm not worried. I'm from Salamis, you know; we can take care of ourselves ..."

A weak cheer from the Salamis contingent, then a quiet time as Ajax checks his weapons and armor. Satisfied, he jams the helmet on his bull-sized head and runs out to face Hektor.

Ajax feels that a little trash-talk is required: "So, Hektor, did you think we'd back down? Do you think Akilles is the only warrior we've got? There are dozens of us who wanted to face you; I just got lucky! So get ready to die, Trojan!"

Hektor is too sad today to bother with talk. He says quietly, "Noble Ajax, we know each other. You don't need to talk to me like that. You know I can fight. I learned a long time ago how to use the shield, work the angles, and you know that's the most important part of fighting. But let's not argue about technique. I must kill you if I can, but I'll do it face to face, with honor."

Hektor throws. The spear hits Ajax's shield and rams through the thin coating of bronze, rips past six layers of folded rawhide. And stops, because Ajax's shield has an extra layer of hide, a seventh layer. Only a giant like him could carry such a heavy shield in a long, hot day of battle. So Ajax hasn't even been touched. And it's his turn to throw. He flips up that heavy spear, ten cubits long, like it was a broom-handle, flings it too fast to follow. It goes right through Hektor's shield without slowing down, slits his linen shirt, and would have opened his belly if he'd stood still. But Hektor leans away from the spear-point, like a bull dancer dodging the horn, and the spearhead goes through his shirt without touching the skin.

Now both men have a spear sticking through their shields. They stare at each other for a second, then rip the spears out of their shields, take them up and charge each other. Hektor, using Ajax's spear, slams it hard into the very center of Ajax's shield, but nothing is going to defeat that shield, with its extra layer of rawhide. The spearhead goes in at an angle, bends.

Ajax stabs at the same moment, and his thrust goes right through Hektor's weaker shield. Hektor gets slashed on the neck, and the gash is bleeding fast down his shirt. But he won't quit. Hektor backs off, scrabbles around for a weapon, and grabs a big rock. He throws it, catches Ajax's shield dead center, right in the bronze boss. You can hear the clang for miles.

But Ajax's shield holds, and he's unhurt. He looks around for a rock of his own, finds a young boulder and lifts it easily, though it would take three of today's weaklings just to pry it from the ground. Ajax grins, lifts the boulder, and tosses it like a little asteroid. The boulder smashes Hektor's shield and slams into his body. He ends up dazed, on his back, with that huge rock on top of him.

Apollo hates to get involved, but Hektor will die unless he does something. So he gives Hektor some of his strength, slaps him back to his senses, and stands him up again, ready to fight on.

Now the two of them are facing off once more, with swords out this time. Suddenly two referees step out, one from the Greek army and another from the Trojan side, both carrying their official staffs. The two referees announce, "Stop! Hektor, Ajax, you've both fought well, but night is falling, and darkness is something we must all obey."

Ajax grumbles, "Make Hektor say it's over for the day." He's not sharp, he's been fooled before.

Hektor: "Ajax, I've seen your strength, your power with a spear. You're the finest Greek I've faced. But darkness is here, and darkness is something we must all obey. So go to the Greek camp, by the ships, and show your followers you're unhurt. And I'll go to feast in Troy, where all my kin will pray to the gods for me. And now, let's give each other a gift, so people can say, 'They fought like lions, but ended the day as friends.'"

This speech is over Ajax's head. But then he hears the cheers, from Greeks as well as Trojans, and realizes that whatever Hektor said, everybody likes it.

The truth is that no one, not even the Greeks, wanted to see Hektor die today. Hektor's a good man, even if he is the enemy. But people like Ajax too; they didn't want him killed either. So everyone's glad the referees stopped this fight. Now, everybody on the field feels noble. They can go back to the campfires and talk about the day's big fight till they pass out.

They all cheer wildly as the two champions exchange gifts. Hektor gives Ajax a sword inlaid with silver, with scabbard. The Trojan herald parades it in front of both armies, so everyone can get a good look. There are appreciative grunts and nods from Greeks as well as the Trojans. Then Ajax has one of his slaves run and get a girdle from his tent, one of those purple things the Levantines make from some creature that lives in the ocean. The Greek referee carries that around and the Trojans show their appreciation. For the first time in years, men in armor from both armies stare at the other side with something besides fear and hate.

It has to end. Darkness is deepening now, and the two armies withdraw.

Ajax is a hero today, and everyone cheers when he comes into camp, unhurt. Agamemnon is feeling generous; after all, didn't Ajax save Menelaos, the only man in the army Agamemnon really cares about? So Agamemnon orders his slaves to butcher a fine ox, five years old, never pulled a plow in its life, meat soft as butter. The slaves hack its head off, take an ax and split the body, and roast all the pieces over a fire.

Agamemnon gives Ajax the finest cut, a long strip of tenderloin, not a bone, nothing but sweet fat and soft red meat.

Everyone gets a good gobbet of meat, even the ordinary spearmen. All the meat a man can force down his throat! There's wine, too, mixed more strongly than usual. Soon every man is feeling fine. The slaves, seeing them half-dazed with wine, sneak in and grab the scraps, to eat them behind the tents before anyone sees.

And now it's time for old Nestor to make another of his speeches. No one minds, not now. Let the old duffer talk.

Nestor turns out to have a suggestion, a good one. "My lords, Agamemnon, Menelaos, and all you chieftains, let's make tomorrow a day for burning our dead, so we can send clean, polished bones home to their families. And then we'll make a big mound, out near the camp perimeter, a bed for those bones until we take them home."

The leaders nod. Nothing wrong with that idea.

Nestor goes on, "And when we have the slaves dig out the dirt for this mound, let's keep them at it! I mean to say, let's build a wall around the camp, and a moat outside it, and fill the moat with spikes, so the Trojans can't break through and burn our ships."

The Greeks all cheer. A day off, a chance to sleep off this wine, and a wall. Everything seems wonderful.

Not for the Trojans, though. No feasts inside those walls. The Trojan chiefs gather by Priam's big stone house, glum and silent. The end is close, and the thought of dying for a selfish fool like Paris is hard to bear. Antenor, an old man but no fool, blurts out what they're all thinking: "We have to return Helen and the goods she brought with her to the Greeks. The gods will never help us while we keep a wife from her lawful master."

The whole room reverberates with cheers. They've all been thinking this for nine long years. They all glare at Paris, finally letting their resentment show.

Paris gets hot, stands up, growls: "Antenor, I don't like these words, and I'm sure you could find more pleasant ones if you tried. If you were serious, then you must be crazy. I say now, and I want every one of you to hear it, that I won't give up Helen, now or ever. But I will return the goods she brought to the Greeks. In fact, I'll add wealth from my own stock to buy her properly."

A long silence, until Priam ends the argument by saying, "Trojans, allies, get your dinners now, and mount a strong watch on the walls tonight. Tomorrow we'll send my herald, Idaeus, to the Greeks, to tell them my son's offer. And tell them also, Idaeus, that we want a day's rest from fighting, so we can burn our dead, who are piling up in the town. After that, we can go back to fighting to the end."

It's a cold dinner for the Trojan fighters, the nobodies. They eat handfuls of old grain by the walls, each contingent muttering in their own weird languages but all saying the same dark things about Paris and his father, Priam, who spoiled the boy.

At dawn Idaeus goes to the Greek camp with a herald's staff. He finds Agamemnon and the rest talking by the ships, and sits with them until they give him the sign to speak. Then he stands and says, "Lords of the Greeks, I've come with an offer from Priam, King of Troy. Paris, who took Helen from your king's brother—if only Paris had died before he ever reached your country!—now says he'll give back all the robes, the jewels, the gold that Helen took away with her, and he'll add his own wealth to it, so that he can purchase her properly, and save our town."

The Greeks don't react. Idaeus goes on, "But ... he says he won't return the woman to Menelaos, her proper husband."

Idaeus lowers his voice and hisses, "The truth is, Paris is in love, like a fool! Like a boy! So he won't give up the woman for anything. Believe me, my lords, we all begged him to! Everyone in Troy begged him to. He's possessed! Afroditi claimed him when he picked her over Athena and her mother. Love is all he thinks about, even if it kills us all!"

Another silence. Idaeus goes on, "And also, Priam asks me to ask you to give us a day of rest today, to let us bury our dead. Then we can go back to fighting, until one side or the other is destroyed."

Still Agamemnon says nothing and the rest of the Greeks wait, watching for his reaction. Then Diomedes jumps up and shouts, "I say no deal! No mercy! A fool can see that Troy is doomed! That's why they're offering this deal, because they know it themselves!"

Agamemnon stands, says, "There, Idaeus; that's the Greeks' answer. There'll be no deal while Troy still stands. But as for burying the dead, you can have your day off from battle, because no one should grudge the dead their rites. I call Zeus to witness this answer." And he raises his king's staff to the sky, to the watching gods.

Idaeus goes back and finds all the Trojan lords and their allied chiefs waiting, hoping for a deal. He tells them there will be no deal—they knew it, really—but that the Greeks agree to a one-day truce, so that the dead can be burned.

So the Trojan slaves disperse through the countryside to find wood for the pyres, while others lay out the dead warriors' corpses in the city square.

When the wood is piled high enough the corpses are laid on it, as many as will fit. Then slaves light the woodpile. Priam has ordered no wailing for the dead, no letting the Greeks know how broken-hearted the Trojans are. So the Trojan dead burn with no sound but the popping of fat and the snap of twigs.

The Greeks spend the day doing the same chore. Slaves scour the dunes for firewood, and when the piles are high enough, the Greek dead are placed on them and the pyres lit. The driftwood is wet and takes a long time to catch. Slaves are sent to collect pine knots, and with their help the pile finally catches. The Greeks watch the bodies burn away to clean bone and go back to the ships.

Next morning, before the sun is even up, the Greeks go to the ashes, take the clean bones from them, lay them all in one shallow pit and raise a huge burial mound over it. Then, before even laying down their shovels, they start building a wall and moat around the camp. They work so fast and so well that the gods are shocked, looking down at them. In fact, Poseidon, who hates newfangled things, complains to Zeus, "Look what these uppity Greeks are doing now! This wall of theirs will be finished in one day, and they haven't even sacrificed to us! If this goes on, nobody will even remember the walls that Apollo and I have built around the great towns of the east!"

But Zeus isn't going to be dragged into any more quarrels. He shrugs, has another gulp of nectar, and says, "Poseidon, what are you worrying about? You control the earthquakes, as well as the ocean. You can shake down that wall as soon as the Greeks leave. Just toss it into the sea and cover it with sand, so no one even remembers it was there."

Poseidon isn't satisfied. He wants these mortals taught a hard lesson. Finally Zeus waves him off, saying, "Here's what I'll do. The Greeks will have a big feast tonight to celebrate this new wall. I'll send a storm right when they're gulping their wine and scoffing down meat. That'll teach them to sacrifice to us next time they build something."

Poseidon subsides, grumbling into his beard.

The Greeks, not knowing they've angered the gods, work all day, warriors and slaves sweating together. By sundown the wall and moat are finished. Then the Greeks hurry down to the sea because a ship has beached, full to the decks with wine from the Black Sea vineyards. Every man who has anything to give—gold, silver, even iron—stands in line to buy as much wine as he can hold. Men with no metal to trade offer hides from slaughtered oxen, or even live cattle captured from Trojan farms; those who have nothing else offer up their captured slave-girls for a jar of that sweet Black Sea vintage.

Then they have a huge drunken feast. Zeus waits till the food is laid out and the wine cups are full, then sends a storm, with plenty of thunder and lightning. Men spill their wine in terror, and beg forgiveness, promising they'll make proper sacrifice next time. Then everyone, Greek and Trojan, lies down to get what rest they can.

8

SLAUGHTER

ZEUS IS SICK OF THIS WAR. Nine years of killing, no results. He calls the family to conference and lays down the law: "No more meddling with the Greeks or Trojans, trying to tilt the battle. No more interference from any of you gods ... or goddesses."

As he says "or goddesses," he looks hard at Hera and Athena. Athena is sulking, refusing to look him in the eye. Zeus says, "Maybe you all need to be reminded that I could throw the whole bunch of you into Tartarus, one layer below Hell. Would you like that? I threw the Titans down there, and all of you put together aren't as strong as they were."

He hunches over the table to let them see his strength. "Suppose we were to play tug-o-war, with all of you dragging me down toward earth. I'd pull you all up into the sky instead, and the whole Earth and ocean with you. I'm the papa here, and don't you forget it."

Athena speaks up: "Papa, we all know you have final say. But you can't blame Mama and me for being sad when we see so many brave Greek warriors dying down there at Troy."

Zeus is about to rage at her when she smiles, suddenly girlish, and pipes up, "Papa, what if we didn't interfere directly, but just made some suggestions to the Greeks, a little advice?"

Zeus can't help laughing. "Just suggestions, huh? Ah, girl, don't worry, I'd never hurt you."

He turns to the rest of them: "But as for the rest of you: No more meddling in the war, or you'll regret it."

Zeus descends to the hill above Troy, leaving his horses and chariot in the clouds to wait for him. He sits in his temple to watch the day's fight. He can see the walls of Troy and the far campfires of the Greeks. If he wants, he can see every pebble in the darkest cellar of Troy, each goat-hair strand of the Greek tents. If he felt like it, he could snake his way through the wet interior of every Greek and Trojan skull, and if he took a dislike to any of the ideas sparking in that wet brain-mush, he could turn the owner of that thought into a carbonized husk with one lightning bolt.

It's time they showed him some respect. You have to knock heads now and then to keep your power. If any of the other gods show up on the battlefield today, he'll knock their heads hard. After all, he made a promise to Thetis, that sweet little sea-goddess, to run the battle, hurt the Greeks, show them they need her doomed son Akilles. Zeus keeps his promises; that's what being god-father is all about.

He sees the two armies getting ready. The Greeks gulp their porridge by the tents and jam on their armor. The Trojans get ready in their houses, then meet up in the streets of Troy, march together out to the dust fields for the day's fight.

When the two hordes run into each other, they charge. No talk today, no courtesies between the two hordes. Today is for killing.

They kill each other all morning, with no advantage to either side.

When noon comes, Zeus is tired of watching this game. He's bored. If you've seen one human punctured with a bronze spearhead, you've seen 'em all.

He decides to force an outcome. So he makes a golden scale, perfectly balanced, gleaming in the noon sun. He takes a pinch of dust and puts it on one of the pans, whispering, "Doom for the Greeks." He takes another pinch of dust, puts it in the other pan, and whispers, "Doom for the Trojans."

The dooms in the scales swarm with life. He can hear the sounds they make, tiny worlds shrieking, oozing, whimpering. Zeus holds them level, then whispers, "Now!" The scales begin to tip. The Trojan pan rises higher and higher, while the Greek pan sinks until it touches the ground. As it touches Earth, the thing in the pan turns back to dust and dribbles off onto the ground.

Zeus smiles. "Death to the Greeks, then; I had a feeling it would be." He laughs at his little joke. Funny how these scientific experiments always turn out the way he wants them to.

Now for the fun part of his job: the lightning. Few pleasures compare to incinerating pesky humans from on high with sizzling, million-volt bolts of lightning. And today's targets are those Greeks who were so rude to Thetis' boy.

Zeus chooses a fine Greek spearman for his first target, tracks the man's every muscle-pulse, and then, with a flick of his mind, sends a bolt down on him. In far less than a second, the man is nothing but melted bronze, charred bone, and burnt meat.

He picks another target, sends another bolt. Another Greek becomes the ground for a million volts of divine annoyance.

Ah, that got their attention. They're running around down there like ants in a rainstorm, wondering where to hide as the drops fall. Now he gets down to business. The bolts fall randomly through the Greek horde, zapping one man and leaving the men next to him unhurt, choking at the smell of roast meat and ozone, wondering if they'll be next.

Zeus is laughing, feeling better than he has in years. He knows the whole god-family is watching his tour de force. It's aimed at them too, them above all. They've been getting very insolent lately. This should remind them who's in charge.

The battlefield is a strobe-lit horror. Compared to the flashes of blue-white electric light from Zeus' lightning, daylight seems like a moonless night. The men are all blinded, frozen in place waiting to be fried alive. Lightning bolts sprout like a forest of white trees, appearing and vanishing in an instant. And at the foot of every one of these trees is a dead Greek, smoking like a bee carbonized with a magnifying glass.

The Greeks break and run for their camp. Agamemnon sets sprint records back to the camp.

The Trojans cheer among the burnt patches, each with its carbonized Greek, still sizzling. Hektor shouts, "Fight like men, now that we have them on the run! We'll smash through that jerry-rigged wall the Greeks have built!

Be sure to bring torches; we'll set their ships on fire! And as the fools stumble through the smoke, I'll kill them all!"

He lashes his horses, yelling, "Pay me for your keep, all four of you! If you carry me fast enough, we'll catch up to old Nestor and Diomedes and I'll hang their armor in Apollo's temple!" Hektor flies over the plain toward the sea, the Greek camp, and his men follow, spearing lightning-blinded Greeks in the back as they run.

It's more than Hera can stand, watching Hektor and the Greeks being slaughtered. She goes in a rage to Poseidon, Zeus' old brother.

"You see what's happening down there, Poseidon? Don't you care about all those Greeks dying, after they offered us so much meat and fat over the years? If all of us stick together, we can push the Trojans back, and my husband won't be able to do a thing but watch!"

Poseidon gives Hera a long hard stare. "Are you crazy, woman? Don't you remember what happened to the Titans when they tried to fight Zeus? He could send us all down where they are now, one layer below Hell. Leave me out of your scheming."

Hera decides to work indirectly, through the mind of Agamemnon, so as not to annoy Zeus. She puts courage into Agamemnon, who's cowering in his tent.

He stands, feeling strong all of a sudden, and starts acting like a king again. He wraps himself in a mantle of royal purple and strides out, to stand in the center of his army penned behind the wall. He climbs onto the wall and shouts down at them, "Greeks! You look like warriors, but you don't act like them! Don't you remember all the bragging you did when we stopped off at Lemnos on our way here? You drank my wine, rivers of it! And ate meat at my expense, and swore each of you could kill a hundred Trojans! And now the whole horde of you is huddled here, frightened of Hektor, run off the field by one man!"

Then he turns and screams at the sky: "And you, Zeus! What did I ever do to you? Every stop we made on the way here, I laid the fattest meat on your altars, and now you turn on me?" His rage is so great that for a moment, it's almost god-like. Zeus watches, fascinated, impressed in spite of himself, as Agamemnon, this coward, this contemptible human, screams up at him.

Then the moment is gone, and Agamemnon is begging again, whining, "Please, Lord Zeus, just let us get away from here with our lives, at least!"

Zeus smiles. He doesn't like Agamemnon very much, but the slaughter today was business, nothing personal. He'll stop when the point has been made. He's been keeping a careful count of every Greek warrior he incinerated today. It's enough; he's made his point. Thetis will be satisfied. He's shown the Greeks they need Akilles; Agamemnon has been humbled, his job is done.

So he won't let the Greeks be wiped out at the ships. For starters, Hera and Athena would make his life a living Hell if he did that.

So Zeus flicks Agamemnon an eagle, his emblem. The big bird with wings like black doors circles above Agamemnon, and the Greeks know they've been spared. Now they'll fight, and the Trojans will pay.

Diomedes is the first to go over the wall, sprinting right at a Trojan and ramming a spear right through the man's armor. Then Ajax lumbers over the wall, through the ditch, to face the Trojans on the plain. What the Trojans can't see is that Teucer, the Greeks' best bowman, is hidden behind Ajax's hulking shoulders and huge shield.

Ajax and Teucer make a deadly sniper team. Ajax hides the little archer with his bulk, then lifts his shield. Teucer peeks out, picks a target, and fires an arrow, then jumps back under Ajax's giant shield like a duckling venturing out from its mother's wing to grab a bug, and squirming back to the shelter of her feathers.

The Trojans can't even figure out who's killing them at first. There's Ajax, looming in front of them, but he doesn't use the bow. Who's firing these lethal darts? Eight times, Teucer steps out to fire an arrow. And eight times, a Trojan drops with an arrow in his neck or chest. Then Teucer aims at Hektor.

Teucer is a good shot, but Apollo won't have Hektor killed, especially not with a bow. The bow is Apollo's weapon; he decides who dies by arrow. So he flicks Teucer's arrow away from Hektor. It burrows into the chest of Hektor's chariot-driver instead, and the man falls dead.

Hektor is angry. That's the second driver he's lost today. He jumps off his chariot, grabs a huge rock and waits for Teucer to sneak out from behind Ajax's shield again. Teucer's head pops out and Hektor flings his stone. It hits little Teucer right above the collarbone, where the neck joins the chest. The rock breaks Teucer's arm as well, and he drops his bow. His big brother Ajax grabs Teucer and hands him over the wall.

With Teucer out of the fight, the Trojans cheer up and charge again.

This time, the Greeks can't hold the wall. The Trojans charge across the ditch, dodging the sharpened stakes, and swarm over the wall like ants. The Greeks stumble back to the ships.

Hektor is everywhere, a terror, a demon. He chases the Greeks, killing the slowest. Now the Greeks are backed right up against the ships, their feet in the surf.

As soon as they can light torches, the Trojans will toss them into the ships. And with the ships on fire, Hektor will hunt through the smoke like a lion on a moonless night, slaughtering the Greeks as they stumble through the smoke.

Hera and Athena can't stand to watch. Hera moans to her daughter, "Look what that Hektor is doing to my Greeks! Oh, I wish that man would hurry up and die!"

Athena fumes, "Oh, Papa makes me so angry! All the times I went here and there doing his errands! 'Athena, go to this man, or that man, give him wise counsel!' or 'Go kill this man or that man for me, Athena!' But now, he doesn't even ask my permission when he kills my favorite warriors! And all because that little flirt Thetis hugged his knees! Well, we'll see what happens the next time he tries to hug me and call me his sweet gray-eyed darling!"

Athena paces furiously as Hektor hacks and stabs his way to the Greek ships. She cries out in rage, a sound to make mountains fall, and tells Hera, "Mama, I'm not standing for this! Get my chariot ready! We'll see how this Hektor feels about meeting me in battle!"

Athena goes into a storeroom to do her switch routine. She went in dressed like a maiden from a royal house; she comes out in gleaming armor, carrying a spear bigger than the tallest pine. Her mother is already at the reins, and their chariot sweeps down in a long parabola to Troy.

Zeus sees them coming, a distant sizzle like a golden meteor, and sighs. This'll be trouble. Better warn them off before he has to hurt them. He flicks a finger, and Iris is before him, kneeling, awaiting orders. She is beautiful enough to distract Zeus for a moment, though time is pressing. Iris is sometimes a young woman with dainty wings sprouting from her milk-white shoulders, but when moved, she dissolves into the rainbow. Now she is in human form ... aside from the wings.

Zeus tells her, "Iris, a task for you, urgent: intercept my wife and daughter—see their chariot burning down to Earth? They're planning to interfere in this human war again. I'm getting very tired of nobody doing what I tell them. These gods think that because they can't be killed, they're untouchable. The idiots forget there are things I can do that are a lot worse than dying."

Iris, frightened, begins to evanesce, shimmering into something more like sun through rain than a human shape.

Zeus says, "No, don't worry, I'm not talking about you! I'm talking about that wife of mine and her daughter—oh, you know what it's like for me at home."

Iris returns to mortal shape, giggling. They all know about Zeus and Hera and their weird daughter. It's a running god-joke.

Zeus winces, goes on, "Anyway, you tell those two that if they go on, I'll start by breaking their chariot-horses' legs, so they can't fly around making more trouble. Got it?"

Iris nods, pleased. Hera is not popular in the family. It will be a pleasure, conveying this message.

Zeus goes on: "In fact, wait, that's not enough. You tell them for me that if they keep this up, I won't stop with their horses. Once the horses are lamed, I'll pull their chariot out of the sky and smash it up to kindling, and then I'll throw the two of them down to Earth, not lightly, but as hard as a mortal would fall. And when they're lying there groaning in pain, that's when I'll throw lightning at them. It'll take that wife and daughter of mine an eon or two to get over the burn scars. You go tell them that!"

Iris vanishes, already halfway across the sky, and Zeus grumbles to himself, "Can't believe it! My little Athena, my gray-eyed darling, acting like this. Can't say I'm surprised at her mother; everybody knows what she's like ..." He sighs, and has some more nectar. It's family; what can you do?

Iris burns into the overworld, and meets the goddess' chariot just as it's preparing to dive toward Earth. Iris shimmers in mid-air before the two goddesses: "Hera, Athena, what are you doing? Have you both gone crazy?"

The two goddesses stop dead, their horses paused in mid-step, the chariot unmoving at the edge of the atmosphere.

Iris blurts: "Father Zeus says that if you two go on, he'll break your horses' legs for you, and take your chariot and break it up into little tiny pieces, and then he'll throw the pieces down to the ground like kindling-wood ..."

Hera is already looking nervous.

Iris continues happily, "Oh, and he said, 'That gray-eyed daughter of mine'— that's you, Athena—'is going to learn a lesson about disobeying her father.'"

Iris allows herself a little giggle. "Oh, I remember he also said, 'It will take those two an eon to get over the bruises.'" Hera is slumping now, trembling a little. As she turns to speak with Athena, Iris adds, "Oh, and he said something about how disappointed he is in you, Athena." Iris sighs, "Yes, how he had soooo much trust in you, which you betrayed like this. He's very angry!"

Hera mutters to Athena, "Daughter, ah, now, perhaps we should let things take their course ..."

Iris adds, as if she just remembered, "And he also said, 'I'm not nearly so surprised at my wife's disobedience, because everyone knows what a harpy she is.' I think his exact words were, 'Is that old battle-ax daring to interfere again?' Oh, he was so angry!"

Hera gulps and says, "Yes, daughter, I do think, after all, it might be better to go home. Let the humans hack at each other! After all, what is it to us? None of our business! Let your father deal with these people if it's so important to him!"

Athena says nothing. Iris has vanished, with one last spiteful laugh. The two goddesses drive their chariot back up to the overworld, more slowly and glumly than they set out. They get out, handing the horses over to the beings that serve the gods, and rejoin the others at the feast. Not even Hera feels like talking.

They wait in silence until they hear Zeus' chariot arriving, and the huge clomp of his feet on the glowing floor. Zeus is throwing his weight around today, deploying his full mass—and he weighs as much as a star. The whole overworld shudders at every step. He slams himself into his golden throne with a sound like mountains falling in an earthquake.

Hera makes a point of getting up and going to a corner to chat with Athena, the two of them keeping their backs to Zeus. Sulking again? He's had enough of it. He yells: "What is it now, you two? Haven't you killed enough men? Are you so desperate to go back and kill more Trojans? I tell you both, right now: If you'd tried to interfere today, I'd have slapped both of you out of the sky and thrown lightning at you as you squirmed in the dirt. You can't die, but believe me, you can be hurt. You have no idea how badly you can hurt."

Athena refuses to speak or even look at her father. But Hera can't resist: "Husband-brother, we know how strong you are! You don't have to keep reminding us! We're just sad for all the brave Greek warriors dying down there. I've been meaning to ask you, how would it be if we, as my daughter suggested, just offered suggestions to the Greeks, a few thoughts to put in their heads—before you destroy them?"

Zeus shrugs: "Well, wife, if seeing Greeks get killed bothers you, you won't want to watch tomorrow's battle, because I'll tell you right now, more Greeks will die, many, many more. I'm going to give Hektor my strength until he's killed so many Greeks that they'll have to beg poor Thetis' son Akilles to return. And that won't happen until Hektor kills Akilles' friend Patroklas.

It's all arranged, and if you don't want to watch it you can go to Hell, or one layer further down, to Tartarus, and lie there where there's not a ray of light or a breath of air. I don't care where you go, because you're the biggest bitch I've ever met."

Hera drops the idea of offering suggestions.

On the dust fields outside Troy, the killing goes on until the sun goes down. Hektor is everywhere, stabbing, slashing, trampling the wounded under his chariot, until it's too dark to see. The Trojans curse the gathering darkness, hoping for a few more minutes of killing light, but the Greeks thank the sun for vanishing, wishing it would fall faster into the sea to end their terrible day.

Hektor takes the Trojans back to a spot near the river where there aren't too many corpses—just so the smell isn't too bad. They all get out of their chariots and sit down. Hektor takes up his spear, tall as a pine tree, plants the spear and says, "Trojans, allies, we've had a great day! Too bad it had to end. I hoped we'd burn the Greek ships and kill them in the surf today. Yes, we'd salt their corpses down with seawater! But the sun betrayed us and sank too fast, hid our prey from us. Nothing else would have saved them! Now we need to get ready to finish them off! Feed your horses well, tether them gently; they'll be hard-driven tomorrow. I want big bonfires around the camp to warm us, and remind the Greeks we're close on them. Let them fear us, let them get no sleep tonight and wake tired!"

The men cheer wildly. Can they actually win? It's been so long since victory was even a possibility. They've been fighting just to hold off the end a little longer. What if they can win, burn the ships and slaughter the Greeks? They begin to imagine it, and their spear hands clench, wishing dawn would come now.

Hektor goes on, "All of you, make sure to get a good sleep, but first we feast! Celebrate today's win! Send your slaves back to town to bring wine, sheep and cattle for the spits. Tell the people inside our walls to have the boys and old men man the walls all night, in case the Greeks try a sneaky night raid."

He plants his spear in the ground. "Tomorrow we end this war. We won't let one single Greek go home unhurt. The few survivors will limp home with an arrow wound or a sword gash that will throb on cold nights to remind him to leave our city alone. The rest will lie here forever."

The men are screaming with joy. They've been afraid so long. They can hardly bear the joy of visiting terror on the men who have hunted them for nine years.

Hektor waves them quiet, goes on: "As soon as the sun comes up, I'll put on my armor and make for their ships, and I have a feeling that Diomedes' swaggering days will end early tomorrow morning ..."

He rips his spear out of the ground, sending clods of dry earth flying. "I wish I were as sure of eternal life as I am that tomorrow will be a terrible day for the Greeks!"

The Trojans cheer until their throats are sore. The Greeks guarding the wall hear it and stare out through the murk at a thousand Trojan campfires. There are fifty warriors sitting around each one, waiting for dawn to finish off the Greeks.

9

EMBASSY

GAMEMNON CALLS THE LEADERS to him. They're shocked when they see him hunched on his throne, big tears running down his cheeks. He snuffles, "My friends ..." Friends? They've never been friends. He goes on, oblivious: "Friends, Zeus hates me. Why is he doing this to me? He promised me I'd pillage Troy! And now we're beaten."

He sniffles some more, then says, "We'll never take this town! I want to go home."

There's a stunned silence.

Finally Diomedes steps forward and says, "I'll be blunt. We're in council, and it's my right. Remember how you called me a coward before the big fight, Agamemnon? Everyone heard you; don't deny it! Well, now look at you, blubbering like a baby! Zeus was playing a prank when he made you; you look like a king, but you were born without courage. But we're not all as cowardly as you. If you want to go home, go! Take your ships and men with you! As for me, I'm staying. Even if everyone else sails off, I stay. Maybe the gods hate you, Agamemnon, but they still like me!"

The others roar with delight. Somebody needed to say it. Nine long years of putting up with Agamemnon's miserable tricks, and now he dissolves in tears like a child! They're ready to toss him in the sea, him and his throne.

Nestor stands up, gives Diomedes a friendly pat on the back, and says, "Well said, my son! You speak nearly as well as you fight. But I'm older than any of you, and I know a few things. Above all, stick together. No fighting among ourselves!"

To cool the men down, Nestor scolds Agamemnon: "And you, my lad, you need to start acting like a king! So do what a king should do! No more talk about surrender! Just give your orders for the night. Put a strong guard on the wall. And have your slaves bring us a proper meal, with plenty of wine! And don't mix it a gallon of water to a pint of wine this time!".

They all laugh. Agamemnon's stinginess is a camp legend.

When they've eaten, Nestor stands and says, "I'll speak freely. It's too late for pleasantries. This war was your idea, Agamemnon. You have no right to quit. You ruined everything when you took that girl from Akilles. I told you not to! But you did it anyway, because you only care about your spite. So we lost our best fighter. Well, we need him back. You have only one option: offer Akilles anything he wants to come back. Without him, we're doomed."

Agamemnon has recovered, and says, "Yes, yes, I see it now. The gods love Akilles, that's why they're killing us! And that makes him as powerful as a whole army. I was wrong to make him angry. It was stupid."

He turns to the group, his shame and tears forgotten: "I've been thinking of what to offer him. Here's my promise, in front of all of you: I'll give him gold, iron, bronze; and horses. I have twelve horses who've won races for me; they're his if he joins the fight. And slave girls, too. I'll send over my seven best girls, good workers and beauties—all from Lesbos! I picked them myself when we sacked the island."

Silence. It's not enough. They all know what he needs to offer Akilles.

Finally Agamemnon says through gritted teeth, "Oh, all right then! I'll return the girl Briseis! And I swear on all the gods that I've never even touched her, let alone bedded her!"

They all know this is a lie. Slaves love to gossip, so everyone knows what Agamemnon has been doing to the girl. But if it will bring Akilles back, they'll all pretend to believe it.

Agamemnon warms up: "And, and, if Zeus lets us take Troy, Akilles can have first pick of the twenty best-looking high-born Trojan women ... except Helen, of course. She goes back to my brother. I'll do better than that! Listen to this: Akilles can have his pick of my daughters! Yes! I have four of them ..."

Odysseus whispers loudly, "Three now, my lord; remember what happened to Iphigenia?"

Agamemnon laughs, claps himself on the forehead: "Ah, you're right! I forgot, I had to sacrifice that one on our way here!"

The laugh makes them flinch a little, but Agamemnon, not noticing, goes on, "Right, three of them now! Well, he can have his pick! I'll make him my son-in-law! My son Orestes is waiting there now, just waiting for his dear father to come home ..."

The Gods, listening, have a good laugh. They know exactly how Orestes will greet his dear long-lost Papa: with a dagger in the belly.

But Agamemnon knows nothing of what awaits him at home, and burbles on: "Akilles will be as dear to me as Orestes! I'll give him seven towns, full of good hardworking serfs. Right on the sea, good harbor! Cattle, sheep, everything! I have so much I'll never miss them!"

Agamemnon is drunk on his own voice, boasting even now, a few hours from ruin.

Nestor tries to make the best of it: "Agamemnon, these are fine gifts you've offered. Now we need to pick a group to see Akilles. I suggest Fenix, Akilles' old tutor, and his friends Odysseus and Ajax, and two heralds to make it official."

Good choices; everyone nods. Nestor finishes up, "We need to hurry, so have the slaves bring us water—you're our host, Agamemnon, so act like it! Then we'll pray to Zeus. Maybe he'll spare us."

The slaves wash the lords' hands, and fill their bowls with wine. Everyone is drinking more than usual tonight. Panic is behind their eyes, and every Greek sees himself floating alone in the trough of a huge, dark wave.

Odysseus leads the group down the beach to Akilles' quarters. He's the brains; the others are there because Akilles likes them.

As they walk, they whisper prayers to Poseidon, who's out there under the waves somewhere. They need all the help they can get.

Akilles is on a couch, playing a lyre. His old friend Patroklas lies near him, listening. It's a relief, seeing Patroklas. He's Akilles' best friend, a little older and steadier than his lord. Akilles takes him for granted a bit, speaks roughly to him sometimes, but they're very close. Patroklas was more like a father to Akilles than old Peleus ever was.

Akilles stands up, still holding the lyre, and says in a flat voice, "You are all welcome. It must be serious business to bring you three, the only Greeks I still consider friends! Patroklas, tell them to bring us more wine, and less water in it this round! We have guests!"

Patroklas, obliging as always, goes to give the slaves their orders, as Akilles leads the party to the couches.

They wait in silence until Patroklas comes back with food. It's a fine spread: a sheep-haunch, a goat-loin, and the fat meat from a pig's back. Akilles and Patroklas play host, spit-roasting the meat for their guests. Akilles puts the meat on wooden trenchers with his own huge hands, and passes bread to each guest.

Then he says "Patroklas, make the sacrifice."

Patroklas picks out the best three hunks of meat and tosses them in the fire. When the sizzle stops; the gods have fed; now the men can eat.

When they've all eaten as much as courtesy demands, Ajax nudges Odysseus, who begins,

"Akilles, you've given us a fine meal. But we're here on serious business. The army's in trouble. Zeus has been blasting us with lightning and Hektor's killing anyone he sees, because he knows Zeus is on his side. The Trojans swear they'll burn our ships tomorrow morning, and I'm afraid they're not just boasting this time. Come back, Akilles. We'll be wiped out if you don't."

Akilles keeps his face neutral, sips his wine. Odysseus leans toward him: "I know you, Akilles. We've been friends a long time. You take things too hard! Your father Peleus used to warn you not to hold a grudge. He knew something like this might happen."

Akilles frowns. Odysseus goes on,

"Agamemnon knows he was wrong. He's made you a fine offer by way of apology: gold, silver, bronze, and slave-girls, the best-looking ones from Lesbos. Horses, too, prize-winners from his stables! And even one of his daughters. He said he'll make you a son-in-law, and give you seven rich seaside towns as dowry!"

Akilles shakes his head. Odysseus pleads, "Well, then, think of your reputation. If you fight tomorrow and drive back the Trojans, you'll be a hero! They'll sing songs about you for thousands of years!"

Akilles says coldly, "Odysseus, stop wheedling like a peddler. I hate fancy talk. I'll tell you all right now, I won't come back. Why should I? For nine long years, I've watched Agamemnon keep to his tent while I did the fighting. I took 12 towns! Where do you think those slave-girls came from? I'm the one who captured them in the first place!"

They nod, laugh nervously. It's true enough.

Akilles waves a huge hand, "Agamemnon always showed up just in time to grab every pretty girl, every gold trinket! You could never find him in a fight, but as soon as I'd killed the enemy, he'd pop up like a camp dog nosing around a spit!"

He mutters, "He only let me keep one thing: that girl Briseis. I liked her. He knew it, too. That's why he took her."

It's true enough. Nobody wants to defend Agamemnon at the moment. But they don't like this sentimentality about a captive girl.

Akilles sees their reaction and shouts, "No, it's not about the girl! It's about respect! He took her back, when he knew I'd quit if he did, so he must value her more than he does me!"

They nod at that; a good point.

He goes on, "Besides ... I've been thinking about things. Why should any of us fight the Trojans? We're no kin to Agamemnon and his cuckold brother. Let them get Helen back themselves. I don't have any grudge against these Trojans! They seem like decent people ... for Easterners, anyway. I suppose they love their wives as much as Menelaos does."

He sneers, "And I bet their wives love their husbands much more than Helen loved him!"

They have a good laugh. You can count on those Menelaos jokes to break the ice.

Akilles relaxes a little, drawls, "I see Agamemnon thinks he's a great general now, a real military planner, with this wall of his! And his little ditch with those oh-so-scary spikes in it! At dawn tomorrow, he'll find out his ditch and his wall won't stop Hektor!"

He turns to Ajax: "Remember when I fought Hektor? He only stood up to me once. Once, in nine years' fighting! Most of the time, he knew better than to front up to me; he always managed to be where I wasn't! Except that one time—remember, Ajax? By the oak tree?"

Ajax nods.

"He tried fighting me ... for about ten breaths! Then he ran back into the city!"

They all remember that moment. They wait, hoping Akilles has vomited up all the bile in his liver.

But there's more. He goes on, "Well, from now on Hektor doesn't need to worry about me, because at dawn I sail for home."

They didn't expect this. He's pleased with their surprise, goes on,

"So you can tell Agamemnon I don't want his gifts. There are beautiful girls at home, and cattle, and iron. There's only one thing you can't buy, and that's life. So tomorrow I go home. Fenix, old friend, come with me—because this army will never take Troy!"

Fenix, oldest and humblest of the three, sobs out, "My Lord Akilles, please take the gifts! For my sake! I used to feed you when you wouldn't eat for anyone else. I helped raise you. I'm begging you, come back. You'll win all sorts of glory, my son!"

Akilles scowls, "I don't need glory. My mother is a goddess, my father's line descends from Zeus, and who are you serving? The filthy Atreus-sons! You all know that family is accursed. Keep serving them and you'll die for nothing. No, Fenix, I won't go back. You stay here tonight, sail with me tomorrow morning."

He turns to Patroklas, who's been sitting quietly at his side: "Patroklas, you're so slow tonight! Go tell the slaves to make a soft bed for Fenix!"

He stands up, gesturing toward the door. The embassy is over.

Ajax sighs, "I guess we'll have to tell everybody that Akilles would rather let us all die than give up his precious grudge. I don't understand you, Akilles! Maybe I'm stupid, but it seems to me that even if a man's own brother gets killed, he'll take the blood-money and give up the feud. But you ... all this fuss about a girl?"

Akilles smiles: "Ajax, we've always been friends and I know you're talking sense, but every time I think of what Agamemnon did to me ... No. I won't fight unless Hektor tries to burn my ships. And I don't think he's stupid enough to try it, even if he burns everyone else's."

The meeting is over. Slaves fill their cups. Each man spills some wine on the fire for the gods. Then they drain their cups and go.

All but Fenix. He stays behind.

As soon as they return, Agamemnon runs up asking, "What'd he say? Is he going to help us?"

Odysseus says bluntly, "No. He said you should save the ships yourself, you and your wall. He and his men are sailing home tomorrow. He says the rest of us should do the same; we'll never take the city. Oh, by the way, Fenix stayed with Akilles."

Odysseus sits down by the fire, tired of talking to people.

After a shocked silence, Diomedes grumbles, "We never should have begged him to come back! It makes us look weak, and it didn't do any good! We just have to do our best without him. Everybody should get a good rest and be ready to fight in the morning."

They go off to sleep, those who can.

10

RAID

αGAMEMNON CAN'T SLEEP. He keeps getting up to have a look at the Trojans' campfires out there on the plain. So many! And there are about fifty warriors around each one. All those Trojans, Lycians, and their outlandish allies, just waiting for the sun to rise. Then they'll swarm over the Greeks' pitiful wall. And the ships will burn, the Greeks will be chased down like pigs in a gully. Everyone will die. And Agamemnon will be remembered as the one to blame.

He paces back and forth, mumbling, groaning. Sometimes he screams and bashes himself on the head; once or twice he grabs his hair and pulls hunks of it out, ranting at the gods, the Trojans, his cuckold brother, himself.

At last he goes into his tent and comes out with a lion's skin over his shoulders, as if he can put on its courage with its pelt. He's putting on his armor when Menelaos steps out of the dark, already dressed. Neither of the Atreus-sons got any sleep tonight.

Menelaos squats by the fire and says, "Why bother getting dressed, brother?

If you're hoping for volunteers to scout the Trojan camp, forget it. They're too scared."

Agamemnon mutters, "They have good reason. Do you know how many men Hektor killed today? And he's not even half-god! One mortal did all that to us! Zeus was with him. The gods are pro-Trojan now."

They watch the fire in silence.

Agamemnon stands up, groaning, says, "We have to do something! I'm in charge here! I'll go wake Nestor, maybe he can think of something. You, brother, go wake the others."

Menelaos stands, but Agamemnon says, "Wait! Menelaos, wake them, but be polite about it. I've been thinking; maybe we've been a little ... high-handed ... with the men. So tonight, greet every man you see, Menelaos. Hail him by name, his and his father's. I want everybody to know that the sons of Atreus are their friends, not just their commanders."

Menelaos trots off on his errand, and Agamemnon heads for Nestor's quarters.

Nestor is awake too. Old men don't sleep much. Nestor sees a monster coming at him in the dark, something with a lion's head and legs like a man. He blurts, "What? Who's that?"

Agamemnon shrugs off the lion-skin, tears off his helmet and says quietly, "Nestor, please help me. I think this could be the end of us. Can't sleep. Did you see all those Trojan fires out there? As soon as they sun comes up, they'll be over that wall like ants."

Nestor pats him on the shoulder. "Agamemnon, Atreus-son, you worry too much. It's not good, either for you or the army. I tell you, I've seen gods play with men a long time; What they give one day, they take back the next! Zeus will pull the rug out from under Hektor soon. That's what the gods are like, my boy! They raise a man up just to knock him down."

Agamemnon is inconsolable. He squats by the fire, shaking his head.

Nestor wrenches up on his creaky joints, grumbling, "Come with me. We'll make the rounds of the camp. A king should be seen at a time like this."

Agamemnon stands to help the old man as Nestor goes on, "Why isn't that dull-witted brother of yours, Menelaos, with us? He has too much of the turtle in him! Slow as honey in winter, that boy!"

Agamemnon says, "It's true, my little brother is a little slow to move sometimes, but tonight he's awake, rousing the others. He came to me tonight on his own."

Nestor nods, scratching his long white beard: "Well, perhaps I was hard on the boy ... Never mind! Now you stand up straight, sir! Act like a king when we meet the others."

They go to wake Odysseus, but he steps from the shadows already dressed. He knows what they have in mind without being told. They move on to the next tent, where Diomedes is snoring by the fire on an ox-hide.

Nestor calls out to him, but it will take more than the old man's reedy voice to wake Diomedes. Nestor kicks the snoring giant in the ribs, growling, "Diomedes! Wake up! What are you snoring for, at a time like this? Why, in my day ..."

Diomedes rolls over, sits on his haunches. He squints at Nestor, sighs, "Old man, don't you ever sleep? You're made out of iron or something."

Nestor chuckles, "You can return the favor by waking up Ajax, Meges, and the rest of them. If they're snoring like you were, give them a good kick in the ribs!"

Diomedes grunts, grabs a lion-skin from his tent, and lumbers off into the shadows like a big cat walking on two feet.

Ajax and the others show up one by one. Some are still sleepy, some nervous and wide awake. Nestor and Agamemnon gesture for silence. Without a sound, the group makes its way over the wall, through the ditch, onto the plain. They find a spot without too many stinking corpses and squat on their haunches to talk.

Nestor speaks first: "My friends, we need to scout the Trojans tonight, see if they're going to attack or withdraw to the town. The man who volunteers to do that will be a hero. Why, we'd each give him a black ewe, oh yes, and her lamb as well, and ..."

Diomedes says quickly, "I'll go. But I'd like someone with me. Two pairs of eyes see better, two brains think better."

Everyone volunteers, including Menelaos. Seeing his brother offer to go on this suicide mission, Agamemnon steps in: "Good man, Diomedes! You've always been brave. Pick anyone you want to go with you, but remember, choose the best man for the job, not just someone with high lineage, like Menelaos."

Diomedes understands what Agamemnon is up to, but he doesn't want dull-witted Menelaos anyway. The choice is obvious: "I want Odysseus with me. He's as brave as any of us, smarter than any of us, and more important, he's Athena's favorite; we all know she loves you, Odysseus!"

The others laugh quietly, but Odysseus winces. It's bad luck to talk about these things. He waves away the joke: "You don't need to introduce me, everyone here knows me. No more talk. We need to go now, before the sky lightens. And we'd better look like them, or their strange friends. So take off that Greek-model helmet and armor, Diomedes. They're a dead giveaway. We'll wear the weird armor those Easterners use."

Slaves run off, coming back with leather helmets. Odysseus puts on the smaller one, a simple skullcap. Diomedes gets the big one, an ox-hide cap with boar's tusks sewn onto it. Odysseus takes a bow as well, the Asians' favorite weapon.

Then the two of them trot out toward the Trojans' camp.

Odysseus can feel Athena with him. He stops, looks up at the stars and says, "Daughter of Zeus! You've helped me through so many hardships; be with me now, and let me and my comrade come back alive, after we've hurt our enemies."

A heron croaks in the dark sky. Athena is here.

Diomedes adds his prayer: "Daughter of Zeus, protect me too! I'll give you the smoke from a one-year-old heifer, never put to the plow, with gilded horns!"

No heron cry this time. Diomedes will have to hope Athena's deal with Odysseus includes him too.

The two of them jog on toward the Trojan campfires, lions' heads pulled over their leather helmets. In the dark, they are two lions running like men.

The Trojans haven't slept either. Hektor has called them together in front of his tent. He says, "I need a volunteer. He'll be well rewarded, because it will be a dangerous mission: going to the Greek ships to see if they're getting ready to sail off."

No one volunteers.

Hektor isn't happy. Not one volunteer? The Trojan force is breaking up, the Asian allies keeping to their own campfires. He needs to destroy the Greeks now, before attrition and despair dissolve the Trojan force.

Finally an ugly churl named Dolon says, "If you promise me Akilles' horses and his chariot, I'll go. I'm a fast runner; I'll make it there and back safe."

Dolon has good reason to take the risk: five sisters, no brothers. That's five dowries to pay. And another, to get himself a wife, ugly as he is. It will take a lot of gold to buy Dolon a bride. He's thinking how much Akilles' godly horses and chariot will bring.

But he's a bad option. Look at him, misshapen, disgusting. The gods hate ugly people. Still, no one else is willing to go, so Hektor raises his royal staff and says, "I swear, and Zeus may hold me to it, that you'll have those horses, no one else."

Dolon puts on a cap of weasel-skin, ties a jackal's skin over his shoulders, and trots off into the darkness. He looks like a jackal with a weasel's head, trotting on man's legs.

He heads for the Greek camp, jumping over the stinking corpses that dot the plain.

Odysseus hears Dolon coming and pulls Diomedes down among the corpses, whispering, "Someone's coming. Maybe a commoner robbing the corpses, but it could be a spy. Let him go by, then we'll grab him."

They lie down on the dust plain like two lions fallen in battle. Dolon trots by.

When Dolon has gone another furlong—a mule-plowed furlong, not one of those short ox furlongs—the two Greeks rise up like lions come to life and sprint after him.

Dolon hears footsteps, sees two lion-men chasing him, and uses all the speed he has. He runs toward the wall, hoping to dodge into the Greek camp and hide among the tents. Odysseus tells Diomedes, "He's getting away from us! Throw that spear of yours!"

Diomedes takes aim, Odysseus grabs his friend's huge arm, yelling, "Don't kill him! Aim ahead of him!"

Diomedes throws, as Odysseus calls, "Stop right there, unless you want to die!"

Diomedes' spear buries itself in the plain just ahead of Dolon. He stops, begging, "Take me alive, please! I'll pay ransom! Anything you want!"

Odysseus answers, "Just tell us the truth. What are you, a grave-robber or a Trojan scout?"

Dolon sobs, "Hektor! He made me come out here! Promised me Akilles' horses and chariot!" Odysseus smiles. "You? You really thought you could drive Akilles' team? Those horses are immortal! Akilles himself can barely control them, and he's half god himself."

He and Diomedes chuckle over the idea of this churl at the reins of Akilles' team.

Odysseus asks, "What did Hektor ask you to find out?"

Dolon says, "He wants to know if you Greeks are loading your ships to sail off!"

Odysseus nods and says, "Yes, I thought he'd send someone to check on us. Now tell us where Hektor and the Trojan leaders are."

Dolon: "By the monument, away from the main body of troops! I can show you!"

Odysseus: "Are there guards? Sentries?"

Dolon: "At the Trojan campfires, yes. But the allies, those crazy barbarians, they don't keep any sentries! They leave all that to us Trojans; after all, their wives and children are safe, far away!"

Odysseus nods again. "Where are the chiefs? Scattered among the soldiers, or on their own? How hard would it be to get at them?"

Dolon: "Priam's sons are well guarded. You'd never reach them alive. Your best bet is the Thracians at the edge of the camp. They don't post sentries. And they're rich! Beautiful horses, white as clouds! And chariots fitted with gold! You'll find their king, Rhesus, sleeping in the middle of their camp."

Dolon raises his hands, looking almost pleased with himself: "There, I've told you everything I know. Now take me to the ships to be ransomed."

But Odysseus shakes his head. He and Diomedes have barely been able to hide their disgust with this traitor. Ransom? He won't live another five minutes.

Dolon stutters, "Well then, tie me up, and untie me when you come back! Please! I swear, everything I told you is true!"

Odysseus smiles, steps back. Now Diomedes looms in front of Dolon. The huge lion-headed silhouette speaks solemnly: "No, I don't think so, spy. You'd just be ransomed and come back spying again. Simpler to kill you."

Dolon screeches and tries to grab Diomedes' beard, claim mercy. But Diomedes saw that one coming. As Dolon lunges, Diomedes' sword scythes right through his neck. Dolon's ugly head rolls in the dust.

Odysseus takes Dolon's weasel-skin cap and jackal pelt and hangs them on a tamarisk branch, calling, "Athena, beloved goddess, these little things are for you. Help us kill some Thracians and we'll be back with better gifts!"

The two of them jog toward the Trojan camp, spot the Thracians' campfire, and watch from the darkness. The Thracians are sleeping off their wine. The fools haven't posted a single sentry. And each Thracian has a string of fine horses tethered by his bed.

Odysseus whispers, "That man in the center, see him? That'll be their king, Rhesus. Kill him, and as many of the rest as you can. I'll grab the horses."

Diomedes hesitates a moment. There are dozens of Thracians sleeping around their king. But Athena touches him, and his heart fills with grim joy.

He runs full speed to the first Thracian, sleeping at the edge of the light. Diomedes raises his spear with both hands like a butter-churn, stabs it down. He moves toward the fire, where the Thracian king is sleeping, stabbing the sleeping men as he goes. Some die without a sound, but others, hit in the guts, wake and writhe, screaming, making wild shadows in the firelight.

Odysseus follows him, pulling dead bodies out of the way so the horses will have a clear path.

Rhesus, the Thracian king, sleeps through the slaughter. Odysseus watches, puzzled; is Rhesus deaf, or too drunk to wake? Then he sees a vile green thing floating over Rhesus' sleeping face, and smiles. Zeus has sent one of his evil dreams to distract the king. Odysseus says a quick prayer of thanks to his godfather.

Diomedes runs left, then right, like a boy playing a skipping game on a rocky stream-bed. Twelve Thracian fighters are dead or dying by the time Diomedes reaches the center and stands over Rhesus. He takes a deep breath, raises his spear, and smashes it through the king's breastbone, crushing his heart. The king dies without waking, still in the web of Zeus' evil dream.

Thirteen dead Thracians! A good accounting. Fourteen, if you count the wretched spy Dolon. Odysseus, seeing that the Thracians' king is dead, whistles to Diomedes to leave. He has the horses tied together, ready to ride off. But Diomedes wants to take the king's armor. He's still hesitating when he hears Athena's voice say, "No. Go now."

Diomedes runs over the corpses he's just made, sliding on blood and innards. He and Odysseus jump onto a couple of horses and lead the whole herd back to the ships, Odysseus using his borrowed bow as a whip.

They stop to pick up their trophies from the tamarisk tree where they killed the spy Dolon.

All the Greeks are waiting for them, cheering wildly. Old Nestor asks Odysseus, "What are these horses, white as clouds? I've never seen one like them!"

Odysseus shouts to the whole army, "Thracian! These are the Thracians' horses! Diomedes killed twelve of them, and smashed their king's heart with his spear! Ah, I forgot: We killed another, a spy, out there by the tamarisk tree, and brought back some souvenirs he gave us!" He laughs, waving Dolon's weasel-skin cap and jackal pelt.

Every Greek is up on the wall, cheering himself hoarse, as Diomedes and Odysseus lead the horses into camp. They hand the captured horses to slaves and walk into the sea, washing the blood and shit off themselves.

Then they go to the baths, where slaves wash them again. Only then does Odysseus put on his finest robe, then take the weasel-skin cap and jackal pelt to the stern of his ship, to be offered in thanks to Athena. He lays the cap and skin there and says, "Athena, beloved goddess, these are for you, with my thanks." Then he goes to drink wine and tell everyone the story of their great raid. But before he tastes his wine, he pours out a good gulp's worth to the goddess who loves him so well.

11

RAGE

TODAY IT WILL BE SETTLED.

Both sides watch the sunrise, looking for clues what the gods have in mind. Then they feel it. All at once. Zeus has sent them Rage.

As the two armies form up, Rage screams like a hawk coming down on a rabbit. Every man holds his spear tighter, grinding his teeth, dreaming of pushing that pointed stick right through a writhing enemy. No envoys, no fine speeches.

The two armies face off. Zeus sends a fine mist of dew down on the fighters' faces. This dew is blood-red.

Both sides charge each other without a word and the killing begins. Rage is the only god Zeus allows on the field today. He's warned all the others not to interfere.

All morning they kill each other face to face, neither side gaining a thing. Then a Greek hero runs forward, climbs up on a Trojan chariot and kills the rider. The driver jumps out to avenge his friend, and the Greek sticks his spear right through the driver's helmet and into the brain.

This hero turns back to the Greeks, and they can see his face. It's Agamemnon. Something's happened to him. Last night he was weeping, lost, a coward; now he's fighting like Akilles.

He runs through the Trojans so fast it's like a man running among statues. Before the Trojans can react, Agamemnon jumps up on another chariot and kills two of King Priam's sons, one a bastard but the other legitimate, a full-blood Trojan prince.

As soon as the two boys are dead, Agamemnon rips their armor off, tosses it back toward the Greek line—roaring, laughing.

The Trojans have never seen anything like this. They never feared Agamemnon in battle, but now they back away from him. He's possessed.

Even the Trojans' horses are afraid of Agamemnon today. He chases another chariot, and the terrified horses rear up. Agamemnon jumps in the car, looks into the faces of the two riders, and laughs: "Why, I know you boys! You're Pisander and Hippolakas, the sons of Antimakhas! Paris bribed your father to make sure Troy never gave Helen back to us!

They beg, "Take us alive! Our father is rich!"

Agamemnon laughs. "Oh, I know your father! He's the reason you're going to die now!" He pushes his spear through Pisander's guts. Hippolakhas tries to flee, but Agamemnon has his sword out. As the boy plants his hands on the chariot rail, his sword chops down, hacking off both arms at the wrist. The boy falls, and Agamemnon chops down again, striking his head off.

Agamemnon jumps down and runs among the Trojans like a brush fire, killing everything in his way.

Trojan chariots are jolting back to the city, horses fleeing toward their stables, while their riders lie on the plain. Those men are no use to their wives now! Only the buzzards circling overhead have any use for them. To the vultures, they look very sweet!

The Trojans run from Agamemnon like cattle from a hungry lion. And like cattle, they're too slow to save themselves. Agamemnon runs after them, faster than their chariot horses, stabbing one after another, tossing riders off their chariots like a farm hand pitching hay from a cart, then running on to the next chariot.

Now Zeus orders the next phase of the day's fight. He calls Iris to him, tells her, "Go to Hektor. Tell him this: 'Don't attack till Agamemnon is wounded. It won't be long till that happens. When it does, you can kill every Greek you see. I'll give you the strength to reach the Greek ships before the sun goes down.'"

Iris finds Hektor and tells him Zeus' orders.

Hektor follows them. Instead of rushing to fight Agamemnon himself, he stays back, rallying the Trojans, pushing them to the front with the shaft of his spear.

Agamemnon is still possessed, killing anything in front of him. Ifidamas, a huge Trojan, challenges him. Agamemnon throws first and misses. The giant grins and throws. The spear hits Agamemnon's silver belt, and bends. He's unhurt, but Ifidamas thinks he's wounded. The Trojan giant runs up to finish him off. Agamemnon whips out his sword and chops his head half off.

That big fool of a Trojan was as dead as bronze before he hit the ground! His wife wouldn't get much joy out of him from now on, even though he'd paid a hundred cattle for her, with the promise of another thousand sheep and goats later. Now big old Ifidamas has lost wife, life, and even his head. You'd think a man can't lose much more than that, but Agamemnon is bending down to take his last possession, his armor! It's always dangerous, stripping a corpse. You're unprotected, you don't see what's around you. Agamemnon doesn't know that Ifidamas has one thing left: a brother. Koun saw Agamemnon kill his big brother. He runs up in a rage, stabs Agamemnon through the forearm.

Then, thinking he's put Agamemnon out of action, Koun grabs his brother's huge corpse by the foot and starts dragging it away.

But Agamemnon grabs his spear with his off-hand and sticks it into Koun's side. Then he stands and cuts off Koun's head with his sword. Crazed with pain, he stands over big brother's corpse, holding little brother's head, and screams, "Look! I've killed them both! Tell their father he has no more sons!"

He tosses the head away and runs into battle again, scattering Trojans like a fox scatters chickens. While the blood flows clear from his arm, Agamemnon doesn't even feel his wound. But as the wound blackens and begins to scab the pain hits him, bad as a woman in labor. His berserk mood fades away, and he's the old, weak Agamemnon again. He croaks, "Greeks, I'm through for the day. Save the ships!" He stumbles into his chariot and heads back to camp.

This is the moment Hektor was waiting for. He shoulders his way to the front through frightened Trojans, turns back to them and shouts, "Now they die! Watch me kill, and do the same!"

He starts killing Greeks, as easily as Agamemnon was slaughtering Trojans a few minutes ago. He slides through the Greek lines like a ship's prow through salt spray, and wherever he passes, men fall, with blood spouting from their necks, or guts spilling from their bellies.

Odysseus has been watching. He grabs Diomedes and yells through the screams, "We have to stop Hektor! He'll burn the ships if we don't push him back!"

Diomedes answers, "I'll fight him, but Zeus is on his side today. I may not live much longer."

Odysseus and Diomedes go on a killing run to match Hektor's. They see two Trojans, the sons of a famous fortune-teller, and kill them both. They didn't know how short their own future would be!

Hektor sees the two Greeks killing his comrades and jumps into his chariot, flying over the dust toward Odysseus and Diomedes. His helmet shines like a comet, and his bronze armor flashes like lightning.

Diomedes yells to Odysseus, "Here comes Hektor. Not much we can do but face him."

Diomedes balances his spear, takes one long quick step and flings it at Hektor's head.

It's a good throw, and it hits the helmet high on the forehead. But Apollo himself gave Hektor that helmet. The spear glances off.

The impact leaves Hektor dazed. His horses head back to the Trojan lines by habit. Those horses have saved Hektor's life. Diomedes and Odysseus can't find him behind the Trojan shields.

Diomedes is furious: "Hektor!" he screams. "You should be dead! I see why you pray to Apollo; that helmet he gave you saved your life today! But I'll find you again!"

And Diomedes begins killing the nearest Trojans, since he can't have Hektor.

Paris has been watching from the shadows, holding his bow. While Diomedes is stripping the armor from a Trojan he just killed, Paris lets fly. The arrow hits Diomedes on the foot and goes right through, pinning it to the ground.

Paris gloats: "Ha! Got you! I just wish it'd hit you in the belly, so your guts could fester and give you a slow death!"

Diomedes grabs his foot and screams, "Aaagh, you Asians and your cowardly arrows! Why can't you fight like a man, wife-stealer? Because I'd skewer you apart in a spear fight, that's why! Never mind, your little sticks can't hurt me! But when my spear just grazes a man, the buzzards invite their friends to dinner, and his wife starts unpacking the funeral robes!"

It's all bluff. Diomedes is badly wounded. Odysseus motions the men up, and they raise their shields high to cover Diomedes. Odysseus pulls the arrow, barb and all, out of Diomedes' foot. Dizzy from the pain, Diomedes limps to his chariot and heads back to camp.

Now Odysseus is on his own. He says to himself, "This is the end. I can't run, and if I stay these Trojans will kill me. All I can do is die well."

Trojan spearmen surround him like a pack of hounds. But this boar has sharp tusks; soon a half-dozen Trojans are dead or wounded, as Odysseus keeps turning, stabbing at any who come too close.

As he stabs one Trojan, the man's brother, a fine fighter named Sokas, screams, "You've killed my brother! Either I kill you or join him!" and he rams his spear right through Odysseus' shield.

Any other man would have died. But Odysseus has Athena watching over him. Sokas' spear rips through his skin and the fat under it, hits the ribcage—but Athena deflects it so it only digs a furrow along Odysseus' ribs and pops out again. It leaves a gash, but his innards aren't punctured.

Odysseus screams at the Trojan, "You won't have long to boast about wounding me, Sokas!" and throws his own spear. It catches the Trojan dead center; he falls without a sound.

Odysseus pulls the spear from his side, and as the pain hits him he screams, "Aaaah, you died too easy, Sokas! I wish you hurt as much as I do now!"

As the spear comes out, the blood stains his side like a crimson girdle. Odysseus tries to hold the Trojans off, but hordes come running to finish him off. He circles, batting down their spears like a buck holding off dogs with his antlers.

It won't work for long. Odysseus forgets his pride and yells, "Menelaos, anyone, help me! I'm alone and hurt!"

Menelaos grabs Ajax, and the two of them smash into the ring of Trojans surrounding Odysseus.

But as Ajax is yanking his spear out of a Trojan's body, something strange happens in his head. Zeus has decided to take Ajax out of the fight by poisoning his mind with fear. The head was always Ajax's weak point. His shoulders are even stronger than Akilles', but a man needs to be strong in the head too. Ajax is weak above the neck. Not slow-witted like Menelaos, but soft. Better to be slow than soft.

Ajax tries to ignore the fear. He runs after the Trojans, stabbing anyone in range with his spear, slipping on blood and guts, moaning to himself, wanting to vomit.

Something is rising inside him, a huge scream that will never stop. Now he can only see burst guts and spraying arteries. His head wants to explode. He grips his helmet and groans.

On the other flank, Hektor is doing some killing of his own. He's killed a dozen Greeks, some of them big men, but so far, the Greek shield wall is holding. Then Paris sees his chance, and picks up his bow.

These bowmen are at their most dangerous when they're standing quietly behind a raging hero like Hektor. Everyone is watching Hektor; they don't even see Paris, waiting for a shot.

Now he sees his chance, as Machaon, the Greeks' famous healer, lowers his shield for a moment. Quicker than a cat batting a fly, Paris raises his bow, aims, fires, all in one motion.

The arrow zips into Machaon's shoulder, and he falls to his knees. The Greeks are horrified. A great healer is worth six fighters. And this is no ordinary healer; Machaon is the son of Aesculapius, the legend who brought back magic salves from the centaurs. With his father's potions, Machaon can wipe away a wound like a woman wipes grease from a pot.

A dozen Greeks turn away from the fight to lift Machaon to the nearest chariot. Nestor drives the healer to safety.

A Trojan chieftain rushes up to tell Hektor, "Quick, on the other flank! Ajax is killing us! He's like one of the Titans come back to life!"

The man pulls Hektor around, points far off and says, "See? That shield, bigger than a cart-wheel? That's Ajax!"

Hektor jumps up, grabs the chariot reins, and rides right through the Greeks, killing as he goes. Some he tramples, others he spits on his spear, others he hacks with his sword in passing, as if he was lopping branches while driving through an orchard.

The chariot bounces over corpses, and the blood and juices splash up, marking the wheels, even the sides of the cart. Bodies pop like gourds, foul gases squirt out with the bile.

Ajax sees Hektor coming, but in his madness it's the wheels, not the driver, he watches. In terror, he sees them rolling over corpses, some fresh, others rotten, green and black. He watches bellies burst as Hektor's wheels roll over them, plopping open like dumplings full of pus and shit. He can hear men screaming as loudly as if they were an inch from his face. He can see men with bone wounds, the most painful of all, rolling around screaming like seals.

And then Rage is all he can see. She's screaming at him, one inch in front of his face. Her face like an old woman who died days ago. He smells her breath, putrid and sweet.

Ajax sees himself completely alone on a plain full of rotting corpses. He lets his huge shield drop to his side, then lets it fall to the dust. Then he falls.

He tries to crawl back to camp on his hands and knees.

The Trojans see him helpless and throw their spears at him. But they're still so scared of him that they stand off and throw short.

Ajax doesn't even notice the spears falling around him. He whimpers, holding his head with both hands, until his followers run out with shields held over their heads to block the Trojans' arrows and spears and drag the big man back to the Greek line.

A KILLES STANDS ON THE STERN of a beached ship, looking toward the fight. He sees Nestor's chariot rumble into the camp carrying a wounded man, and calls, "Patroklas, my friend!"

Patroklas comes out, and Akilles says, "Go see who this wounded man is. I think it was Machaon, but I couldn't see the face."

He hopes it was Machaon. They'll miss a healer like that.

Patroklas finds Nestor taking his meal. Nestor, always courteous, takes Patroklas' hand, leads him to the cushions.

"No, sir," Patroklas says, bowing. "I really can't. You know the man who sent me here, how angry he gets when I waste time. He bid me ask you who that wounded man you brought back might be."

Nestor mutters, "Why would Akilles care about our wounded? Or our dead, for that matter?"

Patroklas has no answer. He's been trying to persuade his lord to rejoin the fight. It shames him, shames all Akilles' people, sitting in the tents while others are dying.

Nestor says, "It's bad, Patroklas. Everyone's wounded. Diomedes was hit with an arrow, Odysseus' side is ripped open, and Ajax—well, the gods have done something to Ajax. I don't understand it myself. He's not wounded, but he can't fight. So no one's left. I'm too old. Not like I was once ..."

Nestor tells a long story about a cattle raid he once led. Patroklas listens politely, gritting his teeth. Akilles will be furious at this delay, but courtesy demands Patroklas listen to the whole long tale.

Nestor concludes, "Yes, that's how I was as a young man, never caring about my own safety! But your lord Akilles is different, eh? He keeps his courage to himself."

Patroklas is embarrassed. Nestor regrets his words, puts an arm around him—everyone likes Patroklas, and this isn't his fault. Nestor begs him, "I knew your father. He told you to give Akilles good advice. Tell your lord to help us now!"

Patroklas can only turn away. He's of lower birth; he can't tell a half-god king like Akilles what to do.

Nestor asks, "Has Akilles had a prophecy? I suspect his goddess-mother told him to stay out of the fight."

The old man chews his beard, "Hmmm ... If he's been warned by a god to stay away, then there's not much we can do. Ah, I have an idea! Patroklas, ask Akilles to lend you his armor! If the Trojans see a man wearing that armor, they'll run! We'll buy some time, at least!"

Patroklas thinks it over, nods, and runs back to ask Akilles. On the way he meets Yuripilas, limping with an arrow in his thigh. "Patroklas, please help me. All the healers are all wounded. Pull this arrow out for me."

Patroklas groans. So many delays! Akilles will be in a rage by the time he gets back. But he can't refuse a wounded man, so he lays Yuripilas down and yanks the arrow out, barb and all, while a slave holds him down.

Patroklas takes his last batch of magic herb, rubs it over the wound, and hurries to Akilles' compound.

12

BREAKTHROUGH

THE GREEKS ARE pent up behind the wall now. If the Trojans break through, they'll burn the ships and slaughter the men as they stumble through the smoke.

The men on the wall watch the Trojan chariots galloping over the plain toward them, dust clouds hiding the infantry behind them.

The chariots clatter up to the wall, and a few try forcing their way through the ditch. It's a disaster. The horses rear and buck, refusing to go into that gully full of sharpened tree branches. A few chariots make it into the ditch, only to crash and tip over. Horses scream as the stakes rip their soft bellies open.

Hektor stands in his chariot, at the edge of the ditch, wondering how to attack the wall. Then Polydamus, a clever man, runs up and yells, "Hektor, this is foolish! We won't get the horses through that ditch, and even if we did we'd be jammed up against the wall! We need to attack on foot!"

Hektor says, "What if the attack fails? How do we get back to Troy on foot?"

"The slaves will wait here, hold the chariots for us!"

Hektor nods and dismounts, calling to the other nobles, "We attack on foot! Dismount!"

By this time the Trojan infantry has come up. Hektor divides the army into five scaling parties. He leads the elite, with Polydamus second in command. His brothers Paris and Helnas are in command of two other parties. Aeneas commands the fourth, and the Lycian allies, under Sarpedon, have their own force, supported by the inland tribes.

The idea is to probe the Greek wall at five points at once, so the Greeks can't concentrate against them. This should work. After all, the Greeks' wall is a weak, improvised barrier. As soon as one Trojan party breaks through, the others will run to the breakthrough, then fan out through the camp, killing anyone in their way as they make for the ships.

But there's always some conceited, well-born young man in a chariot who won't listen to sound military strategy. This time the loudmouth is Asius, a Trojan nobleman. He gallops up in his gold-painted chariot and shouts, "Hektor, what's this nonsense about attacking on foot, like peasants? There's the gate—" and he points to the left, where the Greeks have a huge gate so that their chariots can go in and out of the camp—"I say we charge it at a gallop! What are you waiting for?"

Hektor shakes his head: "No, Asius. We dismount and attack on foot."

Asius is furious: "What? That's what commoners are for! Why should I dismount?"

Hektor begins, "Because there's no room to fight from a chariot. See? No room between the ditch and the wall."

Asius sneers, "Who told you that? Some coward? I'll be through that gate before they can even react!"

Hektor shakes his head again, "No, don't try it. They'll have it blocked; they're not stupid. And then you'll be—" But Asius shouts down at him, "No! You can fight like a peasant if you want, but my chariot and my men will storm that gate!" And he whips his team away, his noble friends following in their chariots, and their doomed foot soldiers trotting after.

But as he comes up to the open gate, he sees the Greeks have laid a big tree-trunk across the opening. Asius' chariots have to wheel off. He leads them in a wide circle over the plain, coming up behind his foot soldiers and shouting, "Up, quick, drag the log away!"

The foot soldiers trot up to the gate, but suddenly the Greeks on the wall stand and throw their spears. Some of Asius' men fall dead, and the rest run back even faster than they advanced.

Asius leads his chariots in a circle, coming back to his surviving infantry, yelling, "Try again, you cowards! They've used up their spears!"

So the commoners charge the gate again. And as they come into range, the Greeks throw—rocks this time as well as spears. Asius' men fall dead under the huge rocks, or writhe with a spear in the belly.

Asius jerks his team to a stop, shakes his fist at the sky and screams, "Zeus! You liar! You told us the wall would fall!"

Zeus chuckles, "Yes, but I promised Hektor, not a fool like you!"

Zeus has nothing but contempt for Asius and his arrogant friends. He has already decided they'll die today and go down to the underworld, where Asius will have a long time to learn patience.

While these hot-headed fools are wasting time at the gate, Hektor's storming parties assemble at five different points along the wall. Hektor raises his arm, and all five parties charge at once.

But Hektor's party sees something that makes them stop dead, halfway across the ditch. It's an eagle flapping slowly over them with a snake in its talons. The snake is blood red.

The eagle hovers right over Hektor. The snake is biting up at its breast, striking again and again until the bird screams and releases it. As the snake falls, the eagle tilts in the wind and glides away.

Polydamus sidles up and says, "Hektor, did you see that? I know you think I'm over-cautious, but you know what it means! The eagle let the snake go! We'll fail!"

Hektor shoves Polydamus back, snarling, "You want me to listen to a bird? I have Zeus' promise that we win today! I don't care if the birds fly north or south!"

Polydamus screams, "It means we'll die!"

All the men listen, infected with Polydamus' fear. So Hektor grabs Polydamus, shakes him, and loud enough for all the men to hear: "There is only one omen, and that's fighting for your city to the death!"

He lifts Polydamus up with one hand, pointing his spear at the man's throat with the other, and says loudly, "As for you, Polydamus, you don't need to worry about being killed by the Greeks. If you won't attack, I'll kill you right now!" The Trojans shout with joy, their fear gone. Hektor leads them at a run through the stakes and up the wall, shields high over their heads to block the Greek spears, rocks, and arrows.

Now the Greeks are sorry they didn't offer proper sacrifices when they built this wall. It's weak, and the gods will not protect it. The Trojans mass around the joins, dozens of men pulling at every weak point, ripping away the buttresses. The Greeks rain rocks and spears down at them, but other Trojans respond by throwing spears at the defenders.

Now the wall is falling apart and Hektor's men are shoving through the gaps, spears first.

Ajax has recovered from his fit of madness. He's trying to make up for his shame, fighting everywhere at once, outdoing himself. He runs from one point to another, dragging men with them, trying to plug the gaps. The Greeks form up behind the wall wherever the Trojans have broken through, using their own shields to make a second wall.

Ajax runs along their line, yelling, "Keep a tight line! Lord or commoner, we're all one shield-wall now!"

But no matter what Ajax does, Hektor's plan is working. As the Greeks collect to contain one breakthrough, other points along the wall are left with no defenders. Sarpedon the Lycian sees a gap and pushes his men into it. The Greeks throw everything they have at him, but he's like a hungry lion hunching toward a sheep pen, paying no mind to the shepherds' shouts or the rocks they throw.

Sarpedon drags his friend Glaukos up to the wall, shouting, "We must break through! Nobles, lead the way! War is when we nobles earn our meat, when we show our peasants why they feed us!"

At that moment, Glaukos falls with an arrow in his shoulder. Then Ajax drops a boulder on the head of Sarpedon's friend, Epikles. Epikles' helmet is crushed as flat as a gold cup lying in a grave. His head is broken; everything goes dark for him.

Sarpedon is so angry he grabs a joint of the wall with his huge hands and pulls it down. He storms into the Greek camp, spear first.

But Teucer the bowman is waiting behind the wall, aiming to put an arrow into the first man through. Sarpedon sees little Teucer grinning at him, bow bent—and the next moment he feels the arrow slice deep into his shoulder.

As he stumbles, Teucer's huge half-brother Ajax slams his spear into Sarpedon's shield. The sheer power of Ajax's spear throws Sarpedon back through the gap, where he lies until his men help him up. As they stand around, he loses patience: "Do I have to do this all by myself? Why aren't you attacking?"

He picks himself up and charges again through the breach. This time his men follow, screaming the Lycian battle cry.

Far down the wall, where Hektor has broken through, the Greek fighters hear Lycian battle cries behind them. They panic and run for the ships. Hektor, seeing them flee, picks up a huge boulder, too big for any three men of our day to lift, and tosses it at the wall. It smashes open a gap like a wasp smashing through a flimsy spider web.

The Trojans cheer, and Hektor calls, "Follow me through!"

He jumps through the gap, a sight so terrifying only a god could have faced him. There are only men facing him today, and they run away, dropping their shields.

Hektor shouts to his men, "Torches! Bring fire! We'll burn the ships!" as he hacks his way toward the beach.

13

FIRE

ZEUS WATCHES THE LITTLE POINTS of light—Trojan torches moving toward the Greek ships. He promised Thetis he'd let the Trojans burn at least one of those ships.

Zeus considers the matter as good as finished. He has other places to deal with, so he turns his mind away from Troy. Seeing Zeus' attention wander, Poseidon grunts in satisfaction. He's been waiting for this chance.

Poseidon is a strange god. Old, solitary. He never feasts with the other gods. He can hardly communicate with the younger ones, Zeus' shiny, quasi-human brats.

No one understands him. Fishermen pray to him as god of the sea, but that's not what he is. Poseidon owns one-third of the universe, the part that lies between Zeus' sky and Hades' nightmare caverns under the earth.

They were three brothers: Zeus, Poseidon, and Hades. They killed their father, naturally. Then, to avoid killing each other, they decided to divide up the universe by drawing straws. Zeus got the long straw and claimed the overworld, the sky and the lightning, all the shiny parts.

Hades got the short straw, and went down under the earth, to the world of the dead.

Poseidon drew the middle straw, the surface. Zeus told him it was the second-best, but Poseidon has been brooding a long time, wondering if he's been cheated. Zeus got the best part; everyone agrees on that. But what if Hades' underworld is second-best? After all, everyone fears Hades, whereas Poseidon gets squeezed between sky and Hell. He feels squashed, slighted.

For example, look at what happened with that Demeter. Even though Poseidon invented horses just to please her, she ended up going down to the underworld with Hades.

Poseidon is always coming in last and he's sick of it. He should be running all the worlds, and here's his chance. He'll take over the war in Troy, now that Zeus has taken his eye off it. He'll save the Greeks, and they'll worship him in place of Zeus.

Poseidon rolls down from the mountaintop, crashing into the sea like a landslide. He translates himself into a wave rushing toward the shore where the Greek ships are beached. All the surface is his, land as well as sea.

When he comes ashore at Troy, Poseidon wrenches himself into something like human form. He's trying to look like Kalkys, the Greek shaman. But he's so old and crazy that he does a very bad imitation of Kalkys, a hulking, fuming god badly crammed into a man's body.

He comes up behind Ajax in the middle of the fight at the wall, tries to talk. But Poseidon's voice sounds nothing like Kalkys or any other human ever born. The two Ajaxes flinch away from this thing and its noises, its fuming semblance of human shape.

In a rage, Poseidon lifts his trident. He'll stop trying to encourage the Greeks with words. He'll do it directly, through the earth itself. He slams the trident into the ground at the two Ajaxes' feet. The pressure wave reverberates through the whole Greek force, up through the earth into their bodies.

As the temblors die away, the two Ajaxes feel Poseidon's power fizzing and trembling through them.

The old god sees he's made his point; he drops all semblance of human shape and melts into the earth.

Clever little Ajax says to big dumb Ajax, "That was no man."

Big dumb Ajax nods, "I know!"

Little Ajax nods toward the ground, whispers, "It was him, the old earth."

Big Ajax flexes his knees: "He did something. I feel stronger ... in the legs."

Little Ajax nods: "From the ground up."

They stand together, shield to shield, helmets almost touching. The best men join them in a tight shield wall. No one needs to speak; the earth itself is bringing them together in an unbroken, unbreakable wall of spears.

And here comes Hektor, at full speed, like a boulder rolling straight toward the Greek shield wall.

Unstoppable boulder meets unbreakable wall, and men die by the dozen.

At first the fights are like wedding dances, two lines facing each other, Greek shields facing Trojan. As long as everyone stays hunched behind his shield, he's likely to stay alive.

But soon the bravest shove their way through the wall, like young men at a wedding dance. Only this time, the dance ends in a man's death. Then the man who got the kill has to try to grab the body, a very dangerous moment. As soon as you lean out to take his armor, you're open to a thrown spear.

Teucer the bowman, Ajax's little brother, jabs his spear into a Trojan's head. The spear goes into the skull; the Trojan falls like a tree.

Teucer wants the Trojan's armor, darts out again, like a quick little fish and tries to grab the corpse by the ankle. But Hektor saw that one coming, and tosses his big spear at the little Greek.

Teucer dodges, but that leaves a gap in the shield wall. Hektor's spear flies through it, into the chest of poor Amfimakas. He falls on his face, dead before he hits the ground.

Amfimakas was Poseidon's grandson. Poseidon can feel the boy dying, his spirit falling through the surface—down, unstoppable, into Hades' world. The earth quakes with the god's rage, and he seethes across the camp looking for an avenger.

Ideomenus the Cretan is limping away from the fight with a gashed knee. Poseidon rears up in front of him, a blurred, grinding shape, almost human, and growls, "Idomenus, why don't you fight?"

The Cretan tries to stammer an answer: "We're all fighting. I'm just hurt."

Poseidon growls, moves in a huge blur—and Ideomenus is healed. New strength and courage surge through him, from the ground up. He heads back to battle, with the old god running beside him almost like a man.

They meet Ideomenus' squire, Meriones, and shout to him, "What are you doing here? Meriones is stunned at the sound, the look of his master. That voice was bigger than a man's. And what's that thing running along next to Ideomenus? Meriones stammers: "I'm looking for a spear. I lost mine."

Ideomenus and the shape beside him speak together, in a huge low groan, "Spear? Any spear you want, from Trojans we killed. Come with us!"

Meriones is offended. Is Ideomenus implying he's dodging the fight? He sputters, "I've killed my share of Trojans! You know that!"

The shape beside Ideomenus trembles with rage, and Ideomenus says in a strange voice, "Humans, always talking! Fight! No more talk!"

The man-shape touches Meriones and he feels it too, this rage burning up from the earth. He runs with them to meet the Trojans.

But Poseidon senses that Zeus' eye is on the battle now. He has to be careful, can't let big brother see him meddling in the war. He works on his semblance, trying to be one of these little humans. But it doesn't fool anyone. What the Greeks see, running along with Ideomenus and Meriones, is a monstrous dust-colored blur that shakes the earth.

The Trojans swarm forward, Zeus' lightning flashing from their spear-heads. Against them come Ideomenus and his men, riding a dusty wave raised by Poseidon. Men die as the two brother-gods play them like pebbles in a child's game.

Ideomenus kills Orthyonus, a big talker from somewhere back in the sticks. He swaggered into Troy and told old Priam he wanted to marry his daughter Kassandra.

Priam said, "What have you brought me for a dowry?"

Orthyonus steps right up to the old man and says, "Oh, I haven't brought you gold or finery. I'll make you a better offer than that: I'll destroy these Greeks who are attacking you!"

He was a big, wild-looking barbarian, and the Trojans needed all the help they could get. So Priam called his daughter over and put her hand in Orthyonus'.

Kassandra was furious, hissing, "Father, don't be foolish! This man will die the first time he goes up against the Greeks! I can see it as clearly as I see your face!"

But Priam is deaf, and no one ever listens to Kassandra. It's done; Kassandra belongs to Orthyonus, though she stares at him as she would a corpse.

And now she's been proved right again. Orthyonus isn't boasting now, lying in the dust with a big hole in his chest from Ideomenus' spear.

Back in the city, Kassandra is weaving at the loom. The very instant Orthyonus falls she says to her maids, "He's dead, my husband. I told them so!" And with a happy smile, she goes back to her weaving. Kassandra likes being right.

Out on the dust plain, Aeneas lunges out and jams his spear right through Afares' cheekbone. The spear takes Afares from sunlight to darkness, Hades' world where there's nothing but fog and silence. But Aeneas' lunge leaves a gap in the Trojans' shields. Fast as a snake, Antilokas sticks his spear through the gap at the Trojan Tho-on. It's only a light jab, but it makes a fine cut in the vein that runs up the side of a man's throat. Tho-on can't believe this little nick is killing him; he watches his life blood hiss out of his neck, pulse by pulse.

Antilokas runs forward to strip the dead man's armor. The Trojans throw every spear they have at him, but old Poseidon is with Antilokas, bending the earth this way and that to save him.

Adamis the Trojan decides to kill Antilokas the one sure way, by running him through. He sprints up and slams his spear two-handed into Antilokas' shield.

But Poseidon won't let his favorite die so soon. He lifts up the earth under Adamis so that the spear bends, then breaks in half. Adamis doesn't understand what's happened, but he knows he's helpless now. He tries to run back behind the Trojan shields, but Meriones sticks his spear right into his groin between the navel and the balls. It's the most painful wound a man can get. Adamis takes a long time to die, screaming and thrashing. The Trojans have thrown all their spears, so they draw their swords—and some of them have those big Thracian swords, powerful blades. Helnas, Kassandra's twin brother, smashes his sword over Deipyrus' helmet. The head is broken like a shaken egg. He falls into the dark even as the sun shines on his body.

Menelaos sees him die and runs toward Helnas, who shrugs a bow into his hand, fits an arrow, fires. But good Greek bronze beats Asian arrows; Helnas' dart bounces off Menelaos' breastplate like a stick thrown by a child.

Menelaos slams into Helnas, spear-first. The point goes right through his hand, nailing it to the bow. Helnas jerks back, with his hand stuck to it.

The Trojans are bringing out all their outlandish weapons today. Pisander runs at Menelaos waving a two-headed battle axe, but Menelaos just waits with his good Greek spear, then sticks it quick at Pisander's face.

It breaks like a clay bowl. His eyes pop out and roll in the dust, as the Greeks laugh and cheer, pointing at the eyes, shouting, "You dropped a couple of eggs!"

Menelaos stands with one foot on Pisander's body gloating: "He got what he deserved, and so will every one of you Trojans! You thought you could steal my wife and my gold? You all laughed at me! Well, better a live cuckold than a corpse!"

Harpalyon runs at Menelaos. He came all the way from the Black Sea to help the Trojans. All that way just to die; Meriones has his bow ready and hits him in the butt-cheek. The arrow punctures Harpalyon's bladder, and he dies writhing in the dirt, as the Greeks point and laugh, "Oh Trojans, your friend is leaking!" Harpalyon's father moans as the Greeks mock his son, calling, "Is it blood or piss leaking out of this Trojan worm?"

Paris watches his friend Harpalyon die and decides the Greeks will pay. He sees that Eukenor the Corinthian is laughing at the death throes. He jams a spear right into Eukenor's jaw, under the ear. The Corinthian falls down dead. But it's no loss, because Eukenor's father has the second sight and told his son long ago: "If you go fight at Troy you'll die in battle; but if you stay home you'll die of a horrible disease. It's your choice." Eukenor said, "I'll go to Troy." So Paris has done Eukenor a favor, giving him a quick easy death, and the Greeks don't waste much time mourning him.

Over where the Greek wall is weakest, Hektor is killing every Greek he sees. The Lokrians over on that flank can't stop him. Those Lokrians fight like Asians, with bows and slings, not with spears like real men. They don't even have helmets. They can't stand up to Hektor's spear, even though the two Ajaxes are fronting for them.

But like all bowmen, the Lokrians are most dangerous when they flee. As they scatter, avoiding Hektor's spear, they turn and shoot. Their arrows pick off one Trojan after another. The Trojans lose heart. Nothing is as demoralizing as getting shot by a cowardly little archer, listening to him hoot at you from a safe distance as you writhe in pain.

Hektor's men thought it would be all over once they breached the wall. But all they've done is to push the Greeks into one compact mass of shields and spears.

The Trojan attack stalls. Polydamus yells to Hektor, "You may be a great fighter, but that doesn't make you a good commander! Look around—see how some of our parties aren't even trying to advance? We're outnumbered, deep inside the Greek camp. And Akilles isn't even fighting yet. What'll happen when we reach his tents?"

Hektor nods. "We need to change strategy. Gather all the chiefs; I'll hold off the Greeks."

Polydamus hurries off. Hektor runs to the front, his tired men slouching after him. They find Paris hanging back, and Hektor takes out all his rage on his brother: "Paris, what are you doing—trying to look handsome, play the warrior? Where's Deiphobus? Our brother Helnas? Where are Asias, Orthy-onus, the rest of them?"

Paris leans on his spear and says, "Brother, don't shout at me. They're all dead except Helnas and Deiphobus—and they're both wounded. I've been fighting all day. Just tell me and my men where you want us to go."

Hektor combines Paris' men with his and leads them straight at Ajax's ships. Ajax's men fall back, but Ajax himself comes barreling out from the shield wall, like a bull pushing through a herd of goats.

He cries, "Hektor, you want to burn my ships? You're welcome to try. Zeus has taken your side today, but I promise Troy will burn before my ships do!"

Hektor roars back, "Ajax, your name means 'sorry,' and you'll be sorrier when I butcher you! Your guts will roll in the dust, and you'll see your ships burning as you die!"

Hektor's party and Ajax's men charge at each other.

14

SLEEP

O LD NESTOR IS DRINKING WINE by his tent when Machaon stumbles
in holding his wounded shoulder. Nestor gives him a seat, saying,
"Sit down, let my women warm up a bath to wash the blood off."

Machaon looks pale and weak. Nestor pokes his head around the tent
and sees Greeks running through the camp in a panic. He mutters, "What's
happening here?" and goes off to find Agamemnon, who's standing with
Odysseus, and Diomedes. All three are wounded, out of the fight, leaning on
their spears as Greek fighters run past, fleeing from Trojans.

Agamemnon sees Nestor coming and calls, "Nestor, why aren't you fighting?"
Then he shakes his head and mutters, "Oh, what does it matter? Hektor will
burn the ships today! Akilles hates me so much he won't even fight!"

Nestor joins the group, saying, "Yes, it looks bad for us! The Trojans have
broken through the wall."

Agamemnon says, "Yes, your wall, Nestor! We all worked to build it, nobles,
commoners, slaves! You said it would protect us, but the Trojans charged
right through it!"

Nestor has nothing to say.

Agamemnon groans, "Zeus must hate me! We have to take to the ships! There's no shame in running when it's your life at stake! Push the ships out to sea!"

Odysseus has had enough. He turns on Agamemnon: "Son of a god-cursed father, what are you gibbering about now?"

Odysseus points toward the shore: "You know what would happen if we started pushing our ships into the water? It'd take all day to get them off properly; they're moored two or three deep! It'd be chaos!"

Agamemnon moans, "But the gods ... they hate me!"

Odysseus yells, "Maybe so, but they don't hate me or my men!"

He shakes his fist at Agamemnon: "You don't deserve to lead an army as fine as this! You should command one full of cowards like you! As for us, we Greeks fight from the first wisp of beard till our last gray hairs go down to the grave!"

After a long moment, Agamemnon says, "You insult me, Odysseus, but you're right. My mind is gone today. I admit it. Someone else will have to lead us."

Diomedes steps up: "That'd be me. I say we go to the fight, wounded though we are, to cheer our men on. That's our job."

And they limp toward the battle, leaning on their spears, with Agamemnon in the lead.

There's someone or something in their path—a hunched figure rising up from the ground like a termite mound. As they move toward it, they recognize Poseidon. His rough old voice darts into their minds, a jolting series of ideas: "Agamemnon ... king ... gods not so angry with you. Akilles will be sorry. You'll fight. Trojans will run."

Then he stops trying to speak words, and becomes a battle-rage that pushes the earth up around them, flinging them forward.

Hera has been watching her big brother Poseidon. She's pleased to see him helping the Greeks. She'd like to help too—but there's her husband and brother, Zeus, watching her, making sure she doesn't meddle. She stares at him, hating him.

So she decides to lie with him. She goes to a secret room her son Hefestos made for her. He inlaid the doorway with spells and metal threads so that no one else can enter, not even Zeus. She gathers weapons: scented olive oil, a fine veil, earrings, her best gown.

She makes ready for battle, first washing all the dirt from her body, then opening the vial of her special scented olive oil. If you even shake the vial, the scent of that oil fills the universe from Olympos down to Hades, where the dead catch a whiff and groan for their lost bodies.

Hera takes that magic oil and smears it over her soft skin. Then she weaves her hair into plaits.

Now for the earrings, three fine gold dangles to slip through her pierced earlobes. She shakes her head and smiles at the tinkle they make. All her magic is working: the waft of scented oil, the soft weight of her plaited hair, the teasing jingle of her earrings.

Now she puts on the miraculous robe her daughter Athena made. It shimmers with this color or that, any color Hera chooses.

And now the veil—to hide her beauty, but not too well.

Now the sandals to set off her shapely feet.

And she's ready. First she goes to find Afroditi. Afroditi flinches away; she and Hera are not friends. But today Hera is all smiles. "Dear girl, may I ask a favor of you?"

Afroditi stammers, "Yes, yes! After all, you're wife-sister of Lord Zeus!"

Hera smiles. It's good the girl remembers who's who. Best to tease her a little anyway. So Hera says, ever so gently, "So you're not peeved with me, dearest? A little peeved at me, perhaps? Because I help the Greeks kill your precious Trojans, mmmm?"

Afroditi shakes her head.

Hera comes closer, murmuring, "You're sure you're not angry, girl? I do so hope not!" Afroditi stutters, "No, not at all! You're our lord's wife!"

Hera purrs, "That's right! So you'll lend me that magic corset of yours, won't you?"

Afroditi blushes; she didn't know her secrets were such common knowledge.

Hera goes on, "You know, the magic corset you wear when you want men to, ah, how shall I put it?—to like you?"

Afroditi nods, and quickly reaches behind her waist, undoing the golden corset and handing it over.

Hera smiles and puts the corset on, under her breasts, hooking it at the back.

If you'd been standing there at that moment, you'd have seen a miracle. As soon as Afroditi took off the corset, her heart-stopping beauty vanished. Her face was the same, her shape didn't change; but somehow she was just a skinny girl, like any other.

And as Hera buckled on the corset, the glory that left Afroditi went into her. All her age and harshness melted away. She was no longer the angry wife, but a fine, warm woman in full bloom, whom any man would ache to hold forever.

Afroditi feels the change and flees into her room, so no one will see her without her magic. Hera feels the change too, stretches out her arms, touches herself, brushes her shoulder with her cheek. Then she sighs; she must get to work, no time for play. She doesn't bother with the pantomime of chariot and horses; she simply wishes herself at her destination, Lemnos, where she has business with Sleep.

Hera likes Lemnos. The Lemnian women once killed every man on the island. It's one of her favorite stories. Sensible Lemnian women!

She floats to Earth on the island. Sleep saw her coming; he sees everything. He never rests. And the sight of her doesn't make him happy. He's her brother, and he has a long memory.

He mutters, "What now, Hera? You must be in a hurry, not to bother with a chariot or horses."

She shrugs: "I have no time for all that. Sweet brother Sleep, do one thing for me!"

He grunts, "I thought you must want something. What is it?"

She touches his arm: "Just do one little thing for me."

He laughs grimly: "I did you a favor a while ago. Remember? I sure do."

Hera strokes his arm, "All I ask you to do is to put my stupid husband to sleep for a little while. I have … things to do … that he wouldn't approve."

Sleep chuckles, shakes his head bitterly: "Oh, I knew it'd be about Zeus! The last time I did you a favor he nearly killed me!"

She begs, "I'll make it worth your while! My boy Hefestos will make you a fine seat, Sleep! You sit and watch, day and night; wouldn't you like to be comfy?"

"Last time I listened to you, Zeus came after me, wanted to toss me in the ocean! No thank you!"

"Noooo, that was a misunderstanding about Herakles, his son! I admit I had a grudge against the boy, but this time it's mere humans I want killed! Just a few thousand Trojans! Zeus won't get upset over humans the way he did about his son!"

Sleep shakes his head, turns away. He's not going to be sweet-talked again.

Hera thinks it over. "All right then, I'll give you that girl Pasitea."

Sleep turns his huge eyes on her, showing real interest for the first time. "Pasitea? Yes?"

She nods, "Yes. Although she's very young."

He's breathing faster. "I get Pasitea?"

She nods again. "Mmmm. She's so pretty, and soooo young."

He asks again, "I get her? Promise?"

She nods.

He bites his lip, then says, "All right. But before I take one step, you're going to swear by the black river. Come on, stretch one hand to the sea—right, like that! And the other on the earth, yes, like that!"

Sleep shouts to the air, "Hades! Do you witness her oath?"

Nothing changes, but both of them flinch at once. They felt it, a pulse from far under the earth. Hades witnesses the oath.

Sleep nods, "Yes, I'll put your Zeus to sleep. But his mind is strong; he won't sleep long. So be quick."

Hera nods, and transports both of them to the summit of Mount Ida. Zeus is sitting there staring down at Troy, making sure his wife and daughter don't meddle in the fight.

As Hera walks toward Zeus, Sleep climbs up a tree. He finds a good branch, changes himself into a buzzard, and settles down to wait.

Zeus hears the sweet little jingling of Hera's earrings and golden belt. He turns toward her, ready to scold—but then something melts inside him. His mouth gapes open, his eyes bulge, and he asks hoarsely, "Hera, I didn't expect you here. Where is your chariot?"

Hera lies, "Oh, I tied the horses down the slope."

Zeus is staring at her the way he did when they were first married. He mutters, "Why'd you come here?"

Hera, all demure, lowers her eyes, traces a pattern in the dirt with her pretty feet, and whispers, "I wanted to get your permission to go see our parents, who are quarreling again. Isn't it sad when husband and wife quarrel? A wife should always be obedient! That's why I came to ask your permission for the journey. I'd so hate for you to be angry with me!"

Zeus is staring at her, breathing through his mouth. He gasps, "I've never wanted a woman as much as I want you right now. And I've had 'em all, goddesses, mortals, demi-goddesses, so many I can't even remember all their names! There was Ixion's wife, what was her name? And Danae, O sweet little Danae, with those ankle bracelets ... Leto ... Semele, O Semele, and Alkmenae, who gave me my son Herakles ..."

"We don't need the whole list! Get to the part about how I surpass them all!"

He says, "That's my point, darling: I never wanted any of them the way I

want you right now. Oh yeah, right here. On this nice sunny mountaintop."
"Certainly not! We can be seen from Olympos! The whole family could be
watching us! I'd never live it down! But there's my room, the one Hefestos
made me, soundproof, triple-locked. Let's go there!"

Zeus whines, "Darling, I don't want to wait that long! I can hide us from
the others right here!"

He whispers something to the air, and all around them, a carpet of flowers
sprouts, flowers so tender that when you roll over them in love-play, it only
frees their perfumes. And above, a golden tent surrounds them, dripping
glints of golden dew.

They fall onto the carpet of flowers in each other's arms. For a long hour
Sleep watches from his buzzard perch, muttering and scowling.

Then he sees Zeus step from the golden shimmer, stretching, yawning,
and brushing flowers off his shoulders.

Sleep hisses, "Always so pleased with himself! Happy as a bull among cows!
Never mind; now I earn my sweet Pasitea!"

He shakes off the buzzard-form, becomes himself—a scrawny husk with
huge, burning, night-hunter's eyes. He leans toward Zeus and whispers, "Sleep!"

Zeus falls into Hera's arms, already snoring. Sleep shouts to Hera, "Remember your promise!" and vanishes. Hera nods, and Sleep carries out his last task,
going down to Poseidon on the battlefield and telling him, "Now, old Earth,
you can do what you want to help the Greeks. That's Hera's solemn promise."

Poseidon mutters, "My brother Zeus ... angry with me?"

Sleep chuckles, "Hera and I took care of him. She made him happy and
I put him to sleep! Zeus is out of action for a while, you can count on that."

Poseidon nods, flows to the front of the Greek host. He roars for their
attention in a voice bigger than thunder: "Greeks, I lead you now! Good men
take the best shields! Weak men take the bad shields! Strong men, take the
best helmets! Little men, take the worst!"

The Greeks obey, eager to please the thing with the voice of a great god and
the blurred outline. Soon the best men are wearing the best armor, carrying
the strongest shields.

Hektor, facing the Greeks, sees what's going on and turns to his men: "They
have a god giving their orders today. I have no god-blood. But no matter; we'll
trade some of our blood for more of theirs."

He runs at the Greeks and throws. His spear catches Ajax right in the
chest. But Poseidon will not let the Greek chiefs die. With Zeus unconscious,

he can bend reality in the Greeks' favor, just as he pleases. So he slows down Hektor's spear, deflects it into the leather straps Ajax wears on his chest, one for his shield, one for his scabbard. It stops short of Ajax's skin, though the force of Hektor's throw knocks Ajax down.

Hektor groans to see his perfect throw ruined by Poseidon's cheating. He turns back to the shelter of the Trojan shields—but not fast enough.

Ajax jumps up with a weapon in his hand. While he was lying stunned on the ground, he picked up a big stone, one of the boulders the Greeks used to keep the beached ships upright. Nowadays, it would take two men just to drag that stone a few feet. But Ajax picks it up with one hand and tosses it sidearm at Hektor without breaking a sweat. The big stone hits Hektor in the perfect spot, just over the rim of his shield, below the bottom of his helmet, on the side of the neck.

He spins like a wooden top, falls flat in the dust.

The Greeks are overjoyed, and swarm toward his body, but the Trojans spread their shields over him as hens fluff their wings out over their chicks.

Polydamus, Hektor's gloomy advisor, takes his master's fall hardest of all. He lunges at Prothenor and rams the spear right through the Greek's shoulder. As Prothenor grabs the dust with both hands, Polydamus screams, "There you are! My spear will make you a nice walking staff for your trip down into the dark!"

The Greeks hate this sort of gloating. These Easterners can't kill a man without trying to be witty. It's unmanly.

Ajax grabs a spear and tosses it after Polydamus, who's scuttling back to the Trojan shields as fast as he can. Polydamus sees the throw and ducks; Ajax's spear whistles over his head and hits Arkelokas, a Trojan warrior who opened his stance to let Polydamus back in. Ajax's spear slams into Arkelokas' neck-bone, lifts him right off the ground and pins him to the ground five paces back, while his feet are still in the air.

Ajax is well pleased with that throw. To show that Greeks can gloat as wittily as Easterners, he calls, "Now, Polydamus, who was your friend that I just pinned to the earth? He looked rich! I'd say he's just as worth killing as my friend Prothenor, wouldn't you?"

Suddenly everyone wants to be witty when they kill a man. Penelos kills Iliones, the richest man in Troy, sticking his spear into Iliones' eye, bursting the eyeball.

Penelos calmly yanks his spear out of the eye, takes out his sword, and chops off Iliones' head and holds it up, showing it to jeering Greeks, then Trojans.

He turns the bloody face close to his own and says, "Why, it's the rich boy, Iliones!" Then he turns the severed head toward the Trojans and says, "Iliones says, 'Tell Mother and Father I won't be coming home! And tell my wife not to make dinner for me!'" As the Greeks laugh, Penelos tosses the head toward the Trojans and roars, "And he says you'll all be joining him any day now!"

The Trojans feel their knees go soft as water.

15

APOLLO

ZEUS WAKES UP in a bad mood. He looks down and sees Hektor lying half-dead, Poseidon openly helping the Greeks.

He glares at Hera. She's pretending to sleep, but he knows better. "Well, wife, I see you've done it again. Taken Hektor out of the fight, tricked me into bed, put me to sleep somehow."

She doesn't react. He goes on, "I'm thinking of giving you a good hard beating. Remember that time you tried to tie me down? Remember what happened when I got free? I had to teach you a lesson. I let you hang by the wrists all night ... couldn't even sleep for your screams. It could happen again."

Hera's scared, remembering that terrible night. She sits up and purrs, "I swear to you, husband, that whatever Poseidon is doing to help the Greeks, it has nothing to do with me. I tried to warn him! 'Poseidon,' I said, 'you silly old fool, you should obey my dear husband Zeus!'"

He laughs. "Sure you did! You know, woman, if you'd just let me run the family's affairs, it'd all go a lot smoother. I've got it all planned. First I order

Poseidon back into the ocean where I won't have to look at him. Then I send Apollo to heal Hektor and put some fight into those Trojans. Then Patroklas, Akilles' friend and vassal, will get himself killed by Hektor. Akilles will go crazy with rage and come back into the fight, and the Greeks will finally sack Troy. See?"

She nods. He goes on, "But I'm not helping the Greeks until Hektor burns at least one Greek ship. That's the promise I made to Thetis."

He stares at her. "So, you understand? Do it my way, or it won't happen."

She nods again, but he can't read her face.

He grunts, "Fine. See if you can help for once instead of getting in my way. Go up to Olympos, find Iris and Apollo and tell them to come to me, here. I have things to arrange."

Hera bows her head, playing the dutiful wife.

She crosses to Olympos in an instant. The gods are drinking as usual. As soon as they see her, they jostle to offer her a goblet of nectar, seeking her favor.

She ignores every one but Themis. Themis always does things just right. In fact, she is the goddess of proper conduct. Themis hugs Hera and asks, "What's wrong? Has your husband been threatening you?"

"Oh, Themis, what that man has put me through! Call all the gods together, so I can tell them his wicked plans."

When everyone's seated, Hera announces, "Kinfolk, we must give up. Zeus is our lord, our tyrant, and we must submit. He's planning to kill many of our favorite humans, and ..." she sighs, "... there's nothing we can do about it."

She turns to Ares, takes his dirty, blood-stained hand, and says, "Poor Ares, did you know those cruel Trojans have killed your son Askalafos?"

Ares goes into a fit, right at the table. He roars, "I'll kill those Trojans! I'll kill every one of them! I don't care what my father says, I don't care if he hits me with a lightning bolt, I'm going down to Troy right now!"

He stomps out to hitch up his foul and eerie horses, Panic and Terror.

Athena says to Hera, "Mother! You know he'll just get hurt!" Hera runs out after Ares. As easily as a mother takes her baby's cap off, she yanks the huge helmet from his head, slides the shield out of his grip, and finally wrenches away his spear. As she undresses him, she scolds, "Stupid boy, have you lost your mind? Father Zeus could squeeze you like a bunch of grapes! And if you make him angry, he'll come here and do the same to all of us!"

Ares whines, "But they killed my son!"

She laughs, "What was his name, if you care so much about him?"

He scratches his filthy, blood-encrusted hair, then mumbles, "It started with an 'a,' I'm pretty sure ..."

She grabs him by the scruff of the neck and leads him back to the banquet hall, saying, "Just forget about your son! Not that it matters, but his name was Askalafos, and he was nothing special. Better men than him have died in battle!"

She pushes him back down onto his couch.

Hera tells Iris and Apollo to go to Zeus. They arc over the horizon, landing on Mount Ida. Zeus is still sitting there, watching the battle by the ships.

He nods, "At least you two show up when I ask you. Iris, I need you to go to my brother Poseidon. Be blunt with him. He's a little slow to understand sometimes, and he can be stubborn. You tell him to stop helping the Greeks, right now. He can go wherever he wants, up to Olympos or better yet down into the ocean where I won't have to see him, but I want him gone from that battlefield immediately."

Iris bows and begins to vanish, but Zeus says, "Wait!" She coalesces again. "And tell him that if he doesn't like my orders he can fight me anytime."

Iris bows, transluces, and flows through the sky to stand before Poseidon on the plain of Troy. How ugly he is, all dirt-dark, wobbling before her.

In her clear girl's voice, she intones, "Poseidon, dark-haired prince of the earth, my lord Zeus brings you a message. You are to go up to the gods' house, or down into your ocean."

Poseidon seethes, his somewhat human shape fluctuating as he thinks of a reply. Poseidon has trouble communicating with these bright young gods. He grunts, "Three brothers! Me, Zeus, Hades!"

She shrugs, "My lord Zeus has instructed me to say that if you do not obey him, he will come down to fight you. He warns you not to challenge him, because he is stronger than you."

Poseidon is hurt. He tries to explain to this luminous girl-god thing: "Three brothers! Equals! We drew straws! Zeus drew sky, brother Hades drew down-world; I, I got this, earth in between!"

She shrugs. He is so ugly, so old!

He fumes, "Tell Zeus he can rule over you little younger gods! I am his equal!"

Iris asks, "Poseidon, sir, do you really want me to return to my lord Zeus with this message? Think of the Furies, who will come for you even if the lightning bolt does not."

The blurred shape shifts, subsides, and Poseidon says, "I obey. But I am angry. And if Zeus spares Troy, then war between us."

Poseidon flows down, seething into the sea like lava.

Apollo has arrived, in his usual effortless way. He stands before Zeus.

Apollo is blinding today. He's always bright, but he seems to know he'll be unleashed on the Greeks he hates, and as a result, he's too bright to look at. If he looks like anything, it's a tall young man. But that's not it either. He looks like the sun at noon. And like the noon sun, he doesn't like to be looked at. Even Zeus finds himself squinting to the side.

Zeus feels the need to boast—Apollo always scares him a little—so he begins, "I just told off your Uncle Poseidon. He was interfering again, helping the Greeks against my orders. So I sent him down into the ocean. Told him, 'If you make me come down to fight you, Poseidon, then the Titans locked in their graves far below Hades will feel the shock when you fall.'"

Apollo says nothing.

Zeus tries again, "Now Apollo, what I want you to do is go down and give the Greeks a good scare. Kill as many as you want, put some courage into those Trojans, drive the Greeks right back to the ships."

Apollo has no comment.

Zeus goes on, "You have free rein. You understand? In fact, you can use Aegis."

For the first time, Apollo shows interest. Zeus sees those eyes of burning magnesium for a moment and goes on, "Use it carefully, it's not a toy!"

Apollo tilts his head, and the name "Aegis" is posed. Not spoken, but presented to Zeus for verification. Zeus nods, "Aegis."

Apollo smiles. A sweet tone, beginning at the horizon, encompasses the two gods and Apollo falls to Earth. As he falls, the sound turns into the scream of a falcon diving on a dove.

Hektor is sitting up, trying to get his breath back.

Then the chaos of battle vanishes. He's in perfect silence. He wonders if he's dying, but instead of going dark, the world becomes sizzling white light. He squints through the glare. This is a god, one of the big ones.

He asks the white glare, "Sir, which of the gods are you?"

In reply, the light blasts Hektor's eyes.

Hektor bows, saying, "Lord Apollo, forgive me for leaving the battle. But as you may have seen, Ajax hit me with a big rock. I expected to go down to Hades' country."

Apollo replies in the tune a sword would make if played on a huge bronze shield. Hektor will be healed and returned to battle, and the Greeks will run from him.

The light strikes Hektor head-on, healing his wound, making his blood boil.

He feels like a stallion let out of its stall. He wants to run, kick, splash through the river and run on again, forever. He stands up, grabs his shield and spear, and goes back to the fight.

The Greeks are advancing until they see Hektor, magically healed, coming right at them. They stop, shields sagging, spears drooping.

Thoas, a good man with a javelin, is the first Greek to recover his wits. He calls to his men, "Yes, it's Hektor. I know he should be dead, but he isn't! So help me hold him off."

Thoas waves his spear toward the weaker men, saying, "You common men, fall back to the ships." They waste no time obeying.

Then he points toward the front rank, to Ajax, Teucer, Ideomenus, all the heroes, and calls, "It's up to us, the best men. We'll form up tight and hold Hektor off, even if all the gods are with him."

Hektor comes on. Next to him is something that runs like a man, a very tall man, but if you try to make out his face it's like looking at the sun.

The tall man has no spear or shield. But as he sprints toward the Greeks, he lifts his right hand. There's something in it, hard to see in the glare. It looks something like a gourd or severed head, with hair or some kind of fringe hanging from it.

The Greeks stare at it, fascinated. And then the tall man flicks his wrist, and a sound comes from the thing in his hand. The sound is terror. In an instant, all the terrors of childhood—before a man learns words to keep the dark at bay—pour into the mind of every Greek on the field. Men who haven't felt fear since their beards sprouted suddenly want to weep.

The Greeks are helpless, dazed and sobbing. Before they can recover, the Trojan front rank strikes them, killing at will. Hektor kills Stikas, king of the Boetians, and Arkesilis, before they can even raise their shields. Aeneas is right behind him; he jabs his spear through the necks of Medon the murderer and Yazis the Athenian. Gloomy Polydamus looks cheerful for once as he takes out his sword and jams it into two stunned Greeks. It's too much. No one can fight the terror Apollo wields. The Greeks turn and run. But running just makes a man a better target. Paris sprints up to a fleeing Greek and punches his spear through the man's back. It comes out high on the Greek's shoulder, and he hangs on the spear for a moment like a spitted goat.

Hektor screams to the Trojans, "Charge the ships! No stopping to loot the dead! If I see a man robbing corpses, I'll kill him myself!"

To help the Trojans, Apollo leaps to the Greek wall. With one kick, he throws up a dirt causeway over the ditch. With another kick, he smashes the Greek wall. It melts like a sand castle hit by a wave.

And then Apollo shakes that thing in his hand, and every Greek is alone in the dark, in terror.

Nestor begs, "Zeus, if we ever pleased you with burning meat or marrow, help us now!"

Zeus replies with a bolt of lightning that falls among the Greeks. Meaning, "No."

The Trojans pour over the causeway like the first wave of a rising tide.

Greeks scramble up into their beached ships in a last-ditch try to keep them from burning. They drop their battle-spears and grab the long pikes they keep for ship-to-ship fights, stabbing them down at the swarming Trojans like butter churns.

Patroklas has been caring for Yuripilas' wound. But he sees the Trojans attacking the ships and runs, calling back to Yuripilas, "I'm sorry, but I have to tell Akilles what's happening. Maybe I can get him to fight!"

The Greeks are packed tight now against the shore. They have nowhere to run, no choice but to stand and fight. Most of them are still stunned with terror. Only a few heroes can resist Aegis' horrible spell.

Ajax steps out and spits an oncoming Trojan on his spear.

Hektor runs at Ajax, throwing a spear that misses him but impales his friend Lykofron. Ajax calls to his brother Teucer, "Get that bow of yours!"

Little Teucer runs up onto the prow of their ship, bow in hand, and lets fly, knocking a Trojan off his chariot. Then he takes aim at Hektor.

If Teucer had hit Hektor, the war would have ended right there. But Zeus is not ready to let the Greeks win just yet. So he flicks a finger and Teucer's bowstring breaks just as he's tracking Hektor. The arrow flies off wildly, and Teucer screams, "I just strung that bow this morning! The gods hate us today!"

Hektor sees Teucer throwing away his useless bow, and calls to the Trojans, "See? Zeus is with us! Now drive to the ships and burn them!"

Big Ajax turns to see most of the Greeks hanging back, shields drooping, and shouts, "You cowards, you better fight! You think we can walk home if they burn the ships?"

The Greeks realize they have no choice, and step forward, shield to shield. But Zeus doesn't want them to win today, so he muddies their minds, drains their courage.

The Trojans are close to the ships now. Soon they'll be able to throw torches onto the decks. Then they can slaughter the Greeks in the chaos.

Zeus is watching, waiting for the glow of fire from the ships. He promised to help the Trojans until the moment he sees one Greek ship on fire. After that, he'll turn the tide. Hektor will die, and Athena will have her way. Troy will fall. But for now, Zeus pours his own strength into Hektor and his Trojans.

Hektor feels Zeus' power sizzle through his veins. It's almost too much for him. After all, he's only mortal, with no god-blood. He burns like a man with fever, his eyes gleam like Apollo's, and white froth bubbles from his mouth.

He sprints at the Greek shield wall, one man against dozens. They hunch behind their shields terrified, as Hektor jabs at them from the front, then the left, then the right. He's everywhere, moving as quickly as a god. The Greeks can only hunker down, like a rock battered by waves.

They're saved by good shields. Only one of them dies: Perifites, who tripped over his neighbor's shield and landed face up, unprotected. Hektor was on him instantly.

The last thing Perifites saw was Hektor's face. Hektor stabbed his spear right through the boy. All the other Greeks could do was hunker down behind their shields. No one dares to fight Hektor man to man.

With their best men penned up by Hektor, the Greeks can't stop the Trojans from reaching the ships. The Trojans shout and cheer as they chase the Greeks along the beach.

Ajax is jumping from ship to ship, calling, "Turn and fight! A running man has no protection! Turn and fight, or you'll never see home!"

Hektor sees that his path to the ships is clear and runs to the stern of the nearest one. He touches the cold, wet hull, overjoyed. This is his goal, and he's touched it with his own hands! Then he has to turn and hold off the Greeks, who are outraged to see a Trojan hand touching one of their ships.

Athena sneaks some of her power to them now, lifting the darkness from their eyes, hoping her father won't notice.

It's a nasty fight at the ships, close combat with whatever weapons come to hand: swords, hatchets, big double-bladed axes. Even the men with spears hold them high up, jabbing them like daggers. There's no room for spear duels.

Hektor swings his sword with one hand, holding the ship's hull with the other as if he's afraid it'll sneak away from him. He screams, "Fire! Bring me fire! Zeus is with us today!"

Zeus is waiting, watching for that fire. The moment he sees a Greek ship burning, he'll abandon the Trojans. But Hektor doesn't know that. He's dreamed for nine long years of burning these ships.

The Trojans are flinging javelins at Ajax as he jumps from ship to ship. Finally, he has to jump down, but he still fights from the lower decks, shouting to the Greeks, "Fight, men, if you want to live! There's no Greek city near us! Do you think you can walk home?"

He leans over the gunwale, stabbing down at the swarming Trojans.

16

PATROKLAS

PATROKLAS AND AKILLES watch as smoke rises from the burning ship. Patroklas turns to his lord with tears in his eyes, silently begging him to help stop the Greeks.

Akilles says, "Crying? Have you had bad news from home? Last I heard, your father is still alive and well, and so is mine."

Patroklas sobs.

Akilles says, "You're crying for Agamemnon's army? They brought this on themselves!"

Patroklas doesn't answer. They listen to the noise of battle.

Akilles growls, "Tell me what you're crying about!"

Patroklas says, "They're all wounded. Yuripilas took an arrow in the thigh. Diomedes has a spear wound. Odysseus was stabbed with a sword and so was Agamemnon ..."

At the mention of Agamemnon, Akilles scowls. Patroklas goes on, "The healers are working on them now."

Akilles shrugs and walks off.

Patroklas calls after him, "May I never nurse a grudge like you do, Akilles! I think your father was the cold sea-cliff, and your mother the gray waves! You have no pity for your comrades lying wounded while the Trojans burn their ships! If you won't help them, let me! Let me wear your armor; they'll think you've returned to battle, and that will be enough to drive them back, give our friends a little breathing room!"

Akilles shakes his head.

"Why not? Is it true what they're saying—you've had a prophecy from your mother, that's why you won't fight?"

"There was no prophecy."

"Then why?"

"Because I'm as great a king as Agamemnon, and a better man! But he took her from me, that girl I won with my own spear! You saw her crying as she left! She thought I could stop them!"

After a while, Akilles says, "You said Diomedes is wounded?"

"Badly wounded. By a spear."

Akilles groans, "That's bad. Agamemnon doesn't matter; he's no fighter. But Diomedes ... we're in trouble without him. Ah, you hear that? That's Hektor, whipping them on. I don't hear a single Greek voice."

The smoke from the burning ship is rising higher.

Akilles puts an arm around Patroklas' shoulder, says, "I wish every one of these Trojans was dead, and all the Greeks but you and me! Then the two of us could share Troy between us."

He walks over to the corner where his armor stands, picks up the helmet and hands it to Patroklas, saying, "I can't stand hearing our men get slaughtered out there. But I can't fight yet, Patroklas; you heard me swear I wouldn't fight till the fire reached my own ships. So I'll give you my armor. You can wear it when you lead our men against the Trojans."

Patroklas jumps up and lays out Akilles' marvelous armor.

Akilles watches, grumbling, "None of this would have happened if Agamemnon had shown me a little respect! Look out there—" he points to the smoke rising from the ship—"The Trojans and their freakish Asian allies hemming up the best men of Greece like goats! It's shameful! And it never should've happened. If Agamemnon had treated me properly, the gullies would be filled with Trojan corpses!"

He's excited now, and strides out, calling, "I'll assemble the men, put them in a good mood for you!"

No sooner has he left than he sticks his head back into the tent and says, "One thing, Patroklas. This is important. You're no match for Hektor. Don't let him draw you into single combat. You'll be wearing my armor, but that doesn't turn you into me."

Patroklas nods, distracted. He's admiring Akilles' armor. He's never dreamed of actually wearing it. He begins putting it on, first the greaves to protect his shins—once you've seen a man's shins raked with a spear-point, you learn the value of a good pair of greaves. Then the slaves fit the breastplate over him, a second, stronger torso. He slings Akilles' sword over one shoulder and his huge shield over the other. Finally he puts on the helmet with its plume of stiff horsehair to make a tall man look even taller.

He tries to lift Akilles' spear, but it's far too heavy for him. No one but Akilles himself can wield that tree trunk. He settles for two ordinary spears and goes out.

Akilles' three chariot horses are hitched up, waiting. Two out of three are immortal creatures born of a harpy and sired by the West Wind. The grooms call them "Blondie" and "Dapple," but those are not their real names. Some say their father was no mere West Wind but Zeus himself. The god-father has mated with mares before, as kings often do. The third horse is mortal, but a fine beast nonetheless. The Greeks call him "Capture" because he was taken from one of the Trojan towns.

Akilles has the men formed up already. They're eager to get into the fight. He brought fifty ships to Troy. Figure about fifty men in each ship, and he can put more than two thousand men into battle, allowing for those who've died in nine years of war. The force is divided into five battalions, each commanded by a hero.

The first battalion is led by Meniste, who was born of a river that flows through the overworld. He has that clean and easy look you see in the god-born.

The second is commanded by Yudor, bastard son of Hermes, most playful and cunning of the great gods. Yudor has his father's sly, easy ways.

The third is under Pisander—a mortal, but a great fighter. Next to Patroklas, he's better with a spear than anyone in the crew. Except Akilles, of course. That goes without saying.

The fourth battalion belongs to Fenix, the grizzled old fighter who pretty much raised Akilles. Alkimedun handles the fifth group.

Akilles stands in front of the ranks and shouts, "You've been complaining, 'O cruel Akilles, why keep us here if you won't let us fight?'—haven't you? Haven't I had to listen to that, day after day?"

They all nod and laugh.

He laughs with them, mimicking their whine, "'O Lord Akilles, we want to fight so much!'" Then he yells, "Well, now you'll get your chance!"

They roar with joy, packed so tight shield-to-shield that their horse-hair plumes brush against each other.

He waves them toward the battle, shouting, "Patroklas will be your commander; obey him like you would me. Show us some of that fighting you promised!"

He goes into his tent and brings out the sacred goblet. Everyone goes quiet as he rubs it clean with sulfur, then rinses it with water. He washes his hands, then pours wine into it.

He raises the wine toward the sky, calling, "Zeus, great king! You who love the lightning! You who rule the cold mountains! You whose priests go barefoot and sleep on straw to honor you! You have heard my prayer and brought ruin to Agamemnon! Now I ask you to grant another prayer! I'm sending my comrade Patroklas to battle; let him fight bravely and return safely!"

Zeus heard that prayer, and granted a part of it.

When Akilles finishes the drink-sacrifice, Patroklas gives the sign. The five captains order their battalions to charge. There's no room for strategy or complicated deployments; the Trojans are already in the camp. Akilles' men simply run at them like a nest of angry wasps kicked by a child—suddenly the wasps are everywhere, stabbing anyone who wanders into their path.

As they charge, Patroklas shouts, "Show that fool Agamemnon what we can do, men! Let him see what he lost when he offended our lord, the best man in the army!"

They slam into the flank of the Trojans attacking the ships. When the Trojans see Akilles' helmet waving at the head of his famous battalions they panic, try to flee. Soon there are gaps in the Trojan shield-wall. Patroklas throws a spear at Pira-Akmes, a Trojan ally from the southern desert where the Orontes flows between sandy banks. The barbarian falls with Patroklas' spear right through his heart.

Trojans scatter like mice in a kitchen when the cook comes in with a torch. Akilles' men pursue, stabbing their spears into the Trojans' vulnerable backs. The weary Greeks who were fighting from the ships jump down and join the pursuit.

The Trojans are in chaos. The brave ones soon stop and turn, ready to fight, but the weaklings run farther. So there are groups of Trojans scattered across the camp, easy pickings.

Patroklas calls to his men, "The Trojans are carrying their shields high, like scared men always do! Hit them low!" And to show what he means, he slams his spear into the thigh of the Trojan Arekile. The spear hits the thigh so hard, you can hear Arekile's femur snap.

Meges, taking Patroklas' advice, jabs Amfikle in the meat of the thigh, and that Trojan dies with the blood fountaining out of his leg.

Now the Trojans try lowering their shields, so the Greeks hit them high. Menelaos sticks Thoas high on the chest. Antilokas hits Atimna in the throat. Atimna's brother Maris screams and lunges at Antilokas, but a man shouldn't lose his head like that in battle. When you lose your head, you forget to watch for danger. Maris forgot to look to his side, where Thrasymid was waiting. Thrasymid slams his spear right onto Maris' shoulder-joint where it attaches to the arm. The spear-point grinds right down into the bone, and Maris falls dead.

They take the Trojan Kleobule alive. But then Ajax jokes, "What use is a live Trojan?" and smashes his sword into Kleobule's cheekbone. The Trojan goes down to Hades' country, and Ajax wipes the blood off his sword.

Trojans are dying in all sorts of strange ways. The Greek Peneleos faces off against a Trojan named Lykon. They throw their spears at the same moment, and both miss. Then they draw swords and charge. Lykon hits Peneleos' helmet, breaking his sword. Peneleos hits Lykon on the side of the neck. It's such a strong blow that Lykon's head is left hanging on by a strip of skin. He goes down to the dark like that, with his head flapping down his back like a mule's saddle-bag.

The Trojans have had enough. They can't resist Akilles' fresh battalions, and try to run to their chariots, to get back to Troy. But the Greeks won't let them get away so easily.

Ideomenus catches a Trojan named Erymas and stabs him in the back of the neck, so hard that the spear-point comes out through Erymas' mouth. His teeth go flying. Blood gushes out of his mouth, nostrils—even his eyes! Erymas has no face left, just a red mush dotted with white teeth.

It's too much for the Trojans. They run like lambs scattered by wolves.

Ajax has Hektor pinned down, jabbing at him from every angle. But Hektor's always been good with his shield, and somehow keeps his wide shoulders under cover. But that's all he can do. Seeing his comrades running away, Hektor jumps into his chariot to flee.

But it's not easy getting a chariot across the ditch. Hektor's fine horses jump it easily, but other Trojan chariots fall in. You can hear the horses screaming as they fall on the sharpened stakes; you can hear wood snapping as chariot poles break. Some of the Trojan teams gallop off, leave their riders behind in the ditch.

Patroklas gets into Akilles' chariot to ride down the fleeing Trojans. He won't let one of them get back to Troy alive.

Some of the Trojan chariots were damaged crossing the ditch. As they bounce over the tussocks, they fall apart. Patroklas runs over their riders. He doesn't want to stop; he wants to catch up to Hektor. What glory it would be for Patroklas if he could put a spear through the Trojans' hero! But Hektor's horses are too fast; he can't catch up.

He settles for cutting off and killing retreating Trojans. It's easy. They have no fight left in them. He sees a Lycian chariot just standing on the plain, not moving. He jumps out and finds a spoiled Lycian named Thestor in the car, whimpering. Patroklas is disgusted. He harpoons Thestor under the jaw, lifts him out of the chariot like a gaffed fish, and throws the miserable corpse onto the dust. Thestor was a catch not worth keeping, a junk fish! Other Lycians come running to avenge Thestor, but Patroklas kills them as easily as a fox kills chickens. A dozen Lycians go down to the dark before Sarpedon the half-god king of the Lycians, gallops up shouting, "Men, why are you running from this Greek? I'll kill him myself!"

Sarpedon leaps from his chariot, spears ready. Patroklas jumps down to meet him. They sprint at each other screaming like eagles fighting in mid-air.

Zeus looks down, groaning, "This is the moment my son Sarpedon dies! I'd like to pick him up and drop him off safe home in Lycia."

Hera frowns, working her needle: "You want to save a mortal from death? It's what they're made for! You know as well as I do that Sarpedon's death has been arranged for ages! But never mind me, do what you want!"

Zeus says, "It's just that Sarpedon is such a good man ..."

Hera throws down her needlework, hissing, "Husband, you're talking nonsense! So what if he's your bastard son? Do you know how many gods' bastards are fighting down there? You and your randy kin have sired half the warriors on the field! If you take your half-breed brat away from death, everyone in the family will be swooping down on Troy, grabbing their sons born on the wrong side of the bed and spiriting them away! There'll be no one left to fight!"

Zeus nods, sighing, "Yes, yes ... it's just a shame he has to die."

Hera takes up her needle again, says, "Well, if you like him so much, once

Patroklas has killed him, send Sleep and Death to float him home through the sky to Lycia to his family home, so they can give him a funeral mound, a memorial stone, and the other rites."

Zeus nods sadly. He mumbles, "But let me give him a memorial of my own, in advance." He flicks his left hand, and a rain of blood falls on the plain of Troy, Zeus' sign of grief for Sarpedon.

Patroklas wipes the blood from his face, runs straight at Sarpedon and makes his throw. The spear hits Sarpedon's driver Thrasidem in the groin, and he falls doubled over.

Sarpedon throws, missing Patroklas but hitting Capture, the only mortal horse on Akilles' chariot team. The horse screams and falls, kicking out, fouling the chariot. Just as the pole is about to break, Patroklas' driver cuts the dying horse loose, and the other two, the god-horses, carry the chariot away to safety, staring sadly back at their mortal comrade.

Sarpedon and Patroklas have their second spears up and ready. Sarpedon throws first, misses. Patroklas throws—and doesn't miss. Sarpedon's hit dead center, between the heart and the guts.

He falls, groaning. He refuses to die, calling to his brother Glaukas, "Bring all our men to protect my body. Don't let the Greeks steal my armor. I swear I'll haunt you forever, brother, if you let the Greeks mutilate my corpse!"

Then he dies. Patroklas walks up and plants a foot on Sarpedon's chest, pulling out his spear like a man pulls a shovel out of wet ground. As the spear rips out of Sarpedon's body, his soul comes with it, then begins its long fall to Hades' country.

Glaukas weeps. He's wounded; he'll need a god's help to avenge his brother. He calls, "Lord Apollo, I have an arrow wound in the hand. My arm is already getting stiff. Your father Zeus let his son—my brother—die here. Please help me defend his body!"

Glaukas feels his hand knitting, as if a thousand tiny needles were darning his ripped hand. And something has been added to his blood, making him fiercer and fresher, ready to fight all day and night.

Glaukas bows his head, whispering, "Thank you, Lord Apollo!" and gathers the Lycian chiefs, calling, "Come with me, fight for my brother's body!"

Then he finds Hektor and yells, "Hektor, have you forgotten your allies? Sarpedon is dead! Patroklas killed him and now the Greeks will steal his armor and hack up the corpse to avenge all the Greeks he killed. Come help me protect the body!"

Hektor asks, "Sarpedon, dead? Are you sure?"

Glaukas nods, still weeping.

Hektor bows his head and moans. The Trojans loved Sarpedon better than any other foreign prince fighting with them. Truth is, they loved him a lot more than some of their own princes. Hektor leads the Trojans toward Sarpedon's corpse.

Patroklas orders his men to fan out around the body. "This corpse is Sarpedon, who was first to break through our wall! Strip his armor and hack up his corpse!"

Hektor comes up just in time to see one of Akilles' men lifting one of Sarpedon's legs to drag the body away. Without breaking stride, he picks up a big rock and flings it at the Greek's head. The rock puts a huge dent in his helmet; his brains are all scrambled and he falls dead. Patroklas runs at Hektor, picking up a rock to return the favor. He misses but hits a Trojan standing close to Hektor, crushing the windpipe, breaking all the little bones that connect the head to the shoulders.

Patroklas is so fierce today that the Trojans back away from him. But Glaukas is only pretending to flee, waiting his chance to avenge his brother. He lures Batykles, Akilles' vassal, into chasing him, then turns suddenly, punching his spear right through the Greek's chest.

The Greeks do some killing of their own. Meriones gets off a good throw, hitting Laogon, son of a priest, right under the ear.

Aeneas throws at Meriones, but Meriones ducks and the spear goes over his head to land quivering in the dirt. Aeneas calls, "I see you're a good dancer, Meriones! If that had hit you, you'd be dead!"

Meriones shouts back, "You'd die just as quick if I hit you!"

Patroklas calls over, "Meriones, stop that chatter! Less talk, more killing! Send some of these Trojans to join Sarpedon underground."

Meriones stops talking, and joins the clash of shields, the clang of swords on armor, and the screams of the wounded as they fight over Sarpedon's body. The crush of fighters around that corpse is as thick as flies around a pig hanging with its throat cut.

You'd have needed fine eyes to recognize Sarpedon lying there with a dozen spears stuck in him and the blood oozing out, mixed with dust.

Zeus is watching, wondering exactly when Patroklas should die. Should he let Hektor kill him now, quickly? Or let Patroklas kill some more Trojans before Hektor kills him?

Zeus decides to give Patroklas one more moment of glory. He takes all Hektor's courage away. Suddenly Hektor finds himself running away. The Lycians see Hektor fleeing, all their friends lying dead around the body of their king. They flee too.

Now the Greeks can do what they want to Sarpedon's corpse. Patroklas rips the helmet off and his men tear off the rest of his armor. When they've stripped the corpse, they'll start hacking it up.

But that's more than Zeus can bear. He begs Apollo, "Take poor Sarpedon's body away, clean the blood from it, bring him home to Lycia for proper rites."

Apollo nods, and stands taller than any mortal over Sarpedon's body. No one interferes as he lifts the corpse, as easily as a man would pick up a shirt. He steps into the sky and takes the body far away to a riverbank where he washes the dust and blood off. Then he carries it to Lycia.

Patroklas sees Hektor fleeing and loses his head, forgets Akilles' order to come back as soon as the Trojans have been driven away from the ships. If you'd just withdrawn now, Patroklas, you'd still be alive. But you let pride delude you, as men do.

Patroklas lashes his horses, heading full speed for Troy. He thinks he can take the town, right now, on his own.

And he came close to doing it! Along the way, he kills Trojans and Lycians as easily as a fisherman spears little fish in the surf. Ten or twelve he kills before he reaches the walls.

He pulls up before the gates of the town, jumps from his chariot and runs up the wall of Troy—right up it like a gecko! He would have been over the walls in a second, if Apollo himself hadn't intervened.

Just as he scrambles to the top, something knocks him back hard, like a mule's kick. It hits him; he's not hurt, but thrown back a dozen paces. He can't see anyone. The wall is deserted, the Trojans have fled in terror. What hit him like that? He can't figure it out, so he picks himself up and scrambles up the wall again. And once again, as soon as he gets to the top, he's hit with a blow like a stallion's kick.

A third time he brushes off the dust, stands up and runs at the wall. And a third time he gets hit as soon as he reaches the top, even harder this time. The force knocks him off the wall once again.

He lies there, catching his breath. Now he sees someone standing on the wall, taller than any man. The figure doesn't speak, but Patroklas understands it well enough; Apollo won't let him take Troy.

He limps away.

Hektor is skulking by the gate. He has never felt fear like this before. Brave men can't handle fear; they don't have the practice. As Hektor huddles there, his cousin Asias comes toward him. But then he sees that this isn't the real Asias. It's a god, pretending to be his cousin. Its feet aren't actually touching the ground. It stands beside him and instantly he feels his fear drain away, replaced by courage and energy. He sees what he has to do, and calls to his charioteer Kebryon, "Drive straight at Patroklas! Ignore the rest!" Patroklas sees the chariot coming and stands to meet it, spear in one hand, rock in the other. He throws the rock first; it hits Kebryon right in the face.

His eyes pop out and he falls stiffly as a diver jumping from a cliff. Patroklas yells, "That was a fine dive your driver made, Hektor! That man would be useful on a ship; he could bring up enough scallops to feed the whole crew!"

Hektor jumps off the careening chariot, falling onto Patroklas. They grapple, too close for weapons. Hektor has his arm around Patroklas' neck and Patroklas is twisting Hektor's leg. Then they spring apart, feeling for the nearest weapon as their men come up to shield them. They both fall back into the shelter of their men's shields as spears and rocks fly in both directions.

The Greeks push forward, driving the scrum over Kebryon's body. They drag it back behind their line and strip the armor. Then they start mutilating the corpse, jabbing it with their spears, spitting on it, kicking it.

Patroklas can't be stopped today. The Trojans' shields are no use against him; he runs through their lines as easily as a lion among sheep.

But Apollo has been watching and waiting. He will never forgive Patroklas for trying to push past him over the wall of Troy. Three times this miserable mortal tried to climb past him! It can't, won't be forgiven.

In fact, Apollo decides to take his revenge right now. Patroklas sees a blur moving to his side, then feels a huge blow on his back, as if a tree had fallen on him. Apollo only struck him with the flat of his hand, but that blow would have killed anyone else. Patroklas is alive, but badly hurt, lying stunned in the dust. Apollo reaches down to slap him again, this time in the head. He loses consciousness, and Akilles' helmet rolls away in the dust.

Apollo is playing with him. When Patroklas finally manages to stand up, Apollo takes his spear-arm in one huge hand and breaks the spear in half. Then he tears his shirt off and rips Patroklas' shield from his hand, flings it away.

Patroklas is standing dazed, half naked, a perfect target. A Trojan named Yuforbas runs up behind him, pushing his spear into Patroklas' back. But

Yuforbas can't believe he managed to spear the Greek hero so easily, so he runs back behind the Trojan shields.

Patroklas stumbles back to the shelter of the Greek shield-wall, but Hektor has seen that he's hurt, and smashes his way through to finish him off. He slams his spear into Patroklas' belly so hard that it punches out the other side and pins him to the ground.

The Greeks flee; Hektor has time to lean all his weight on the spear. He gloats, "You were going to steal our women, weren't you, Patroklas? But Hektor was hunting you! Where's your hero Akilles? He can't help you now. You'll feed the buzzards out here. Your master Akilles sent you after me. Told you, 'Don't come back without Hektor's bloody shirt.' Didn't he, dead man?"

Patroklas whispers, "It was Apollo who killed me, not you. The god hit me first, then Yuforbas. You were only third, Hektor. You, on your own, I could have killed twenty times."

He coughs up blood, pats the dirt, and whispers, "Besides, soon you'll be joining me down there."

He dies. Hektor shouts at the corpse, "How do you know? Maybe I'll kill Akilles before he kills me!"

He plants his foot on the body, yanks the spear out, and goes looking for Patroklas' charioteer Otomedon. But Otomedon has already driven off to tell the Greeks that Patroklas is dead.

17

AEGIS

AKILLES' HORSES WILL not move. The god-horses Dapple and Blondie are weeping huge tears. Otomedon tries sweet-talking them, then cursing them, but nothing works. They won't move away from Patroklas' body. They are immortal; death appalls them. They can't understand why their beloved driver has left them.

Zeus, staring down at the battle, has eyes only for the two god-horses. He moans, "Never love a mortal, noble horses! They just die on you. But I won't let the Trojans steal you."

He bends his will; the two horses shake the salt tears from their manes and let Otomedon drive them back into battle.

Hektor has stripped Akilles' armor off Patroklas, who lies naked in the dust as Trojans and Greeks kill each other over his corpse. It's a sunny day, but Zeus has sent a dark cloud over the spot where Patroklas died.

Menelaos sees Patroklas lying in the dust, all torn and bloody. He stares at his dead friend like a cow mourning her stillborn calf.

Yuforbas wants to claim the corpse and pushes through the Trojan ranks shouting "Menelaos, get away from that corpse. It's mine! I was the first to put a spear in him. Step back or I'll kill you."

Menelaos says, "You Trojans are always boasting. Aren't you Panthoos' son? Your brother Hyperenor was a braggart too. That is, until I killed him."

Yuforbas yells, "I'll bring your head home to my parents, to comfort their grief!"

He sprints and throws. His spear hits Menelaos' shield and bends. Menelaos runs at him, driving his spear through Yuforbas' neck. He falls in a heap of rattling bronze. His armor is as good as ever, but the man it sheltered is dead meat.

Menelaos jumps on the body like a hungry lion, ripping off the armor and stacking it, piece by piece.

Apollo is annoyed. He takes a business interest in Yuforbas' family. The father, Panthoos, is one of Apollo's highest priests. Now the Greeks have killed both his sons. He goes looking for Hektor, who's foolishly ridden himself out of the fight in a hopeless attempt to steal Akilles' god-horses. Apollo grabs the nearest human, Mentes, leader of a Thracian tribe, and makes him shout, "Hektor, you're wasting time! Akilles' horses are already back in the Greeks' camp. And Menelaos is stripping Yuforbas' body!"

Hektor gallops back, sees the Trojan's body flopping this way and that as Menelaos rips off his armor. He charges, with Apollo's fire streaming from him and the bravest Trojans close behind.

Menelaos has to make up his mind quickly. He frets, "If I run now, the Greeks will laugh at me again! But if I stay I'll die; Hektor's got a whole army with him."

Menelaos is not the swiftest thinker, but he reaches the correct conclusion, "Death is worse than being laughed at!" and runs away.

As he flees, he has an idea: "What if I get Ajax and bring him here? The two of us might be able to save Patroklas' body."

He runs to find Ajax, who's over on the left flank. The two of them jog back together, their armor clanging, their breath coming hard.

They're too late to save Akilles' armor. Hektor has already stripped it. Now he's dragging Patroklas' corpse back toward the Trojan shield wall, so he can cut the head off and toss the body to the jackals of the plain.

Ajax charges at Hektor, roaring with rage. Hektor drops the body and retreats behind the Trojan shields. Now Ajax stands over the body, spread out wide and low, like an eagle hissing at a lion who wants her nestlings.

Glaukas, still grieving for Sarpedon, shouts, "I wish my brother had stayed in sweet Lycia, instead of dying for you ungrateful Trojans! If you'd held on to Patroklas' corpse, we could have traded it to the Greeks for my brother's armor, and maybe his corpse too. But you wouldn't even fight Ajax!"

Hektor sighs, "Glaukas, you know better than that. Ajax had Menelaos with him; I was right to step back. Two-on-one is bad odds. If you'll come with me, we'll face them together!"

He calls to the Trojans, "I'm putting on Akilles' armor now! Make sure everyone knows it; I don't want any spears from my own men."

Hektor runs back to where his slaves have piled Akilles' armor. He jams it on piece by piece, flinging off his own armor, telling the slaves, "Take this back to the town."

Zeus watches, shaking his head sadly, muttering, "No, Hektor, you shouldn't wear poor Akilles' armor. No good'll come of it. You mortals should show each other a little respect."

Hektor pulls Akilles' helmet on. With it come the thoughts of Ares, god of slaughter and rape and flies. If Hektor had put on his own helmet, his thoughts would have come from a nobler god. Now Ares' filthy thoughts fill his head, and Ares' thoughts are all bad. Whatever power they give has to be paid for, many times over.

Thinking like Ares, Hektor shouts savagely, "Lycians, Thracians, allies! You've bankrupted Troy with your eating and drinking; now repay us and I'll make it worth your while. Whoever grabs Patroklas' corpse and brings it back behind our shield wall gets half of all I've grabbed from the Greeks!"

Ares' vile thoughts spread from Hektor's head to the Trojans and Lycians. They form up and charge, every man's mind full of greed and bloodlust.

Menelaos and Ajax watch this snarling horde run at them. Ajax says calmly, "My friend, I don't think we'll live through this. I'm not so worried about Patroklas; he's past helping. I'm worried, to be precise, about this dear head of mine! And yours too, of course. Personally, I prefer my head attached to my shoulders. "

Menelaos, gloomy and slow as ever, answers, "Yes, I suppose we'll be killed."

Ajax says patiently, "Yes, but I was thinking, old comrade, that perhaps if we called for help we might be able to avoid dying."

Menelaos brightens up: "Yes, we'll call for help!"

Ajax nods, "Yes, use that big voice of yours."

Menelaos bellows, "Greeks! Over here! Hektor is charging us! Save Patroklas from the jackals!" Ajax adds, "And us too, if it's convenient!"

A few Greeks hear and come running, standing shield to shield with Menelaos and Ajax over Patroklas' body. But Hektor slams into them with a much stronger pack.

The Trojan shields push the Greek ones back, and expose the body. Hektor would have carried it off, but Zeus took pity on Patroklas, telling the dead man, "I never had any grudge against you, Patroklas. You had to die to bring Akilles back into the fight, but I won't let the Trojans feed you to their dogs."

Zeus fogs the Trojans' minds and eyes. They can only see a few inches, like old men with milky cataracts. They're easy pickings for Ajax. He sees a Trojan ally named Hippotoas trying to drag the body away on a rawhide strap.

With Hippotoas suddenly half-blind, stumbling awkwardly, Ajax has time for a perfect spear-thrust into the head. The spearhead punches through helmet, skull, and brain, so hard that Ajax's spear hand slams into Hippotoas' helmet.

Hippotoas' parents never got any return on all the food they gave their boy. You can spend all that money raising a young man and then lose your profit in one moment to an enemy spear. There's no riskier investment.

Hektor kills a Greek in revenge, but when the scrum is finished it's the Greeks who have Patroklas' body, their shields covering it like eagles defending a dead nestling with their wings.

The Greeks are ripping the armor off Hippotoas' corpse, jeering at the Trojans. Apollo loses patience again; what does it take to put some fight in his Trojans? Again he takes human form, this time appearing to Aeneas as Perifas, an old slave of the family. Aeneas steps back as he sees this hunched figure blazing with light, radiating the heat of the sun. The old slave-shape speaks in a voice that has nothing to do with age or servility, a voice that crackles with rage: "Aeneas, why do you hang back? There are gods who wish you well. Fight harder!"

Aeneas shouts, "Trojans! A god is here, urging us to fight!"

He sets an example, impaling Leyokritus on his spear. But Ajax keeps his men safe, reminding them, "No stepping out from the shield wall! Keep it tight as turtles sunning on a rock! Hold your spears near the head, and stab as they come close!"

So the Trojans charge again and again but lose more men than the Greeks, because Ajax kept the wall tight, knowing the worst thing a man can do is be too brave and jump forward or too cowardly and step back.

All day they fight over Patroklas' corpse, pulling at it like slaves stretching an ox hide. The Greeks keep their spirits up by calling to each other, "If we let them have the corpse, we can't show our faces at the ships!" while the Trojans call out, "Grab the body, even if it kills us!"

The sky, bright and sunny everywhere else, is dark over Patroklas' corpse.

Akilles is still expecting Patroklas to ride back to camp victorious. He paces, waiting. He's beginning to realize something has gone wrong, and whispers, "Mother, can you tell me what's happened to Patroklas?" But Thetis doesn't answer. It's beginning to sink in: his most loyal friend will not come home alive.

Hektor has been watching for Akilles' god-horses. Now he sees them coming, with Otomedon and Alkemedon in the car. He calls to Aeneas, "See? The god-horses, and weak men driving them. We can take them now!" He grabs Aeneas, Aretus, and Kromias, and the three of them try to corral the chariot, kill the riders and grab the team. But Otomedon prays to Zeus for strength. Zeus grants his prayer; Hektor throws and misses, and Otomedon throws at Aretus. With Zeus' help, the spear slips through Aretus' shield and slices into his belly. Aretus jumps up like an ox that takes one last step after the ax splits its spine, and lies still.

The Trojans draw back in horror. Otomedon has time to jump down and grab Aretus' armor. Then he drives off shouting, "That doesn't make us even, Trojans! Patroklas was worth more than the man I just killed!"

Zeus agrees. His grief for Patroklas is building, and he tells Athena, "I'm giving you free rein, daughter. Go help the Greeks."

She wastes no time with chariots or wings; she wills herself on the field, appearing among the Greeks as old Fenix, Akilles' foster-father. In an old man's voice, she sighs, "Menelaos, are you going to let Patroklas feed the stray dogs in a Trojan alley?"

He says wearily, "Hektor's fighting like a god today! But still, I'll stop them if Athena lends me her strength."

Athena is pleased that he invoked her. She touches him on the knees and shoulders, giving him the strength of a fly. A fly is the bravest warrior of all. It will attack over and over, no matter how many times you swat it away. With a fly's strength and speed Menelaos sees an opening and throws, bringing down Podas, a rich Trojan with fine armor.

Menelaos grabs his corpse and yanks it back behind the Greek shields.

Now Apollo must work as hard as his sister on the Trojan side. He takes human form again—as Fanops, a favorite of Hektor's—and stands before him, crying, "Hektor, Agamemnon's cuckold brother has killed your friend Podas and dragged away his corpse! Are you going to let a cuckold like Menelaos shame you?"

Hektor runs to fight Menelaos. Now Zeus decides he's given the Greeks enough luck. In the end, today will go to the Trojans.

Zeus pours black clouds over the Greeks and sends lightning bolts into the ground at their feet. Then he takes Aegis in his hand and shakes it at them. They cringe in terror.

Hektor kills at will now. He stabs Leytas' spear-arm. Leytas runs away, staring down at his ruined hand. He'll never hold a spear again.

Hektor sprints after Leytas to finish him off, but Ideomenus leaps out at him, spearing Hektor in the chest. That should've been a lethal strike, but Zeus won't let Hektor be hurt yet. The spearhead breaks off and the Trojans cheer, because they know the gods are on their side now.

Hektor throws at Ideomenus and misses. But the spear, flying high, brings down Koyranos, who galloped up in his chariot to help Ideomenus. Koyranos takes the spear right in the jaw. It shatters his teeth and cuts out his tongue.

Meriones grabs the reins and yells, "Ideomenus, get on, quickly! It's the Trojans' day, and there's nothing we can do!"

Ideomenus scrambles into the chariot and whips the horses with all his strength, because now the terror streaming from Zeus' aegis has spread to him, flowing across the Greek ranks like flood water.

Ajax and Menelaos are still fighting to protect Patroklas' dead body, but they see the Greeks fleeing and start to fret, the first little streams of terror trickling around their feet.

Ajax leans toward Menelaos, holding his huge shield to cover them both, and says, "You see how Zeus sends the Trojans' spears into our men every time?"

"Yes, even when a weak man is throwing!"

"And ours always fall short or long or off to the side?"

"He's given today to them."

"We need Akilles! Somebody should find him and tell him his friend is dead!"

Menelaos looks around, "But who? I can't see anyone in this darkness."

Ajax looks to the sky, calling, "Zeus, father, if we have to die, let us die with the sunlight on us!"

Instantly the sky is clear.

Ajax leans over Patroklas' body and shouts to Menelaos, "Now go find

Antilokas! He's a fast runner and a fine talker too. He's the one to tell Akilles his friend is dead."

Menelaos is a slow, stubborn man; he doesn't like to leave the body. But he knows Ajax is right, so he steps out from the shield-wall to find Antilokas. Trojan spears hit his shield, and he knocks them off with his own spear, backing away, calling to his friends, "Yes, I'll go, but don't let them have the body! Remember what a good man Patroklas was!"

Then he turns and runs hard, looking for Antilokas.

He catches up with him way out on the flank, pulls him out of the shield wall, and tells him, "Patroklas is dead."

Antilokas can't speak. His spear falls from his hand, his shield sags to the ground.

Menelaos goes on, "Zeus is helping the Trojans. We need Akilles. Find him, tell him to hurry out here to save Patroklas' body."

Antilokas says, "What happened to Akilles' armor?"

"Hektor took it."

Antilokas starts to sob. He goes on weeping as he takes off his armor so he can run faster. He gives the armor to a friend, and runs off toward the ships.

Menelaos trots back to Patroklas' body. The Greeks can't keep it safe much longer. More and more Trojans are joining the scrum, and every Greek shield is stuck full of Trojan spears, like teeth on a comb.

Menelaos falls in next to Ajax, shield to shield, saying, "I found Antilokas; he's gone to the camp."

"You've done well!"

"Yes, but Akilles can't fight today! He has no armor, remember?"

Ajax groans.

"So we have to do something now before they have us surrounded."

Ajax grunts, "All right, then. You and Meriones lift up the body, carry it back."

Menelaos gestures toward the Trojans, "But they'll be on us in a second."

Ajax pulls his little namesake, Ajax Oyeleas-son, out of the wall and says, "No, the Ajaxes will hold them off. Big Ajax—" slapping his own breastplate, "—and Little Ajax," tapping the small man's helmet.

The strange funeral procession sets off. As soon as the Trojans see the Greeks lifting Patroklas' corpse onto their shoulders, they're furious, grabbing at the body. But the two Ajaxes, one huge and one small, face them like wild boars turning at bay, and the Trojans scatter like hounds.

Menelaos and Meriones stumble over corpses, duck Trojan spears, and drip sweat. But they never drop the body, even though Patroklas was a big, heavy man.

And as these two carry Patroklas home, the other pair—the two Ajaxes, big and little—protect the pallbearers, holding their shields high to catch the Trojans' spears, keeping Hektor's men at bay.

All the other Greeks have run off like deer. As the four heroes stumble toward the camp they have to step over shields, spears, and helmets dropped by fleeing Greeks.

18

SHIELD

AKILLES IS STANDING on the stern of his ship, looking out over the plain. A little while ago he saw dark clouds and lightning. Now he sees thousands of Greeks fleeing wildly toward the ships without armor or weapons.

He mutters, "What are they doing, running like rabbits? I sent Patroklas in my own armor! Oh, if he—" He stops, muttering, "My mother told me our bravest would die ..."

Then he stops and clutches his head, moaning, "'The bravest of us' —She didn't mean me!"

He kicks the gunwale, howling, "I told him not to follow Hektor onto the plain!"

But it's no good trying to justify himself. He groans, "I sent him out there! I promised his father I'd bring him home safe!"

Antilokas runs in, climbs up beside Akilles, wipes the sweat from his face and intones, "Akilles, Peleus-son—"

Akilles knows very well what the news will be.

Antilokas blurts, "Patroklas is dead!"

Akilles stumbles to the gunwale and half-falls, half-jumps to the ground, landing on his hands and knees.

Antilokas calls down, "I wish it weren't true!"

Akilles grabs two huge handfuls of dust and pours them onto his head. He smears the dust into his skin, over his clothes.

Antilokas calls down to him, "They're fighting over his body out on the plain!"

Akilles' mouth is open, but no sound comes out.

The slave girls have come out of the tents. Antilokas calls to them, "Patroklas is dead!"

They begin the mourning rite, beating their breasts, wailing, falling down in fits.

But they're only doing what is expected of them. It's different with Akilles. He's in agony. He gets up off his hands and knees, falls face-first in the dust. His huge body hits the ground like a tree. Then he stands up, tearing out clumps of his yellow hair.

Antilokas clambers down off the ship and tries to restrain him for fear he'll stab himself.

Akilles throws him off as easily as a handful of straw, takes a deep breath and howls.

That sound blasts every ear in the camp. They can even hear it in Troy. If the Trojans knew what it boded for them, they'd have died of fear the second they heard it.

Far out in the sea, Thetis is sitting beside Father Ocean. Her sisters are seated in ranks around her. They are holding court; all is respectful silence.

Then Akilles' cry comes blasting down to them.

Thetis screams. Her scream rebounds through the ocean. Her maidens catch her grief and begin screaming too. Old man Ocean's court vibrates with their cries.

As the rest of the ocean-daughters hear her grief, they pour into Ocean's palace. Soon there are hundreds of them, beating their breasts, weaving from side to side, chanting their grief.

Now Thetis calls to them, "Sisters, listen! There is no grief like mine!"

They moan in rhythm as she sings, "My sorrow is my son; his grief is his greatness! The finest mortal ever born, he shot up like a sapling! I tended him like a loving gardener, till off he went, in fifty fine ships, to Troy, to fight!"

She chants, "But welcome him back I will not, I will never, welcome him back, he will die! Soon, so soon, he will die!"

They moan as one, weaving side to side among the seaweed.

She sings, "Only a little time he was given, less than most mortals, and even that life, that tiny sliver, even that life has been bitter, envenomed by envy! Bad it was then, but worse it is now! His best friend is dead, his little time left is nothing but grief, and then dead forever! Grief in his last days, darkness forever!"

She raises her head, her tears salting the sea, and sobs, "But I will see him—with what comfort? None, no comfort, but I must see him!"

As she finishes her song, she flows up from old Ocean's palace and all her sisters follow, like dolphins in a fast ship's wake.

She flows straight to the Greek ships and steps out of the waves, walking sadly to her son's tents. Behind her stream her sisters in single file, all moaning as one.

Akilles is lying on his couch, tears streaming from his eyes.

Thetis flows to him and embraces him, murmuring, "Tell me your sorrows, my son!"

He only sobs in her arms.

She asks, "Did father Zeus not grant your prayer? I saw the Trojans burn a ship; wasn't that the sign you asked? We in the deeps could see that flame!"

He sighs, "He granted my prayer, and Patroklas is dead. What's a king-quarrel compared to a friend's death? He's dead, mother, dead—in my armor, in my stead!"

"Then where is your armor, my son?"

"Hektor has it! He stripped Patroklas' body!"

"Zeus gave me that armor when he sent me to a mortal's bed ..."

"If only you'd never met that mortal, my father! Soon you'll have eternity to grieve for your mortal son!"

"What will you do, dear son?" "Do? Spit Hektor on my spear, a funeral gift for Patroklas!"

"Then your end is not far off, my son. You know the story: When Hektor dies, you follow."

"I know it, mother, you've told me often enough. It doesn't matter. I'd die now if it would bring Patroklas back! I sent him out there and he's dead—in my armor, in my stead!"

He chants, "Can't save myself, couldn't save my friend! What use am

I? I can kill any man, but I let my vassal die. My hate was so sweet I let it distract me!"

He sighs, "At least I can end this stupid quarrel. I'll make peace with that pig Agamemnon, for Patroklas' sake. And then I'll take the army out and make some company for myself in Hades. Many a Trojan wife, Dardanian mother, Lycian sister, will learn to weep, weep for her men, with my help!"

Thetis whispered to her son, "Yes, but not just yet, son. Your armor is on Hektor's shoulders; your own skin unguarded, soft as a molting crab."

He's outraged: "I'd fight naked! Patroklas is lying there, food for stray dogs! Let me bring home his body, grant me that!"

She shakes her head, "Not without armor. Let Hektor wear it, and bad luck seep from it. I promise you: he dies before you. But neither dies today. Wait till dawn, my poor son, when the sun comes up you'll see what I bring you—god-armor, hot from the forge!"

She hugs him once more—how many more times will she have?—flows down to the beach and tells her hundred sisters, "Go tell my father Ocean I've gone to see the blacksmith." They nod, flow into the waves, down to the old man's palace. Thetis leaps into the sky on her bright metal feet.

Hektor is sweating into Akilles' armor, attacking the Greeks again and again, trying to grab Patroklas' corpse and take it back to Troy, a trophy.

The Greeks are carrying Patroklas on their shoulders, making their way back to camp slowly, with the two Ajaxes, big and little, fending off the Trojans. Hektor is as hungry for Patroklas' cold flesh as a lion for the haunch of a sheep it can smell upwind. Three times he bashes through the Greeks' shields and grabs the cold feet; three times they form up in a scrum and push him back.

The two Ajaxes are tired. They've been stumbling backward all day, fending off Trojans, sliding on blood and entrails. They're wounded in a dozen places, stiff and sore from bending this way and that to duck Trojan spears. They can't last much longer.

Akilles can hear the battle, far away as he is. His ears are finer than any mere mortal's, and he knows what every sound means. He can hear the hoarse breaths of the two Ajaxes, the scraping sound a shield-wall makes when the men are too tired to hold the oxhide disks high any longer. He wants more than anything in the world to run onto the field and help bring back Patroklas' body home, but he promised his mother he wouldn't fight today.

And as he thinks that, there is suddenly a pearly young woman next to him, who says, "But you must fight today, Akilles."

He turns and sees Iris, herald of the great gods.

She says, "Patroklas was your vassal; will you let him feed the jackals? Do your duty, recover his body!"

Akilles asks politely, "Madam, may I ask which of the gods sent you?"

"Hera sent me."

"And Zeus?"

"Zeus doesn't know."

A man must be very careful when the gods involve him in these palace intrigues. Akilles asks, "How can I fight without armor? They stripped my armor from Patroklas. My mother is bringing me a new set from the blacksmith."

She's annoyed at quibbling from a mere half-god; "You must fight, now!"

"My mother told me not to fight without armor."

"Wear another man's armor!"

He shakes his head, "I can't, Madam. Not all mortals are alike. Look at me; only Big Ajax is anywhere near my size. An ordinary man's armor would be far too small for me."

She goes silent, and her human figure blurs. That means she's discussing the matter with Hera. After a moment, she coalesces again and says, "Hera and her daughter have decided that you need not fight today. But you are ordered to go to the wall and show yourself, to frighten the Trojans. This will buy the Greeks a little time."

She blurs and disappears. He feels Athena's mantle being draped over his shoulders. She doesn't show herself or speak to him—she's not happy that he disobeyed Hera's order—but she needs him. He can feel her steely mind weaving a sphere of hard light around his head. He walks out of the tent, his grief almost forgotten in this borrowed god-strength. Everyone stares as he walks to the wall; his head is ablaze, flaring like the bonfires that besieged cities light to call for help.

His feet don't even touch the dust as he walks through the gate and out to the edge of the ditch around the camp. He opens his mouth and Athena's mantle works the bellows of his lungs for him, compressing them and then releasing a sound no mere human could make. Athena joins her voice to it from the far horizons and it blasts the Trojans like the giant wave that smashes towns after an earthquake.

Akilles' head is a comet, his voice is a landslide. The Trojans hunker down in terror. Their horses have more sense and turn instantly, heading back for the safety of their stables. The drivers can only hunch in the cars, hands over their ears.

The bravest Trojans have endured that blast and are trying to gather their wits, take up their weapons again, when Akilles roars a second time. Again Athena shrieks with him from the edge of the horizon. This time weaker Trojans simply flee. Some are so terrified that they stab themselves with their own spears.

Only Hektor and a few of the bravest Trojans are still pursuing Patroklas' pallbearers when Akilles shouts a third time. Even Hektor can't bear it; he and his comrades break and run. The Greeks cheer, taking Patroklas' body back into the camp unmolested.

As they come through the gate, Akilles sees the body for the first time. He sent Patroklas off alive, cheerful and modest as ever. He remembers how he scolded his friend. He'll never get the chance to make amends. This corpse is on his head. This death is his doing.

Hera pauses the sunset, lets the red disk linger above the horizon a few moments, so that Akilles can get a good look at Patroklas' corpse. She wants him in a killing mood tomorrow morning.

Then she whispers, "Fall!" and the sun sinks into the sea.

The Trojans don't stop running from Akilles' great roar until they're so tired they have to stop. They make camp out on the plain, too scared to sit down or take off their armor. They keep looking westward, afraid Akilles will chase them down.

Polydamus has more sense than the rest. He says, "Comrades, we should go back to Troy right now. If we stay here till morning, we'll see more of Akilles than we want. And the survivors will be glad to get back to the town. So the smart move is to go there now, before we lose another man. We'll fight from the walls; they've never been able to break through our walls."

Hektor stomps into the firelight, twice Polydamus' size, and growls, "I don't like that kind of talk. It stinks of cowardice. Haven't you had enough of hiding behind the walls?"

"Prince Hektor, the Greeks can't match our bows; fighting from the walls, we can pick them off at will."

"We've lost all our gold already, lost most of our best men—but now that Zeus has shown me his favor, you want to run and hide? I won't allow it. We fight on the plain."

He turns to the others: "Get some food in you now. I want every man ready by dawn. If you're worried about your treasure, send a slave back to the city with orders to give it all away. We settle this tomorrow."

He holds his spear high, crying, "And let Akilles fight me! He'll be the one who takes a spear in the belly!"

They cheer, warming their hands at Hektor's foolish words like half-frozen men at a fire.

Polydamus walks off. He was right, but Hektor won't realize it until it's too late. Akilles stays awake all night, watching over his friend's body.

He puts his huge hands on Patroklas' chest, crying, "Forgive me! I sent you off to die. Forgive me, Menoetius! I sent your son Patroklas to die."

He stands back as the slaves wash the body with hot water, cleaning off the dust-clotted blood.

Then he puts his hands on Patroklas' chest once more, sighing, "The only amends I can make you, my friend, is to join you in this Trojan dust. Soon, soon, I promise. We'll lie together soon. And I'll make you a gift before we lie together: twelve Trojan warriors' heads for decoration around your grave, and Hektor's armor as a trophy. You'll have dead Trojans' wives for a chorus of singers, and their burning city for a hearth."

He steps back. The slaves smear the corpse with perfumed olive oil, then wrap it in strips of linen. Akilles leads his five battalions in a death chant.

Zeus knows where all this is leading. He grumbles to Hera, "I hope you're happy now! Sometimes I think Agamemnon must be your bastard son."

Hera sniffs, "Well, I don't see why I shouldn't help these mortals if I happen to like them! They may not be as clever or strong as we are, but I can still do them a good turn now and then, can't I?"

Zeus grunts and turns away.

Thetis' shining feet have carried her into the sky. Now she flies toward a golden tangle of stars and pillars—the miraculous palace of the blacksmith god.

His name is Hefestos, and the main thing about him is that he's ugly, the one cripple in a family that values good looks. That's why his mother Hera threw him out of the sky as soon as she saw his twisted legs and wry-wrung face. But Hefestos was a tough little fellow, and now he's the cleverest of the gods, tolerated for his wondrous gadgets. And through it all he kept his sweet nature, ugliest and the kindest of the family.

He's always making some new marvel—magic platters that travel on their own, or golden slaves who move like they're alive.

He made this palace for his wife, Charis. She is beauty, as he is ugliness. They make quite a couple, but the marriage is a happy one.

Charis sees Thetis coming a thousand miles off and floats down through the glowing stairways to meet her guest: "You're always welcome in our house, Thetis. Come and take some food. It's not often you come to see us."

They sit, and the golden slaves serve them. After courtesy is satisfied, Charis asks, "Why have you come up from the sea, Thetis?"

"I need your husband's help."

Charis calls, "Husband, come and speak to our guest!"

Hefestos pokes his grinning, ugly head through the door: "Thetis! You're always welcome! But let me wash off all this smithy grime before I say hello!"

He limps off, a bull's shoulders on wobbly heron legs. First he puts his tools away, each in its proper place in the big silver box.

Then one of the golden slaves hands him a wet sponge. He scrubs his chest and head, his ugly face and gnarled, greasy hands.

Another slave hands him a clean shirt; a third holds out his crutch. Tucking it under his arm, he limps back to see Thetis. He beams at the sight of her: "I owe you my life, dear Thetis; I'll do anything for you."

He turns to Charis, "My dear, do you know that our guest saved my life?" Charis shakes her head. She's heard the story a dozen times, but she's being polite.

He tells it again: "Well, when I was born, there was a little trouble; I came out a bit twisted up, you know, and my mother didn't like my looks ..."

Charis scowls, "In fact she threw you away, the monster!"

Hefestos waves his hand, "A misunderstanding, that's all! You can't blame her! They're very strict about appearances on Olympos! But it's true, she threw me away. I fell ..."

He stares, his jaw tightening as he remembers: "Yes, I fell a long way, kept falling for a long, long time ..."

Charis coughs, and he goes on, "Ah, right! Well, I fell into the ocean at last. And there, Ocean's daughters Thetis and Yurinoma found me and took pity on this poor cripple. They cradled me like a twisted-up dolly, didn't you, Thetis!"

She smiles at the memory. He stares fondly at her, sighing, "Seven years, eh Thetis?" Turning to Charis, he marvels, "Seven years those two girls took care of me as well as my own mo—"

He stops, blushing. Better not to mention his mother. He starts again, "None of the others even noticed I was missing; who misses a cripple? But Thetis and her sister cared for me like a pet goat with a bad hoof!"

Thetis says, "Charis, your husband is being far too modest. From the moment we took him in, he made himself useful. Hefestos, you paid your keep a thousand times over with the fine things you made: goblets of gold, silver armlets! I'll always remember your magical toys—"

She turns to Charis, "They were wonderful! There was one that could swim through the sea as if it were alive!"

Hefestos blushes, "Oh, I was just learning back then. I'm a real smith now. So whatever it is you want, I can make it for you. Just name it!"

She starts to explain, then draws the veil over her face to hide her tears. Wiping her eyes, she says: "My friends, Zeus tortures me. He gave me to a human, Peleus. I never wanted to be married to a creature that lives only a few years, but I obeyed—and now my husband is too old to do anything but sleep, while I'm as young as I was at our marriage."

She sighs, "But there was one comfort, my fine son Akilles. He grew like a tree, stronger, taller than any mortal. And then—well, perhaps you already know what happened to him at Troy?"

They shake their heads, "No, we haven't heard." Of course they've heard, but they are courteous hosts.

She weeps again, "It started with that vile Agamemnon! These little human kings, their jealousies! He took back a slave girl my son had won fairly. He did it in front of the whole Greek army! My son was shamed—and he liked the girl too, poor boy. So he refused to fight, and then ... You've heard what happened to Patroklas yesterday?"

They know; they nod.

"You see, he was wearing my son's armor. Now Hektor has it. So I come to ask you to make my son new armor, to protect the little life he has left."

Hefestos takes Thetis' hands and says, "Thetis, he will have armor to amaze gods and humans alike. I only wish I could save him from—"

Charis gestures to him, and he changes tone quickly: "Right! It will be ready by dawn. I'll go get started."

Now he limps to his furnace, and calls to his bellows, twenty of them. They obey him like living creatures, and blow any way he wants, soft as a breath or hard as hurricanes.

When the fire is hot, he takes lumps of every kind of metal—red copper, soft tin, bright silver and honey-colored gold—and tosses them into the pot as easy as a cook slicing onions into a cauldron. When the metal melts, he takes the tongs and pours it into a shield-frame.

As soon as one layer cools in the frame, he pours in another. At last he knocks it out of the frame and admires his work: a three-layered disk of bright metal, big enough to protect even a giant like Akilles.

Next Hefestos crafts the face of the shield, the part that men will see in battle. For many, it will be the last thing they ever see. He wants it to be his best work, a way of showing his gratitude to Thetis.

He decides to put the whole world on this shield-face. A few taps of his hammer, and there on the metal is Ocean: waves rocking, birds flying, fish leaping. You can even hear the cry of the gulls. He taps again and the sea is dark; now there's a full moon on the waves, with the stars burning around it. There are the Seven Sisters glowing, almost winking; there's Orion, the glowing bones of the hunter. And fleeing him forever, but never escaping, is the Great Bear, the stars that twist and turn, but never sink into Ocean.

Hefestos smiles. It will please his dear Thetis, this metal ocean of his. He takes down a different hammer, gives a single tap on the shield-face; now the sun shines. By the light of this metal sun, you can see two cities. And if you look closer, you can see the people in each town. There's a big wedding going on in one of them. Men are delivering the bride to her husband's house, and women are peeking out to watch the procession.

You can even see the bride. You'd fall in love with her if you looked too close. There's her veil moving in the breeze. You can hear the boys singing a wedding chant in her honor.

Now you can see men gathered to judge a quarrel about blood-money. The murderer says he already paid it, but the dead man's relations say they never got a penny. Both families have friends who are yelling at the other side, so the heralds have to keep pushing everybody back with their staffs. Two silver coins lying on the marble bench, to be given to whoever makes the best speech.

The other city is dying. Two armies are camped outside it, arguing about whether to sack it or accept a bribe to spare it. You can see the hard faces of the warriors as they gulp unmixed wine and argue about who gets a bigger share of the loot.

But the city isn't ready to give up yet. The defenders have set a trap. They've left a few old men, women, and big children on the walls to fool the attackers, while the strong young men slip out by the back gate to ambush the besiegers.

Athena is leading the defenders, with her brother Ares in tow beside her. She gleams from the shield, as if the metal Hefestos used to make her figure were still molten. She's twice the height of the warriors following her. Ares lurks near her, dull, crafted of lesser metal. Looking at his figure in the shield, you see him shift, as you turn your head; one moment he's fearsome and terrifying, the next disgusting and cowardly. You can see the trail of blood he leaves behind and the flies swarming around his head.

The defenders follow a respectful distance behind their two patron gods. If you stare at the marching men for a moment, they don't move, but if you watch longer, you see them flow, like metal in a forge, down to a riverbed where the besieging forces water their cattle. The defenders hide themselves and wait for the slaves to lead the herd down to the water.

If you watch long enough you'll see the battle. First, scouts run up to tell the men waiting in ambush that herders are bringing the attackers' livestock to the river.

Here come those stupid herd boys, oblivious, singing along as one of them plays a flute. They walk right into the ambush. The defenders jump out from the brush, drive off the livestock and chop the herders' heads off before they can call for help.

But the cattle start bellowing at the smell of blood; the besiegers realize they're under attack. They put on their armor and rush to the river, where the two sides face off shield to shield.

If you keep watching, you'll see the battle. You'll see Strife and Chaos bouncing among mortal men like evil clowns, making the fighters hate and kill each other, then lapping up their blood as they giggle at the terror in dying warriors' eyes. And if you look down into the shield-face long enough, you'll see Fate herself, hammered out of the hardest, darkest metal in Hefestos' storeroom, dragging three men after her on a rope.

The first of the three is already dead. She's dragging him along by one heel like a butcher drags a dead goat. Next is a wounded man, coughing up blood, trying to hold his guts inside his ribs. Last in Fate's coffle is a man still unhurt. He walks along staring at Fate, who strides uncaring, her skirt stained with men's blood.

You don't want to look too long at that scene. Better to shift your eyes to what the blacksmith god makes next: a fine field, already plowed three times. Serfs are furrowing it; they work with a will, because as soon as one of them reaches the end of a furrow, there's a slave waiting with a full cup of good strong wine. Hefestos has made the furrows dark as wet earth, even though they're crafted from bright metal.

Keep staring at this happy scene and you can watch the crop come up, golden heads of wheat waving in the breeze. It's harvest-time. Scythes are the only weapons in this battle, and the serfs are singing as they slice bundle after bundle of sweet bread-in-the-making. The landowner watches his workers with a smile. He doesn't grudge them their noon meal, not today. You can almost smell the barley porridge the women are cooking under a big oak in the middle of the field. And it won't be just porridge, either, because the master has ordered a big ox killed. His house slaves are busy with their cleavers, cutting up the beast for the cauldron.

But what will they drink? Just look a little longer, and you'll see! The blacksmith god has made a vineyard of fat black grapes, so many the branches would break if the men didn't prop them up with big sticks. These sticks are made of silver; they glow on the shield-face. The owners are worried about grape-thieves, so Hefestos has made them a fence of shiny tin, with a ditch of dark metal beyond it. Children are running back and forth among the vines, piling up the makings of next year's wine while a boy sings harvest songs.

Now you see a herd of cattle, some gold, some of tin, or spotted with different metals. You could watch those fine fat cattle forever as they munch the weeds along a riverbank. Oh, how the cattle enjoy those fragrant water-weeds! The cattle boys have an easy time of it, till the reeds part suddenly and two huge lionesses ambush the lead bull. One clamps her claws on his throat while the other hoists herself onto his back to deliver the death bite. When they've killed him, they settle down to feed, tearing chunks of hot meat from his body. Those cowardly herd boys aren't doing anything but tossing rocks and siccing their dogs at the huge lionesses. The dogs are just as cowardly as their masters; all they do is bark, their rumps backed up against their masters' shins.

Keep looking at the shield-face and the scene changes. Now it's a mountain pasture where nothing is moving but a few sheep.

Then the meadow comes alive with fine boys and beautiful girls dancing and courting, unashamed. The boys are wearing oiled linen robes so you can see every muscle. The girls have made flower garlands for their hair, and they wear only light linen dresses. When the sun shines through the linen, you can see their sweet curves. Sometimes boys and girls dance separately, sometimes together. No one minds, no one scolds them; the whole village watches happily and a minstrel plays for the dancers.

Now your eye has wandered to the edge of the shield, and you're in Ocean again, among the waves that circle and enclose this metal world.

Hefestos made other things for Akilles, of course: a fine breastplate that no spear could pierce, a helmet that shapes itself to the wearer's head as soon as he pulls it on; light, strong greaves to protect the shins.

But it was into that marvelous, ever-changing shield that the lame god poured all his skill, and all his love for Akilles' mother. When it was finished and all the armor he made had cooled, he hobbled into the room where Thetis waited with his wife.

He lays the miraculous shield before her like a platter, with the armor piled on it. She stares at his marvelous works, and then—too moved to speak her thanks—she bows in gratitude, takes up his gifts, and steps into the air, falling to the plain of Troy to give her son his last, best armor.

19

RECONCILED

THETIS ᵮALLS ƓENTLY through the dawn, bringing her son his armor. She finds him kneeling by Patroklas' body. He's been there all night.

She touches his shoulder, whispering, "Leave him in peace, son. Put on the armor Hefestos has made for you."

She shows him the shield, then the helmet, breastplate, and greaves.

The shield frightens the captive women. They hide their faces with their veils. After trying to stare boldly at the moving images on it, Akilles' men look away too. No man can look at that shield-face for long.

No one except Akilles. He stares at the blacksmith's gifts like a starving man stares at a table piled with food. Then he goes over, caressing each piece. He looks long and fondly into the shield-face, then slips it onto his shoulder.

"Mother, these gifts are a miracle! I'll test them on the Trojans. Let me get ready now."

Then he stops and runs back to the body, moaning, "No, I can't go! If I leave him alone like this—"

She hugs him, murmuring, "He's dead, my son; what can happen to him?"

He moans, "The flies! If I don't keep them off, they'll lay their eggs in him!"

"Leave that to me. Just watch."

She takes a tiny bottle from her robes and pours a single drop on Patroklas. Suddenly the smell of decaying meat is gone; everyone inhales deeply for the first time in hours. He looks like a sleeping man, not a dead one.

She turns back to Akilles: "You see? He'll stay fresh for a year if need be."

He nods, wiping his eyes. She says, "Now call an assembly and take back what you said to Agamemnon."

He nods. For Patroklas' sake, he'll do it.

He goes to the beach and calls the men. Everyone knows that giant voice and comes running. Even the sailors who've spent the whole war just lounging on the decks climb down off their ships to hear what Akilles has to say.

The fighters come too, though many move slowly, limping, pale with infected wounds that won't heal. Odysseus and Diomedes are both moving a little slowly, wincing in pain. Agamemnon is the last to arrive. It's not his wound slowing him down, though; he's wary, not sure what to expect.

Akilles has decided to get it over with quickly, pride be damned. He says, "King Agamemnon, I wish the girl Briseis had died the day we took her city. What sense does it make, the two of us fighting over a girl? Many of our best men have tasted this dust because of our feud. It was good for Hektor and the Trojans, a disaster for us."

He holds up one huge hand and shouts, "So I say now, in front of everyone, I'm putting away my anger forever."

There; that's the worst of it, done. He goes on eagerly, "So, if you'll give the order to arm, my lord Agamemnon, you'll soon see Akilles killing Trojans once again!"

The men cheer wildly; the chiefs nod and smile at him. Odysseus gives him a comradely wink; he knows it wasn't easy for the boy.

The only man who isn't satisfied is Agamemnon. All he needs to do is embrace Akilles and say something conciliatory. That's what a good king would do, but this is Agamemnon, who never drops a grudge. He stands, arranging himself for a long speech. Instead of smiling and ordering wine for all, he starts solemnly:

"Fighters, Craftsmen of Ares, I have always believed in letting a man speak his piece. No good comes of interruptions, so though it will take me a while to explain things, I hope I'll have your full attention."

They settle in, a few of the men rolling their eyes and muttering. Not again! But Agamemnon begins.

"Some of you—" and he stares hard at Odysseus—"have been scolding me about this, ah ... this matter between me and Akilles. And I grant that I was wrong to insult our best man, weakening the army. But why did I do such a foolish thing, I who have always shown good judgment?"

Odysseus has to bite his tongue. He bows his head so Agamemnon won't see his scowl.

Agamemnon doesn't notice; he's been rehearsing his speech all day. He assumes a thoughtful look and says, "I have thought long and hard about my lapse in judgment, and I think I know what happened: The Furies must have possessed me! What else could it be? I was possessed by Folly, and you all know that Folly is Zeus' firstborn daughter! She's older and stronger than any man!"

He tells a long, long story, longer than any he's ever inflicted on the army, about how Folly, aided by Hera, once fooled Zeus himself. They all listen politely.

Finally he gets to the point: "And just as Zeus grieved that day, so I grieved when I saw Hektor killing Greeks at the ships—and all because Folly blinded me!"

He spreads his arms wide for the dramatic ending: "And so, noble Akilles, I offer you now all the prizes Odysseus offered you in your tent, to which I'll add some of my own treasure."

Everyone cheers. This is more like it. But Agamemnon has to ruin the moment by saying spitefully, "So, Akilles, why don't you send your battalions into battle—or would you rather spend today checking on me, overseeing the deliveries just to be sure you haven't been cheated?"

The men grumble. That's an insult, a foolish one. But Akilles grits his teeth and waves it off.

"Presents? My dear lord Agamemnon, you are free to give me any presents you like, or none at all."

Everyone cheers. This is how a man should act. Akilles turns away from Agamemnon and addresses the men directly: "Remember, all of you, that Akilles is fighting with you today. I'll deal with Hektor, but I expect every man to stay up with me! No hanging back!"

They shout themselves hoarse, clanging spear and sword against their shield-bosses.

Agamemnon is not pleased. His big speech was barely noticed. Odysseus sees Agamemnon's spite building. The truce could crumble unless he acts now.

So he stands up and shouts, "Akilles, have mercy on us mortals! You're half god, you don't need to eat like us poor critters do. If you send us all out now, with empty stomachs, we'll be too weak to hold up our shields by afternoon. Let us get some food in our bellies! And then—I speak for every man here, don't I, boys?—with lunch inside us, we'll stand with you all day long!"

More cheering.

But Akilles is scandalized: "Eat, while the flies are buzzing around Patroklas' body? I don't understand you people. Agamemnon talks to me about prizes, and you talk about food, Odysseus? It's not right!"

Odysseus can see Akilles' anger rising, so he moves to another topic: "And in the meantime, King Agamemnon will have his slaves bring all the gifts here, so we can all see Akilles has been treated properly."

Akilles shrugs. Prizes, lunch ... a lot of shameful distractions.

Odysseus goes on, "And King Agamemnon will also swear, in front of us all, that he's never bedded the girl Briseis."

The mention of Briseis makes Akilles angrier than ever, so Odysseus goes on, "And let this be a lesson for you, Agamemnon! Treat your fellow kings with some respect!"

Then he turns to Akilles, holding out both hands, "And you, Akilles, show yourself the better man; let Agamemnon give you a feast in his tent."

Akilles starts to object, then stops and nods. It has to be done.

Agamemnon likes this part. Akilles, his guest! He'll enjoy that. So he answers, "Odysseus, you always know what to say! I'll swear that oath and have my men bring the prizes and sacrifice a fat boar to Zeus."

Akilles grumbles, "We're wasting time talking about trifles. Patroklas' body is lying in my tent, all hacked and torn up, while we talk about feasts, and food, and oratory."

He's getting angrier by the second: "And while you're blathering, all I can hear—" His voice is rising, a bad sign.

"—is Patroklas' death rattle! And I wasn't there to help him!"

He starts to shake; soon he'll be out of control. Odysseus hugs him hard, pushes him back down on his seat: "Akilles, listen now. You know I'm your friend."

Akilles stares at the fierce broad face, the fire-red beard, the sharp fox eyes. Friend? Finally he nods.

Odysseus goes on, "And we both know you're better than me in battle. And by no small margin, either. But I'm a little older than you, and I see things more clearly than you do. We're just mortals, Akilles; we can't fast forever in

Patroklas' honor. We'd starve if we tried to honor the dead that way, because people die every day."

He stares hard at Akilles, whispering, "People die every day. Not just Patroklas, and—" leaning in close, he whispers more quietly, "—not just you, either. All of us will die."

Then he leans back and laughs, patting his tummy, playing the glutton. "So grief or no grief, a man has to eat! The trouble with you, Akilles, isn't just the god half; it's that the half that isn't god is pure hero! There's no mere mortal about you, on either side of the family!"

Akilles smiles bashfully, amused in spite of himself.

Odysseus pooches out his own belly and slaps it, puffs out his cheeks like a fat man and says, "But the rest of us, we're mere flesh and blood, and we'd like to eat some other flesh and blood from an ox or sheep today!"

He taps Akilles' magic shield and says, "You could hold that new three-layer shield of yours all day, but we mortals get tired holding up our ox-hide shields and big spears! So let us eat a little and we won't let you down out there!"

Akilles feels as grim as ever, but he has to work with these men. He waves a hand, submitting.

"Good! I knew you'd be reasonable. Now we'll look over your gifts, make the sacrifice, and have a good meal. Just be patient!"

The gifts from Agamemnon are laid out for inspection: seven tripods, twenty big metal cauldrons, twelve horses, and seven slave women, guaranteed to be good with a needle. And Briseis, making eight women in all.

Odysseus makes a big show of weighing out the gold, then gives the signal; the slaves pick everything up and take it away. It's time for the sacrifice.

Agamemnon presides over the ceremony. His herald Talthibyas, a pompous fat man with a loud, clear voice, drags a huge boar in front of the men, intoning, "Lord King Agamemnon offers this fine boar in sacrifice, that Lord King Zeus may look kindly on our fight!"

He ties the boar to a stake. Agamemnon steps up, draws his dagger and slices off some of the bristles on the boar's back. It grunts, puzzled, then goes back to snuffling for scraps.

Agamemnon looks up to the sky, holding the dagger in one hand and the bristles in the other. He calls, "Zeus, you are my witness! Earth, you are my witness! Sun, you are my witness! You Furies, who take revenge on liars, you are my witnesses! I swear before all of you that I never so much as touched the girl Briseis! May all my witnesses punish me if I'm lying!"

And as he says "I'm lying," he cuts the boar's throat. It squeals, jumps a little, then falls dead, its thick blood pooling around Agamemnon's feet.

He calls his herald over, points toward the sea. Talbithyas slings the boar over his shoulders and trots down to the beach. He spins three times like a discus thrower and flings the pig into the surf to feed the fish.

Akilles has to say something now. All he can manage is, "Zeus, you made us humans fools. Why else would my fellow king—" he gestures toward Agamemnon—"have stolen that girl when he knew it would make me angry? So much harm came of it! Good men died. Patroklas ..." Agamemnon gestures; the meeting is over. Men disperse to eat before battle.

Akilles walks back to his compound, Briseis following warily a few paces back. When she sees Patroklas' body, she throws herself on it, keening, "Patroklas! My only friend! When I left you were alive; I come back to find you dead!"

She tears at her hair, scratches her face, goes on in that high voice, "Sorrow, sorrow, one follows another! My husband spitted on a spear, I saw it! My three brothers killed, I watched! Sorrow, sorrow, nothing but sorrow! My one comfort was you, Patroklas! I sorrowed, sorrowed, but you comforted me!"

She turns slyly toward Akilles and keens, "Patroklas, you comforted me! You said you'd make my lord Akilles marry me! You said we'd have a wedding feast in Phthia! You said, 'Don't weep, dear girl; Akilles will marry you, and you'll reign in Peleus' house!'"

Akilles ignores her. He is very weary of humans. The men want lunch, the girl wants marriage, Agamemnon wants to make speeches. He wishes he were among wolves or lions, beasts with more fang than tongue.

She throws herself on the corpse again, shaking her hair from side to side, tearing her nails on Patroklas' cold flesh. The other slave women join in at the top of their voices. They pretend to be weeping for Patroklas, but Akilles knows it doesn't take much to make a slave woman weep. They're weeping for themselves. Their whole lives are grief.

The men wander in and out, stuffing their faces as they watch the women play at grief. They all want Akilles to have a bite with them. It's all these spearmen can do, eat and talk—and then talk about eating. "My Lord Akilles, have some of this flank-steak! You need to feed up for the battle!"

Finally he lashes out: "Will you stop this talk about eating? Everyone out!"

Only a few have the courage to stay: Odysseus, Nestor, Ideomenus, and old Fenix.

He kneels beside the corpse again and tells Patroklas, "You were the one man who always made sure I had a good meal before I went into battle. So I'll fast for you today."

He strokes Patroklas' cold arm. "I didn't know there was pain like this, Patroklas. If they told me that my father was dead, or even my son, I could bear it. But I can't bear your death. I can't bear that you died in my armor, in my stead, in this dust, fighting for Agamemnon's cuckold brother, that wretched Atreus-son clan ..."

He strokes the dead man's arm, muttering, "Remember when you promised that when I die here, you'd bring back all my treasure and show it to my son so he could be proud of his father?"

He sighs, "But you died before me. In my armor, in my stead. Now who'll tell my poor old father about my death? Because I'll be joining you soon, my friend. That's the only comfort I can offer; wait a little while, and we'll be together in the dust."

Odysseus has begun to cry. Even Zeus, staring down at the scene, feels a catch in his throat. He snarls at Athena, "You've got your mother's hard heart, girl! Your champion Akilles is weeping his heart out down there and you don't even watch! At least drop some ambrosia on his skin so he won't get hungry!"

Athena obeys. Becoming a falcon, she dives onto the plain and swerves toward Akilles, brushing a drop of ambrosia on his neck as he bends over the corpse. He feels a rush of air, then a surge of strength. In fact, he feels so good it shames him. Is he no better than the rest of them, feeling good when he should be grieving? At last the others have finished stuffing themselves and put on their armor. A forest of spears, a boulder-stream of shields, they form up and march out of the camp. The army has never been so strong and united. The sunlight bounces off the soldiers as if their bronze armor has defeated it. Their steps are like Poseidon shaking the earth.

Akilles rushes back to his quarters to put on his new armor. But as he takes up Hefestos' gifts, he realizes what things of beauty and power the blacksmith has made for him. Forgetting Patroklas for a moment, he runs a hand down the greaves, then feels the curves of the helmet. What marvels! They move with his hand, eager to cover and protect him. So light, but so strong! Every inch swarms with living metal, too beautiful to be mere armor but too effective to be mere jewelry.

He puts the armor on as reverently as a priest arranging his vestments. First the greaves. A good pair of these is a true gift from the gods. These are the best

Akilles has ever seen, molded precisely to his legs—how did the blacksmith know?—and fitted with strong clasps across the ankles.

Then the breastplate. A slave holds it up to him, ties it in the back. It feels as comfortable as a second skin.

Now the helmet; he pulls it on, and feels it warp to the shape of his head, caressing his temples like a lover.

Then he takes up the great shield. While it lay there in the tent, the shield seemed dark. But as soon as Akilles picks it up it begins to flash, not from the sun but its own infinite depths.

Akilles lunges and twists to see if he can move in this new armor. It's superb. Light as linen and more flexible. And warm somehow, eager. It seems to want to go into battle as much as he does.

He grabs his spear, big as a tree. The centaurs made it for their battles; no two-legs but Akilles could ever lift it, never mind wield it.

The chariot is ready and waiting, with Otomedon holding the reins.

Seeing the god-horses who drove Patroklas to his death, Akilles scolds, "Dapple, Blondie, make sure you bring your driver back alive this time."

Dapple in a low, throaty voice: "We'll bring you home safe today, Akilles. What happened to Patroklas wasn't our fault. Apollo killed him."

"Just be more careful! I don't want to die yet."

Dapple shakes his mane, saying, "Your death day is known. It won't be today, but it's not far off. And we can't save you, no matter how fast we run."

The Furies squeeze Dapple's throat to make him stop talking.

Akilles hugs the horse's huge head and whispers, "Why do you all love to tell me I'm going to die? I know it already. You don't need to keep reminding me."

Then he jumps into the car and drives off shouting, "But a lot of Trojans will die before me!"

20

TOURNAMENT

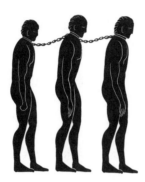

THE GODS HAVE DECIDED to watch Akilles' return to battle. It will be a great performance and everyone shows up—not just Zeus' clan but all kinds of immortals: tree-women, ocean-girls, and river-men dripping mud.

Themis, Zeus' secretary, made sure to invite everyone. Even Poseidon shows up—and it's not every day, or even every century, that he deigns to visit his brother. While the little gods are filing quietly into their seats, Poseidon stomps up to Zeus and growls, "Well, brother, why bring us here? Something about this Trojan war?"

Zeus says, "Of course it's the war. Today I give all of you permission to help whichever side you want. You can just watch, or go down to join one side or the other. As for me, I'm just going to sit here and watch."

Hera and Athena are overjoyed; they can meddle to their hearts' content today! They huddle with the other pro-Greek gods Poseidon, Hermes, and Hefestos. The Trojans have a weaker clique backing them. Apollo is on their side—but though he has great power, he hates to use it. His wild sister Artemis is with him, but she's a strange one, fickle. Their mother Leto loves Troy too, but she's too gentle to go up against Hera. Ares supports the Trojans, more or less—but would you want him on your side? He's a murderer and a coward. Stupid, too. Afroditi favors the Trojans—one of them anyway, her toy prince Paris. But Afroditi has already demonstrated she's not much use in battle.

The Trojans have a few river-gods on their side, especially those rivers that flow through Trojan lands. But mere river-gods can't do much against great gods like Hera and Athena, Hermes and Poseidon.

Athena, as always, is the first to join the fight. She floats over the sea near the Greek camp and sings a war song. It would make a chicken attack a lion. Every Greek who hears it sprints to battle, eager to kill Trojans.

Athena seems to be everywhere at once. Every Greek hears her war song as if she were singing into his ear.

Ares tries to use his own god-voice to cheer the Trojans, roaring a war chant from the temple mount of Troy. The Trojans feel Ares' spirit come over them, wanting to hurt someone as long as there's no risk they'll be hurt in return. Ares moves his song from the acropolis to the river so that his voice seems to come up from the water. It's a good trick, but it's no match for Athena's cold, clear battle cry.

The Greeks don't even need Athena's help today. Akilles is back; that's enough to make them all fight like heroes. He races through the shield wall to the front, taller than any mere mortal, and comes out facing the Trojan shields. Seeing him back on the field, the Trojans feel weak and sick. He's not just huge but terrifyingly fast, faster than men half his size. You can't beat him face to face and you can't outrun him. If he singles you out, you're dead.

He stands between the two armies, waiting for Hektor to step out from the Trojan side. It's a fine sight, and the gods all cheer.

Their cheering is so loud that it shakes the earth. Hades, lord of the underworld, is bumped off his dark throne by the noise and stares up, afraid that all the gods' cheers will crack the earth and let the sunlight play on his awful realm, caverns full of things that even Zeus shudders to remember.

The gods are so excited that the two factions are ready to fight each other.

Apollo faces off against Poseidon, with his deadly bow ready, a poison arrow in place. Poseidon needs no weapon; he owns the earth and can snap it like a whip.

Athena goes head-to-head with Ares. He's twice her size, scarred, covered with blood, trailing a cloud of corpse-flies, and armored from head to foot.

But Athena isn't worried. She'd love nothing better than single combat against her brother, and no sane man would bet against her.

The next match is a tricky one for a gambler: Hera versus Artemis. Some say Artemis is more dangerous than her brother. After all, they say, the moon sees more wet work than the sun. Artemis is a more enthusiastic killer than Apollo, as well. But she's up against Hera, the toughest of all the gods. Not even a night killer like Artemis has much chance against her. Hera's weapon is her will.

Apollo flinches first in the confrontation with Poseidon. He vanishes, goes down to the battlefield in the form of Likaon, one of Priam's sons. Likaon says to Aeneas, "Didn't you swear you'd face Akilles in single combat? Or was that just the wine talking?"

Aeneas mutters, "There's no fighting Akilles; you should know that. He's always got those two goddesses, mother and daughter, watching over him."

"Or maybe he's just a better man than you are."

Aeneas shrugs: "Yes, since you put it that way. He's a better man than me, or Hektor, or anyone. We all know that."

Apollo is annoyed. If shame won't work, he'll use more direct methods to make Aeneas fight. He sends a jolt of rage into the Trojan's mind. Suddenly Aeneas says, "Sure I'll fight him! Or I would, if it weren't for Athena always deflecting any weapon that comes near him. I'd fight him right now!"

Likaon taunts, "I thought you were Afroditi's son! She's one of the great gods. Thetis is just a sea-girl! You have more god blood than Akilles!"

Apollo sends poisonous ideas into Aeneas' brain, heating it with the kind of swagger that gets men killed. Aeneas shoves his way through the shield wall, to face off against Akilles.

Hera is delighted: "Athena, Poseidon, look! Apollo is up to his old tricks, pushing humans to do his fighting for him! Shall we send poor Aeneas back into the ranks? He's not a bad fellow for a Trojan."

Athena shakes her head. No half measures for her: "No, let's give Akilles our strength and help him kill Aeneas. The Trojans will see that their patron gods are weaklings and we're the strong ones."

Poseidon grunts, "But Akilles—he dies soon, yes? Maybe today?"

Hera pats his wrist. Poor old fellow, he's a little slow. "No, no, Lord Poseidon, not today! Soon, but not today!"

She bustles about happily, getting ready to help the Greeks. Athena is putting on armor too, delighted to be back on the field.

Then Poseidon stamps his foot. The world shakes. Hera almost falls. Even Athena stumbles.

Poseidon growls, "Listen to me! No fighting for you! If you go down there, Apollo and Ares will join in. Gods hurting gods. Not proper!"

He rolls Hera and Athena up in Earth's carpet, carrying them to the top of the hill Kallikolona with their feet sticking out, their pretty slippers kicking angrily. There he unrolls the carpet, sending mother and daughter spilling out among the other gods. They fix themselves up after their carpet ride and join the Greek-loving gods, who are sitting together next to the Trojan-loving faction. All is courtesy between the two groups; no one wants to anger Poseidon.

Besides, it's a joy to watch, the showdown between Akilles and Aeneas.

Akilles sees a man step out from the Trojan ranks, assuming it'll be Hektor. When he sees it's Aeneas, he's annoyed.

He calls, "Aeneas, you poor fool, who talked you into facing me? Did the Priam-sons tell you you'd inherit? They were lying to you! You're a side branch of the family, and they'll cheat you. Besides, have you forgotten what happened last time we met? I can still see you running down Mount Ida, throwing your shield away to flee faster."

Aeneas yells back, "Don't you dare talk to me like that, Akilles. My lineage is as noble as Priam's, or yours. Your mother is a mere sea-nymph; mine is great Afroditi. And as for courage, the gods hand it out as they please. So no more talking like women arguing about the price of fish—"

He runs at Akilles and throws his spear: "—We'll settle it like men, with pointed bronze!"

It's a beautiful throw. Akilles himself is surprised at the impact it makes on his shield. For a second, he wonders if it'll go through, into his guts. But this is Hefestos' masterpiece, this shield. No human spear can pierce it. Aeneas' spear smashes through the first two layers of metal, but the third, pure gold, bends it. The shield's surface moves strangely; pictures change, darken—but the spear sticks harmlessly in it.

Now it's Akilles' throw. Aeneas holds out his shield to catch the spear, but it flies right through and sticks in the ground behind him, still quivering. Aeneas knows Akilles' power now. That spear went right through a seven-layer shield as if it were a linen shirt! Aeneas feels fear crawling over his skin. Akilles sees Aeneas' terror and draws his sword. In one leap, he's on the Trojan. No lion could have leaped faster or farther. His sword is out, ready to slice open Aeneas' head—

But Poseidon steps in. He stands up among the gods and yells, "No! Aeneas is a good boy! This is Apollo's fault! Always getting someone else to die for him, too good to work up a sweat! No, we stop this now! Aeneas must live to make sons!"

Hera sniffs, "You can do what you like, Lord Poseidon. My daughter and I have made our position very clear. We won't lift one little finger, and she holds up an elegant, jeweled finger—

"To help the Trojans, not until every single one of them is dead or enslaved."

Poseidon thuds down into the earth, flings a handful of dirt at Akilles' face, and freezes the world so he can save Aeneas.

First he takes Akilles' spear out of Aeneas' shield. He places it at Akilles' feet, good as new. Then he picks up Aeneas and carries the Trojan far off to the left wing, where the wild Kaukonian allies are fighting.

Poseidon puts Aeneas down there, takes the spell off him, and says, "Aeneas, I like you; I help you. But you were foolish, listening to Apollo! Never listen to that pretty boy!"

He pats Aeneas roughly on the shoulder. "We like you; even Hera doesn't hate you, boy. But never fight Akilles! Wait till he's dead—won't be long—and then fight any other Greek. Just not Akilles!"

Aeneas, dazed, bows his head to the god. Poseidon returns to Akilles, takes the blindness off him.

Akilles blinks, puzzled, and mumbles, "What? Where did Aeneas go? I was just about to kill him. And why is my spear lying here, when I threw it hard enough to fly a mile?"

He shakes his head, "Some god must love him. I guess he was telling the truth about his lineage. Ah well, there are plenty of other Trojans to kill."

He runs along the Greek shield wall shouting, "Every man forward! I can't fight them all myself! But I'll be in front of you, and any Trojan in range of this spear—" he holds up the huge spear—"—will be dead before he can do you any harm! Now advance!"

Hektor has the much tougher job of putting some fight into the Trojans. He runs along the shield-wall making his own speech: "Akilles can talk, but we'll see what the bronze decides. I'll face him myself. All you need to do is keep your shields high. I'll do the rest. I'll kill Akilles even if—" Apollo doesn't like this talk about facing Akilles. Hektor is his last useful proxy. So he stops Hektor, puts him in a little worldlet outside of time, and comes to him in his real form. Hektor stares in awe as Apollo tells him, "Do not face Akilles. Do you understand?"

Hektor nods, and he's on the field again, at the head of the Trojan shield wall. Dazed by what he's just seen, he slinks back into the ranks.

He can only watch as Akilles kills his comrades one after another. He's making a sport of it, finding new ways to kill. He splits a man's head in two with his sword, then tosses the corpse under the Greek chariots. They roll over the body; Akilles grins.

Without even looking, he tosses his spear at a Trojan chariot. The spear seems to speed up as it flies; the driver is hit in the belly. He dies bellowing like a bull being sacrificed.

Then Akilles sees young Polydoros, Priam's youngest boy, his old father's favorite. Priam told him over and over not to fight, but you can't stop boys from playing war.

Polydoros is a fast runner. He thinks he's too fast to be hit as he dodges this way and that. Akilles sees him showing off and waits until the boy sprints into range. Then he lunges, sticking his spear right through the boy's back so it punches out by the navel. Polydoros, who thought he was going to be a great hero, dies on his knees trying to stuff his guts back into his belly.

Hektor can't bear it. His little brother, everyone's favorite! How they all spoiled him, because they all doted on him! He's seen many of his brothers die, but he can't stand seeing little Polydoros die like this. He forgets Apollo's warning and steps out for single combat.

Akilles is overjoyed: "There you are at last, the dog who killed my friend!"

Hektor yells, "You talk too much, Akilles. You're a better fighter than me, but anything can happen in battle."

He throws, but Athena is hovering over her champion. In a playful mood, she breathes on the spear so that it stops dead in mid-air, falling to the ground right in front of Hektor. He can hear her laugh in the air around him.

And then Akilles is on him, sword ready to smash his head.

But this is too much for Apollo. Much as he dislikes direct intervention, he can't let Athena get away with a prank like this. He can play pranks too; she needs to see that.

So he vanishes Hektor. Akilles ends his lunge with a fearsome swipe, but his sword only cuts air. Hektor is gone.

Now he sees Hektor to his left. Puzzled, he lunges again, sweeping his sword sideways this time, but hitting only empty air.

Trojans are actually laughing at him.

Hektor appears on his right now, and one more time Akilles lunges.

But once again he hits nothing but air. And now even some of the Greeks are laughing at him.

He shouts, "Filthy dog, you've played some trick with your friend Apollo! Never mind, you'll meet me again! And in the meantime I'll kill the rest of your family!"

Akilles plays his own deadly pranks on the Trojans, killing each in a new way. He kills a Trojan just to lure others into rescuing the body; when one comes up, Akilles casually sticks his spear through the man's kneecap, then strolls over to stop the screams by chopping off his head. Then he runs down a fleeing Trojan chariot—it's amazing how fast he is for a giant—jumps on the car, kills both riders, then reins up next to a terrified Trojan who drops his spear and shield and goes down on his knees, trying to grab Akilles' knees with both hands to beg for mercy.

Akilles takes his time. He leans over the sobbing Trojan, finds the perfect angle, stabs down and flicks the man's liver out onto the dust. The coward dies covered with his own black bile.

He kills and kills all day. Now he kills with spear-jabs to the back, because the Trojans won't face him. He mounts his chariot and drives off looking for more men to kill, wheels splashing through fresh blood.

21

RIVER

THE TROJANS HAVE BROKEN, running like goats. Some run toward Troy, but Hera sends a fog to confuse them. The rest stumble to the river and flail in the shallows, sloshing into the current as they turn to see if Akilles is following them. They drown and float downstream like a swarm of locusts driven into a river by a grass fire.

Akilles can take his time. He gallops up and reins in by the bank, wades in with his sword, hacking away. The Trojans cower in the shallows, too frightened to resist. Corpses float downstream and blood makes red clouds in the current.

Soon Akilles' sword-arm is tired, so he takes a dozen young Trojans alive to be sacrificed at Patroklas' funeral. They're as easy to herd as fawns, cringing and whimpering as he ties them in a coffle with their own shirts.

He leaves his captives on the high bank and jumps down into the water again for some more killing. He sees a Trojan struggling to climb out of the water and yanks him down by his hair. Turning him over, Akilles sees his face, and kicks him, saying, "I remember you! I captured you on a raid years ago, sold you off as a slave! To Lemnos, I think. What are you doing back here?"

The man tries to grab Akilles' knees, but he says, "No, no mercy today. What's your name?"

"Likaon. I am Likaon, Priam-son."

"One of Priam's, eh? But what are you doing back here? You're supposed to be a slave in Lemnos! I got a good price for you."

"Eetyon, Priam's guest-friend, paid my ransom."

Akilles laughs, "Well, we can't let this sort of thing go on! If a coward like you can come back from slavery, next thing you know all the men I've skewered will come slithering up out of the ground!"

He jabs, but Likaon cringes low against the dust, and the spear misses. The Trojan shrieks, "Have mercy! My father will pay twice what you sold me for!"

Akilles stabs again and again, as Likaon dodges. He could kill this miserable wretch any time he pleases, but he's enjoying the game.

As he dodges, Likaon tries to find words to save his life. He screams, "Spare me! I paid you a hundred oxen last time; this time Priam will give you three hundred!"

The spear stabs into the mud an inch from his belly. He screams, "No! Please! I'm only a half-brother!"

Akilles laughs, "Go on, worm! Tell me how you fit in Priam's family tree!"

As the spear stabs out his outline in the mud, Likaon screeches, "I'm no real relation to Hektor!"

The spear cuts him slightly and he screeches, "Different mothers! Priam married my mother Lathoye! My only full brother is Polydoros! You've already killed him! You don't need to kill me! I'll pay!"

Akilles kicks him, snarling, "Stop talking about money! I used to take ransom for you Trojan dogs before you killed Patroklas. No more, especially Priam's sons. You may have crawled out of a different womb but the same seed put you in it and I won't leave the old man a single son."

"Have mercy!"

"Mercy? I'll be following you down to the darkness soon. I'm not wasting my last days showing mercy."

Likaon understands at last that he's going to die. He drops his arms and goes silent. Akilles stands over him, picking his spot. He's fascinated by the big sobbing breaths; catching their rhythm, he darts the sword-point inside the collarbone just as the lungs are expanding, to pop the heart like a wine-skin.

The sword slides in so easily that the hilt hits Likaon's collarbone. Akilles pulls it out and Likaon crumples. He picks him up by one heel and tosses the body into the river and watches it float downstream muttering, "The fish will nibble your wounds. They like the fat under a man's skin!"

He kicks dust into the current, shouting, "Your river won't help you, Trojans! How many bulls did you sacrifice to this current? How many horses did you lead down to bleed into this stream? But it didn't help you!"

Yellow heard him, and was angry. Humans call that river Scamander, but his real name is Yellow, for his color after a rain. Yellow went looking for an avenger for these insults.

He slithers and slides upstream, feeling for a kinsman. And he finds Asterapayos, a river-son. Yellow sends tendrils of rage all through the man, and he suddenly turns from his flight and faces Akilles in the shallows.

Akilles asks, "Who's this man too stupid to run?"

Asterapayos has a spear in each hand. He calls, "You want my lineage? I am the grandson of a river called Vardar. And now this river Yellow asks me to kill you, because you insulted him."

Asterapayos feels the river's strength flow into his arms like flaming water. He throws both spears; he can throw with either hand.

The first hits Akilles' shield dead center, but Hefestos' glowing gold turns it away.

The second one nicks some skin off Akilles' elbow. His blood drips into the river.

Now it's Akilles' turn. He throws, but the river bats up his giant spear, and it flies over Asterapayos and sticks in the bank.

He draws his sword. Asterapayos has no sword, so he splashes to the bank and tries to pull Akilles' spear out of the mud. But it's buried too deep. He can't yank it out in time.

Akilles jumps up next to him, chuckling, and flicks Asterapayos' belly open. The Thracian sees his guts slither out onto the mud, and falls onto them, gasping like a fish.

Akilles tears off the dead man's armor snarling, "So you were the son of a river; so what? My father descends from Zeus, who rules every stream that reaches the sea! Your river didn't help you!"

Then he kicks the body into the river, where little fish swarm happily over it, starting at the sword wound where the fat is easiest to reach.

He stares at the fish tasting Asterapayos' flesh, then turns to see the Thracian's men frozen halfway up the steep banks. He laughs at them,

"You stuck around to see if your master could beat me? Should've run while you had the chance."

They try to scramble up the bank, grabbing at any brush or rock they can find, but Akilles is too fast. With one leap he's across the river, sword slashing left and right, killing as easily as a man knocks the heads off thistles.

Then the river surface shivers and a groan comes up from the depths. The water shouts, "Akilles, you go too far! You're dirtying my water with my own people's blood! If you want to kill all the Trojans, do it on land!"

Akilles laughs, "I decide who dies and where! I won't stop till Hektor is looking at his own intestines at my feet."

And he jumps into the shallows to provoke the river, kicking at the stream.

Yellow lashes up into a fist of water and knocks him onto the bank. Then the river calls, "Apollo, I know you're watching all this! Where's your bow? You always leave your people in the lurch!"

Akilles is getting to his feet on the bank, but the river swells into a flood that flows uphill at him, uprooting brush and trees.

Yellow crawls out of its banks, tossing Trojan corpses from its streams, surging toward Akilles.

He sees a wave, another fist of water, rising up to hit him, and grabs at a tree. But the water-fist slams into him so hard that it rips the tree out by the roots. Akilles is knocked flying, and as he tries to get to his feet, Yellow forms another giant water-fist and sends him flying again.

Akilles has never been afraid, but he is now. He runs away.

He's fast, but Yellow is faster. It falls on him like a flail, tossing him as easily as a stream in flood sends a tree trunk bouncing downstream.

He swallows water, feels himself drowning, and shrieks, "Zeus! Don't let me die like this! My mother swore I'd die by an arrow, not like a cattle herder caught in a flash flood!"

Poseidon and Athena won't let him drown. They take him up, each one taking a hand to lift him from the flood. Athena says coldly, "Stop being a coward, Akilles. You aren't going to die now. The water's spent, see? Yellow's going back to his bed."

Akilles sees the river retreating by a thousand gullies back into its banks. Yellow is still hissing and gurgling in a thousand angry voices, but he's worn out with the chase.

Athena tells Akilles, "Now return to the business at hand: killing Trojans. We have decided you will kill Hektor. Go and do so."

Ashamed and relieved all at once, he wades through the flood, pushing aside corpses, some fresh, some old, flooded out of their graves.

Athena and Poseidon fly off, and Yellow makes another attempt to kill Akilles. He calls to his neighbor-river Simoyis, "Little brother, give me all your flow! If we don't kill this man he'll destroy our city and there'll be no more sacrifices on our banks!"

Simoyis agrees and sends his flood from the hills.

Yellow roars, "Yes! Fill your flood with dead trees, boulders, cold mountain rain! I'll vomit sand and gravel into it! We'll bury Akilles under twenty feet of silt!"

The rivers aim their flow, heavy with rocks and trees, at Akilles.

Hera sighs, "This won't do, it really won't." She calls, "Hey there, Cripple! Where's that crippled brat of mine?"

Hefestos limps up eagerly. The worse she treats him, the harder he tries to please his mother.

She grumbles, "Where were you? I need you to set Yellow's stream-bed on fire."

He scratches his huge head, "Burn a river, Mother? Why?"

"Stupid boy, just do what I tell you! Burn every clod of earth, cook all the fish, even the beasts that burrow in Yellow's banks. Kill everything that lives in that river!"

"Yes Mother!" He limps off to set fire to the banks. He sets his bellows working, and soon the air is full of the smell of burnt flesh and melting bronze as the dead warriors on Yellow's banks are consumed. Then Hefestos pushes his sky-fires closer, until the river starts to boil. Eels try to wriggle away from the flames, fish leap out of the scalding soup, and at last Yellow groans, "Stop, blacksmith! Your fires are killing my fish!"

Hefestos damps his fires and Yellow submits: "I can't fight you, blacksmith; you'll turn my whole stream into a cauldron. I'll leave Akilles alone."

Hera won't let Yellow off so easily. She signals Hefestos to scorch the stream again. Fish lash their tails and die, their eyes turning into white pebbles as they cook.

Yellow screams in pain, "Hera! Tell your clubfoot boy to stop! I'll leave Akilles alone! Have mercy!"

Hera says, "Hefestos dear boy, you can stop now."

He waves his hand, and the fires vanish.

Yellow mutters through the steam, "What business is it of mine anyway? Let Akilles kill all the Trojans."

His voice fades as his waters cool: "They're only people, and people are no business of mine." You can hear his mutter fading into the gurgle of a quiet stream.

Saved from the flood, Akilles runs off after the Trojans.

Hera sits happily on the hilltop, looking forward to more slaughter. But trouble breaks out behind her.

Ares has been glaring at Athena. That girl thinks she's so clever! He runs a hand along his groin where she guided Diomedes' spear. It still hurts when he pees or gets excited. She's gonna pay.

There she is, gloating as usual, smiling, watching Akilles wipe out the Trojans. Ares' Trojans.

Ares is never far from murder. He feels a murder coming on right now.

He reaches for his spear.

She's ignoring him, as usual. Well, she'll be sorry this time. He feels the ash-wood shaft of the spear and grasps it, brings it down on her with all his strength.

But Ares is as stupid as he is brutal. He forgot that Athena is wearing an Aegis draped over her shoulder, its claws falling over her arm. Nothing can penetrate an Aegis, not even Zeus' lightning. The spear slides off her, sticks in the ground. Ares just stands there, confused.

Athena grabs a boundary stone, tall as a man, lifts it with one hand and brings it down on Ares' head. His eyes cross, he stumbles like a drunk, then falls.

Longer than the biggest ship, Ares falls. The earth shakes as he hits the dust.

Athena tosses the stone away and laughs, "You always were stupid, brother! Don't you know by now I'm stronger than you? This is what you get for siding with the Trojans!"

Afroditi runs to help Ares, who's up on one elbow, groaning. She gets him to his feet, and the two of them stumble down the hill.

Hera points toward them, taunting, "Daughter, look! Your slut of a sister is helping that big fool get away!"

Athena takes the hint and floats down the hill, fingernails out. She lands on Afroditi's back like a lioness and rakes her nails down the love-goddess' soft skin. Afroditi screams and Athena silences her with a fist behind the ear.

Afroditi falls, out cold. Without her help, Ares falls too. The two of them lie face down in the grass of the hillside.

Athena yells, "That's what you get, both of you! If you traitors hadn't gone over to the Trojans, the Greeks would have burnt the town by now!"

Poseidon wants to take on somebody from the pro-Trojan faction too. He stomps over to Apollo and says, "You, archer! We should fight, you and me, now! You're young, you hit first! Come on!"

Apollo answers, "Why should I fight over humans? They come out like flies in May, and in a little while they die. I'd as soon fight for the leaves of a tree in Autumn."

And he turns his back, leaving old Poseidon standing there, puzzled.

But Apollo's lynx-eyed sister Artemis has had enough of this hands-off approach.

She scolds Apollo, "Running away again, brother? You're good at that. You said you'd fight Poseidon!"

Apollo ignores her, but Hera has enough pretext to attack Artemis.

She clamps a big, strong hand on Artemis' fragile bow, shouting, "You like to hunt, do you? You like to kill women in childbirth with your toy bow? Now see how it feels!"

She rips the bow out of Artemis' hand and starts spanking the Huntress with it.

Artemis writhes and screams while the other gods laugh themselves breathless at the beating. All Artemis' arrows tumble out of her quiver, and her bowstring makes a twanging tune as Hera whacks her with it.

She runs sobbing to hide in her mother Leto's robe. Leto strokes her daughter's bruises.

Hera waves a hand, saying, "Don't worry, Leto, I won't beat you. You're a good mother. Just take your insolent daughter away. And both of you better remember, I'm Zeus' first wife and always will be."

Leto gathers up Artemis' fallen weapons as Hera and Athena watch, sneering. Artemis runs to Zeus, who takes her on his lap asking, "Who's been beating you, girl?"

"Your wife Hera! She's always the one starting trouble!"

Zeus chuckles, "You don't say." He strokes Artemis' hair, lets her cry her fill.

Apollo has his own plans. He walks, tall as a fir, silent as winter, through the gates of Troy, staring coldly at the weak defenses. He will have to help these humans again.

He looks over the city's walls and sees Akilles drive up to the gates with a crowd of frightened Trojans fleeing, throwing away their shields and armor.

Old King Priam looks down from the wall and croaks, "Don't shut the gates yet! Our men are still coming in!"

The gatekeepers call back, "But Akilles is coming!"

Priam mumbles, "Well, keep the gates open as long as you can! If we leave any men out there with him, they're finished!"

Apollo grimaces in disgust. If they leave the gate open, Akilles will follow these fleeing men right into the town and kill everyone. He will have to act, and quickly. He slips into the mind of Antenor, one of the fleeing Trojans, and places this thought there: "If I keep running, Akilles will catch me—he's faster than all of us—and I'll die a coward. If I try to hide, he'll find me and kill me. So I might as well turn and fight him. I'll face him and take my chances."

He stops running, turns and hunches behind his shield, spear ready.

Akilles trots to a stop just out of range, amazed that one of the Trojans is ready to fight.

Antenor yells, "You're too proud, Akilles! You're not a god! I'd rather die facing you than live to see my children sold as slaves!"

He throws, thinking of his beloved children. The spear hits Akilles on the shin, but Hefestos' wondrous greaves stop it; it falls to the ground like a twig.

Akilles chuckles and runs straight at the Trojan.

Apollo sighs. He can't quite leave this man to be killed. The rest of the family would laugh at him. So he lifts a finger, and Antenor is gone, in an egg of darkness outside the world.

Then Apollo does what he hates most, assuming human form—Antenor's form. He dodges and weaves, fleeing across the plain, drawing Akilles away from Troy.

Over trampled grain fields, empty sheep pens, stinking corpses, they run, Apollo teasing Akilles, staying just out of reach.

Inside the town, the gates slam shut and the Trojan warriors collapse, pull off their helmets and catch their breath.

22

HEKTOR

T HE GREEKS ARE so close to Troy that they hold their shields high to block arrows and rocks launched by the women and old men on the walls. The Trojan men are clustered around the wells, drinking in huge gulps.

Apollo has led Akilles far across the plains. Bored with the game, he turns and shows his true form. Akilles skids to a stop in front of a shape only vaguely like a man, far taller than any human, with a burning metallic face.

He feels Apollo's chilly amusement and says, "Yes, you fooled me. I've wasted precious time chasing you, when I could have killed dozens of real men."

Apollo opens his arms, as if to say, "Here I am."

Akilles says, "I know I can't kill you. I wish I could! You're the worst of the gods, because you hate humans."

Apollo's amusement sparkles in the air. Akilles runs off to see if there are any Trojans he can head off.

Old Priam, standing on the walls, sees someone coming. It can't be a Trojan; all the survivors are inside the walls. He sees it's a giant. There are only two Greeks that big: Ajax and Akilles. And the figure comes on so fast it must be Akilles.

Priam grabs Hekuba's arm, groaning, "It's Akilles, coming on like the Dog Star, just as bright and deadly!"

Hekuba doesn't even look. She's trying to find her sons in the crowd around the city wells. She has many sons—or she did before the war—and it's not always easy to keep track of them all. She frets, "I can't see Likaon! And where's little Polydoros? I begged him not to fight!"

Priam sees something terrifying: Hektor is still out there on the plain. He calls, "My son, come inside the walls!"

Hekuba turns and sees Hektor out there, waiting for Akilles. She screams, "Son, come inside!"

Hektor stands like a statue, watching Akilles sprint toward him. How can a giant run so fast? Priam sobs, "Son, don't make me watch you die! If you die, I'll have to see my daughters fondled by Greeks, my grandchildren sold like livestock!"

Hektor doesn't move. The sun glints off Akilles' huge shield as he runs.

Hekuba screams, ripping handfuls of hair from her head. She tears open her robe and holds up her breasts, calling, "Hektor, these breasts fed you, warmed you; for their sake, come inside the walls!"

Hektor has heard his parents' cries, but he can't go in. He stands alone on the plain, watching his death come running. Fast as Akilles is approaching, Hektor seems to have all the time in the world to decide what to do. He thinks, "If I go inside now, Polydamus will say, 'I told you so!' That's the worst part. I was a fool, strutting around talking about bravery and honor. He said we should fight from the walls, and he was right."

Akilles is close now. Hektor can see his snarling white teeth.

He thinks, "How can I face the widows? I'm the man who got their husbands killed. We could have fought with bows from the walls. The Greeks fear our archers; we could have picked them off. Now their husbands are lying dead out here. If I go in, the widows will glare at me, and they'll be right."

Akilles is in throwing range now. Hektor thinks, "If I can kill Akilles, the widows will forgive me. Polydamus will forgive me."

Then he looks at Akilles and realizes he doesn't have a chance in single combat.

So he thinks, "What if I slid off my shield, dropped my spear, took off my helmet, walked up to him unarmed, and offered to make a deal? I'll offer half our wealth, plus Helen and everything Paris brought from Sparta."

Akilles is close now, holding his spear low for a belly stab.

Hektor thinks desperately, "I could make every man in Troy swear to give Akilles half their wealth!"

Akilles is only a few paces off now.

Hektor realizes, "I'm talking nonsense! He won't make a deal, he wants my life!"

His courage fails; he turns and runs.

Akilles follows, watching the angles so he can cut Hektor off if he breaks for the town gates.

Hektor runs well, for a man in full armor. Not as fast as Akilles, of course. Hektor is only human; Akilles is more than half god. It's no contest.

They run over the fields where men have been killing each other for nine long years. They run past the fig tree where so many men have died, and on, past the two springs, the source of the river Yellow. One spring flows cold, the other hot; even on a warm day like this you can see the steam-cloud rising from it. Hektor vanishes for a moment in the mist, but Akilles runs through it and spots him just ahead.

They run on, over the flat rocks by the pool. Once, Trojan women and girls brought their washing down to these rocks. They'd sing happy songs as they beat clothes clean against them. It's been a long time since anyone sang those songs.

Akilles chases Hektor around the walls for two long laps, as Priam and Hekuba scream and tear their hair, begging Hektor to come inside. It's too late for that now; they know it, but they can't stop.

Akilles is enjoying the game. He's in no hurry.

As the two of them start their third lap, he's smiling, barely sweating. Hektor is breathing through his mouth and he can hardly lift his feet. It won't be long now.

Zeus shakes his head and grumbles, "I hate to watch this. Hektor never missed a sacrifice to me, or any of us. He did everything a man is supposed to do. Now we leave him to go against Akilles alone? That's not even a fair fight."

Hera and Athena scowl. They expected him to weaken like this.

He goes on, "You know, I've got half a mind to save Hektor! Why not?"

He looks around for support, but none of the other gods say anything. No one wants to offend Hera and her daughter.

He suggests, "Why don't we see what the scales have to say? Find out where the balance lies? Athena turns to him, fuming: "Father, you know yourself Hektor's death was decided long ago. We've been over this a million times. But go ahead! Do whatever you want! Just as long as you're ready for the consequences!"

He sighs, "Yes, you're right, daughter. I was only wondering ... but you're right. I give you free rein. Go down there and meddle to your heart's content."

Athena swoops down on Hektor and Akilles. Akilles is matching Hektor turn for turn, as a falcon mirrors every swerve of the dove it's chasing.

He's herded Hektor away from Troy, out onto the plain. The rest of the Greeks have come up, so Hektor is within spear-throw of many Greek warriors. A few raise their spears, but Akilles roars, "No one touches him! His death belongs to me!"

Apollo has been lending Hektor a bit of strength, but he's tired of wasting energy on a doomed human. As the two warriors run past the hot and cold springs for the fourth time, Apollo is deciding when to pull the plug and let Hektor fend for himself.

Now that Athena's gone, Zeus brings out the scales to see if he can get the others to call off Hektor's death. He doesn't have much hope, but it's worth a try.

He lifts the two golden pans, showing all the gods that the balance is true. Then he takes a grain of sand and puts it in one pan, grunting, "That's Hektor," and another in the other, saying, "And that's Akilles."

He lets go, hoping that Hektor's pan will rise. If it does, he can intervene.

Hektor's pan falls all the way down to Hades, into those monstrous abscesses under the earth.

Apollo shrugs and disengages; Hektor stumbles, more tired than he's ever been in his life.

Zeus sighs and puts away the scales. All he can do now is watch the poor man die.

Athena flutters to Akilles' ear, eager to help with the kill. She's giddy with the thrill of this hunt, stroking Akilles' arm, whispering hoarsely, "Brave Akilles, your triumph is almost here! Rest a moment, my champion! Rest and get your breath, while I trick Hektor into fighting you."

Athena assumes the shape of Hektor's bravest brother, Deiphobus. She loves these games, and throws herself into the role, striding toward Hektor and saying in Deiphobus' voice, "Brother, I see you're having a hard time. I'll stand with you. If the two of us stick together, we can kill Akilles."

Hektor sobs with relief, "Deiphobus, you've always been my favorite brother! But after this I'll do anything for you! No one else has the courage to come out and help me! They just look down from the walls and leave me on my own!"

Athena can hardly hide her laughter. She says in Deiphobus' voice, "Oh, they begged me not to come out and help you, but I couldn't stand to see you face this Greek by yourself. Together, brother, we're invincible, just the two of us!"

Hektor clasps his brother's shoulder, weeping with relief, and calls to Akilles, "I won't run from you any farther, Greek! My brother and I will face you together!" Akilles smirks. He knows who that brother really is.

Hektor holds up a hand: "Let's agree on terms first. If I win, I'll treat your body with respect. No mutilation. And if you win, you treat my corpse with respect."

Akilles says coldly, "You're a fool, Hektor. Athena has fooled you to your death."

Hektor shrugs, "If I die, I die. But let's agree to treat the loser's body respectfully."

"You're dead already, Hektor. You'll die a fool. No terms."

Hektor tries again, "Who knows which of us will die? You would want your body treated properly, just as I do."

Akilles screams, "That's my armor you're wearing! You tore it off Patroklas' body! No terms! I'll drag your carcass through the dust, that's a promise I'll make freely."

He hefts his spear up on his shoulder and goes into his run, yelling, "But first there's the little matter of killing you!"

He throws. Hektor sees it coming and ducks. The spear buries itself in the ground and Hektor feels something like hope.

He circles, taunting, "You missed me! How could that happen, O great hero? Perhaps you're just an ordinary man! We can make a deal, end the war, once you're dead!"

He throws on the word "dead." A good throw! It hits Akilles' shield dead center. The shield-face writhes with the impact, but absorbs the blow. The spear falls harmlessly, as if spat out by Hefestos' wondrous gift.

Akilles has his spear back. Hektor sees it but can't believe it. He saw that spear fly far over his head, and now it's back in the Greek's hand? It's impossible!

He doesn't know that Athena, feeling playful, wanting to take part in this deadly game, has pulled Akilles' spear out of the ground and brought it back to him.

Hektor has no spear, so he turns to ask Deiphobus for one. And there is no Deiphobus. There's no one with him. That's when he realizes two things: Athena has been playing one of her pranks, and he is a dead man.

He draws his only weapon, the sword, and says, "This is the end, then. But I won't die groveling or trying to run away. His spear will hit me in the chest, not the back."

And he leaps, sword high.

Akilles leaps at the same moment, his helmet burning like a comet. His spear flashes as he aims. He knows that armor Hektor's wearing; it used to be his. The one vulnerable spot in it is the neck, between helmet and breastplate.

He stabs. Hektor falls, his neck gashed wide open. The blood is pulsing out where the big vein has been cut.

Akilles stands over him gloating, "That armor didn't save Patroklas, and it didn't save you. But Patroklas had a friend to avenge him. Who'll avenge you? Your people left you to die alone out here."

He watches Hektor die, pulse by pulse. He talks to the dying man quickly; there's so much to say: "I'm going to give Patroklas a fine funeral by the ships—but you, you'll be food for dogs, for buzzards! For the worms!"

Hektor whispers, "Akilles, I beg you—I'd clasp your knees if I could get up—please, return my body, take a ransom for it, so my poor parents can burn me properly.

Akilles kicks him, gloating, "Begging, ransom! I'll give you better than that; I'll give you dogs, buzzards, worms!'"

Hektor lies on his back and stares at the sky, whispering, "I knew it was no use asking you for pity."

He says in a voice suddenly clear and loud, "Paris and Apollo will kill you right over there, by the main gate."

Then he dies. We say a man falls because that's what happens. As long as he lives, his body holds his soul inside. When he dies, the soul pours out like water and starts its long fall, down through the grass, then the dirt, then the rocks and caves. It falls for a long time until it lands in Hades. And as it falls it moans, grieving for all it has lost, the sun and women and strength, all the joy of having a body.

Akilles sees Hektor's dead eyes staring at the sky. He plants a foot on the torso and yanks his spear out, muttering, "I don't care where they kill me or how, at least I got you first."

He tears the armor off: "I'll take what they have in mind for me! I don't care!"

The Greeks have gathered around, taunting the dead man—cautiously at first, then talking more boldly: "He's not as big as I thought he'd be!" Finally one of them works up the nerve to jam his spear right through Hektor's belly.

The rest of them rush in like a pack of dogs. The spears rise and fall over Hektor's corpse like harvesters threshing grain.

When they've hacked up the body sufficiently, they kick, piss on it, spit on it, making up jokes: "Hektor, my prince! Wake up! You've got some dirt on your lovely face! Excuse me, Prince, someone is pissing on your wounds!"

Some of the men ask Akilles, "Lord, shouldn't we storm the town? Listen to them wailing for their dead princeling! They'll be easy pickings!"

He stares hard at the man and says, "While Patroklas lies unburied? Not while I'm alive. If you attack, it'll be over my dead body."

The man stutters, "Yes, lord, of course; I only—"

Akilles shakes his head bitterly, "Men forget the dead before they're even cold. It'll be the same with me. I know you people. But as long as I'm alive, we'll show a little respect. I'll show Patroklas this corpse, so he knows he's been avenged."

He takes out his sword and jabs it through Hektor's heels, then takes a leather thong and pushes it through the holes. He loops the thong to the back of his chariot.

Then he tosses the armor that both Patroklas and Hektor died wearing into the car and shakes the reins. The god-horses break into a slow canter. He's in no hurry. He wants the Trojans on the walls to get a good long look at Hektor's naked, mutilated corpse bouncing along in the dust. He drives slowly along the walls, enjoying the cries of horror.

When he's heard enough of their weeping and screams, he wheels off toward the Greek camp, Hektor's body flying up as it strikes each tussock.

Hekuba moans as she watches her son's body abused. She rips off her veil, tearing her cheeks with her fingernails, pulling hunks of hair from her head.

Priam runs down to the gates, trying to open them himself so he can take his son's body from the Greeks. The soldiers at the gate have to hold him back. He beats weakly at their shoulders, groaning, "Let me go! I'll offer Akilles anything he wants! He'll have pity on me!"

The soldiers know better; they pull the old man away from the gates.

Priam falls on his knees and rolls in the mud and dung moaning, "So many of my sons have died, but none of those deaths hurt like this one!"

They lift him out of the mud and dung, weeping with him.

He moans, "Hektor dead means we're all dead! No, worse than dead! My daughters will be sold! My grandsons will slave in the fields! Dead or sold, sold or dead!"

They weep with him. They all know it's true.

Hekuba sings over the wall, to the plain where her son's body was defiled, "Hektor, you were the city! Your death is our death, but your death hurts more than ours! You walked through our streets like a god, but a god can't die! Your death is our death!"

Hektor's wondrous wife, Andromakhe, finest of women, has been weaving in her room, tracing a pattern of flowers onto the cloth. A slave girl comes in and Andromakhe tells her, "Go heat some water for my husband's bath. He'll be all hot and sweaty when he comes home from fighting those Greeks!"

The girl bows and goes for a cauldron.

At that moment Andromakhe hears a roar of grief. She knows in a moment what it means, and stumbles over the loom, calls to her women, "Come with me now!"

They veil themselves, wrap up properly, and run into the street. As they run toward the walls, Andromakhe moans, "There's only one man they'd cry like that for! Oh, he was always too brave! He stayed out on the plain too long this time!"

She stumbles, and her women pull her up. She staggers on, moaning, "Please, gods, kill me now, before I have to hear this news! Kill me before I see my son killed, before they sell me as a bed slave—" She shrieks, and they lift her by the arms, leading her onward, crying, "You were always too brave, Hektor! I warned you to fight from the walls!"

They've reached the walls. She shrugs off her women and runs up to look out onto the plain, just in time to see the naked corpse being dragged through the dust behind Akilles' chariot.

She faints. Her women pick her up, stand her against the wall. She practices breathing again, steadies herself. She has a duty, a widow's duty, no matter how she feels. She takes a deep breath and chants, "Nothing but grief, for both of us, forever! You were born in these walls, unlucky! And I in Thebes, unlucky! Eetyon had seven sons, but all unlucky! I grew up in the shadow of a dark mountain; you are falling through dark rocks! You will fall, fall, all the way to Hades, darkest place of all! And you are still the lucky one; I'm left alive, with a son I love! A curse, this love! I'll suffer for that love as I watch him beg from his father's friends! Cuffed away from the table, fighting with the dogs for scraps. But only if he lives, if he is unlucky! His father's friend, deep in his wine, may feel a moment's pity and give the boy a sip, but he'll get the back of a man's hand if he drinks enough to wet his palate. 'Get out, beggar,' they say, 'Run with the dogs, orphan! You're no kin to us!'"

She takes a breath and sings again, for her son, to make them promise: "He'll take a scrap of bread and wander out to sleep in the cow sheds, the boy you all called 'Little Lord'! The boy you used to love to spoil, who slept every night in the arms of his nurse, who lived to play and sleep when play had wearied him!"

She turns again, toward the shore where the Greek ships are beached, and cries, "Hektor, you were the walls of the city, and it dies with you! The writhing worms will have what's left of you, when the dogs have torn the meat from your bones. The Greeks will look on your body unclothed, though you have rooms full of fine robes in our quarters. I'll burn your robes, then, husband! I go now to burn them, since we can never have your body to burn! We can never bury you, all of us who loved you, men and women, old, young, all!"

The women moan quietly while she sings. When she finishes, their moan rises to a wail that goes on and on, all night.

23

GAMES

KILLES DRIVES BACK to the camp with Hektor's body bumping along behind his chariot. He drives around Patroklas' body for hours. His men are tired, but he keeps them marching after him. All the other Greeks are drinking wine in their tents, but Akilles' men stir up the dust all afternoon, doing laps around the corpse.

At last he waves the men to a stop, unties Hektor's body, and drags it over to the bier. He puts a huge hand on Patroklas' chest and says, "My friend, I did as I promised. Here's Hektor, you see? I took him down and brought him here face down in the dust. The camp dogs will gulp his meat, while you get a fine funeral. There'll be twelve Trojans, noble-born, sacrificed at your funeral pyre."

The men go off to their tents to clean up for the funeral feast. It's a fine meal. Akilles has gone all-out. Oxen, sheep, even a big boar get their throats sliced in front of Patroklas' body. Then the slaves carry the kicking, dying beasts around his bier until all their blood has flowed out.

They're cut up and roasted on spits. The men can smell roast boar, roast ox; they're drooling in spite of themselves. It's not that they don't grieve for Patroklas, but they can't match Akilles' grief.

They can't even get him to wash up and go to the feast. He just shakes his head, repeating, "No water touches me until Patroklas has been burned properly. The rest of you, go eat and drink; I'm waiting for dawn, when we light the pyre."

Everyone goes off to stuff themselves. They can't resist all that free meat, and there'll be wine too, not just for the lords, either.

Akilles doesn't take even a sip of water, just paces back and forth along the beach, finally lying down on the sand.

He wakes to find Patroklas standing by him. The dead man sighs, "You've forgotten me already? Burn my body then, so I can cross the river. The dead won't let me in the ferry until my body is burned. I never thought it would be so hard to get into Hades' country."

Akilles sits up and reaches for Patroklas' hand. The ghost says, "No. We'll be together soon enough. All the dead say so; they're waiting for you."

Akilles cries out, "Why do you say that to me? Why does everyone tell me this over and over?"

Patroklas says, "Tell the men to bury me with you, when your time has come."

Akilles tries to hug the ghost, but his arms touch nothing. Patroklas' form trembles and dissolves.

Before dawn, he stumbles back, telling the sentries, "Patroklas came to me! He's a ghost—less than a ghost. He can't even get into Hades' land."

And he stumbles off again, to pace the shore until the pyre is ready.

At last dawn comes and they can burn the body.

Firewood is scarce after nine years of war. The ax-men have to go a long way to find the big logs they need for a good hot pyre. Mule teams drag the trunks back to the beach and slaves pile up a platform a hundred feet square.

Akilles has shaved his head, all but one blond lock.

He orders all his men to put on their armor and march with him to the pyre.

The men are uneasy; he's strange this morning. He grabs the one lock left on his head and starts sawing it off with his sword blade, puts the lock in Patroklas' hand and points to a stream, the Sperkyas, that flows near the camp, saying, "Little river, this last lock was supposed to be for you. My father said I should promise the river nearest our camp a big sacrifice to send me safe to the sea when the war was over. But you won't help me; no one can help me. So I give this lock to Patroklas instead."

He steps away from the bier and calls, "King Agamemnon, please begin the rites. I know our men want to eat. I'll stay with the body. Patroklas' friends can stay too if they like."

Agamemnon dismisses the common soldiers, while the kings carry Patroklas' body to the center of the woodpile and lay it down gently.

The butchers have saved big chunks of fat from all the slaughtered beasts. Akilles places them lovingly around the body to help it burn.

Then he brings all the things a dead man might want on his last journey. Two big jars of honey and ointment; Hades' land is cold and dry. Then four horses. Akilles kills the horses himself, picking each one up and tossing it on the pyre near Patroklas. Then a pair of dogs, Patroklas' favorites; he grabs each one, pricks its skull with the tip of his sword, and tosses it onto the pyre, one on each side of the corpse.

Then the Trojans, human sacrifices. Some of the others are uneasy about this. It's a little old-fashioned, extreme. But no one feels like quarreling with Akilles at the moment. The twelve Trojans he took alive are fine boys—just boys; Troy, short on manpower, has been filling its ranks with children. The boys stare terrified at the giant who drags them, roped at the neck, to the pyre. He stabs each one in the heart, chops the rope that tied him to the coffle, and throws the body onto the edge of the woodpile. The boys die silently.

By the time he's finished, twelve Trojans' corpses are lying around the edge of the woodpile, with Patroklas at the very center, the dogs beside him, the horses around him. Everything is ready for the fire.

Akilles holds up a hand wet with blood and calls, "See, Patroklas? I've done all I could for you! Twelve Trojans will burn in your honor, while Hektor feeds the dogs!"

He points to Hektor's body, lying in the dirt. He's ordered a slave to drag two hungry dogs over to it, make them feed. But no matter how the slave pushes their snouts at the body, they won't touch it. They whine and hunch away. And even after all this time, Hektor doesn't stink. He still has friends among the gods.

This angers Akilles. He wanted everyone to see the dogs gulping gobbets of Hektor's body. Worse, the fire won't start. These are very bad signs, and some of the men are muttering that Akilles went too far, sacrificing those Trojans.

Odysseus strolls over and whispers, "Maybe if you pray to the winds …"

Akilles nods, calls to the slaves, "Wine, here! That gold goblet!"

When the wine is ready, he dashes it out of the cup so the winds can taste it, begging their help, promising them more drink if they'll help the pyre kindle.

Iris drags the two winds—Boreas, the cold northerly, and Zephyr, the sweet little breeze—back from a banquet and puts them to work.

You can see the two winds coming in from the sea. Boreas swoops down hard, lashing the waves, while Zephyr flutters the crests into foamy banners. The two converge near shore and come up the beach with a roar, hitting the pyre like all of Hefestos' bellows at once.

The flames start low, running under the lattice of tree-trunks, skittering from the torch to the center of the pile and fanning out. Soon the air is choked with the smell of meat. Horse meat, dog meat, and the flesh of thirteen boys all burning at once. It's like a second feast, but no one is eating.

Akilles guards the fire all day and all night, tossing wine from a cup on the flames so the gods can drink. As he paces, he begs Patroklas' pardon, over and over, moaning and muttering.

It's dawn again before the pyre has burnt all the meat off Patroklas' bones and all the marrow out of them, cleaning him up for Hades. As the sun comes up, the flames go down. The winds go home, their job done.

At last Akilles can sleep. He lies on the hot sand near the pyre and dozes until the crunch of Agamemnon's entourage wakes him. He stands and says, "Atreus-son and the rest of you, take Patroklas' bones out when they're cool enough. You'll find them at the very center."

They bow and nod. He goes on, "Put the bones in a good-size urn, and pack it with fat. Leave room, though, because I'll be going in there with him soon. Don't make Patroklas a big mound just yet. A small one for now. Build the big one when you can put both of us in it. It won't be long."

He gestures toward dozens of jars of wine he's piled near the pyre: "Now douse the fire with wine."

Slaves come running with shovels and poles to mark out the barrow around the pyre. Other slaves are pouring wine on the ashes. The smell of wet ash, burned meat, and boiled wine spreads over the camp.

Agamemnon's herald brings Patroklas' whitened bones from the center of the pyre. Women are waiting with an urn, ox fat, and linen strips. They massage fat onto the warm bones. When they're well greased, the bones are eased into the jar, the skull last. Then the urn is wrapped in linen.

Akilles watches it all for any mistake, any sign of disrespect.

It's done. Everyone turns to go, but he says, "Now we'll have the funeral games."

His slaves run out with prizes: iron cauldrons, burners, slave women, oxen and sheep.

Nobody expected this, but in a moment they go from weeping to excited squabbling, betting on the games, shouting at each other.

Akilles grabs the first prize and shows her to everyone: a slave woman who can embroider all sorts of fancy things. The fastest charioteer gets her, and a cauldron too, big enough to hold a stewed ox. Second prize in the chariot race is a mare in foal; third is a smaller cauldron.

He says, "You all know I'd win if my team was running. My horses are immortals. But they're mourning Patroklas now—"

He points to the two god-horses weeping huge tears as they stare at the pyre—

"They've lost the man who loved to bathe them in the river; they don't get over things as quickly as people do."

He points to the prizes again, "But when a man is killed, his people have to show they're still strong. So the rest of you, go out there and ride hard!"

T HE CHARIOT RACE is soon underway. It's a classic: broken axles, cheating, threats and recriminations.

Athena and Apollo duel with each other to hobble the chariots. The gods enjoy playing with humans; a chariot race isn't much different from a war to them. Athena smashes Yumelos' chariot to spite Apollo, while Ajax and Ideomenus, drinking wine as they watch the race, nearly come to blows over who's in the lead. The rest of the fighters laugh till their ribs hurt, listening to Ideomenus and Ajax arguing about which cloud of dust is in the lead.

Antilokas beats Menelaos at the turn with a move he learned from his sly old father, Nestor. Menelaos comes running out shouting, ready to fight; but Antilokas, a smooth talker, calms him down. They exchange courtesies and it's all forgotten.

Akilles gives a special prize to old Nestor, who's been going on and on about what a great driver he used to be. And a great boxer too, and wrestler, and everything else. The old man is touched, and makes another long speech. Everyone's happy to listen, sipping their wine, rejoicing in being alive, young, and strong.

Then it's time for the boxing. A rough sport, not for the chiefs, but they enjoy watching the lower ranks knock some teeth out. The prize this time is only a mule. Two soldiers smash each other's faces in with leather-wrapped fists for a few minutes. Yurilas, the boaster who swore he'd take that mule, gets hit hard enough to send him flying. The mule goes to his opponent, and Yurilas is dragged off, a bloody mess.

Now the wrestling. This is a sport worthy of the chieftains—more useful in a real fight and less likely to ruin a man's face than boxing. So two of the greatest chiefs stand up to compete: Ajax, biggest and strongest in the army (except Akilles, of course) and Odysseus, two heads shorter but strong as a bull and smarter than anyone else.

It's a great match. The two of them heave, grunt, and sweat while everyone looks on, drinking wine and screaming encouragement. Finally Ajax uses his size, lifting Odysseus right up off his feet, planning to body-slam him to the dust. But Odysseus always has a trick ready; he kicks Ajax right in the back of the knee. The big man's leg buckles and he goes down with Odysseus on top of him.

All Odysseus has to do now is lift Ajax off the ground to win. But he can't do it! Ajax is just too big, heavy as an ox. So Akilles pushes them apart and announces, "You both win. No more; someone will get really hurt. You both get a prize." Everyone cheers; they're both popular with the men.

The foot race is next, and Odysseus toes the line for this one too, still breathing hard from his wrestling match. He's facing the other Ajax, Little Ajax, Ajax Oyleas-son. Antilokas is in this one too—he's young, skinny and fast. He looks like a winner up against tiny Ajax Oyleas-son and short, thick Odysseus, who's old enough to be his father.

But Athena's watching, and it's no secret she's soft on Odysseus. He gasps out a prayer, mid-race: "Athena, beloved goddess, lift my feet!" She pulses new strength into his old legs, and he wins going away.

But Athena isn't done with her pranks. She's so offended with Ajax for daring to race against her dear Odysseus, that she trips him near the finish line. He falls face-first into a pile of cow guts left over from the sacrifices. The men fall over themselves laughing at the sight of him skidding through half-digested grass, popping gut-tubes and getting up spitting cow dung out of his mouth.

When he's finally washed his mouth out with wine, Ajax himself joins the laughter, shouting, "Not as bad as some of the food around here!" He slaps Odysseus on the back, saying, "That Athena! She watches over you like you were her own child!"

Antilokas comes in third but wins everyone over with a smooth speech: "You see, the gods too respect the aged! Ajax is older than me, and as for Odysseus, he is from another time entirely—yet he's carried off the prize. Only

Akilles could outdistance him."

Akilles slaps Antilokas on the back and says, "You can flatter with the best of them, my boy! Here's another chunk of gold!"

They're all a little drunk, and some of the contests have to be stopped early. Play-fighting with shield and spear, always a dangerous event, gets called early because Diomedes keeps aiming at big Ajax's throat. The goal is to draw a little blood without hurting your opponent too badly, but Diomedes is playing too hard. So Akilles pushes them apart and divides the prize, calling it a draw.

Discus throwing comes next. Everybody's relieved; you can't kill anyone with a discus. In fact, half the competitors are too drunk to throw the thing in the right direction. Epeyas tosses it right at the spectators, who all fall flat and come up laughing, as Epeyas finishes off his big throw by spinning himself right into the ground.

There's only one man in the army who's really good at this event: tall, quiet Polypoetes. He takes the disk and sends it flying so far it's lost in the tussocks. Everyone cheers and he gets the prize, enough iron to last a man five years.

Now the bowmen show what they can do. The Greeks don't like facing archers in battle; it's no way for a real man to fight, they think. Besides, it's Apollo's weapon, and he hates them. But they can appreciate a good bowman when his target is only a pigeon. Akilles holds up a pretty speckled bird, shows it to everyone, then points to a post a hundred paces away, saying, "I'm going to tie this pigeon to the post. If you hit the bird, you get the fine double-bladed axes; if you hit the string, you get the single-bladed ones."

Teucer shoots first. But he forgot to pray to Apollo, who sends a breeze and the arrow goes low, hitting the string, not the bird. The bird flaps free. Meriones, next competitor, grabs the bow, makes a quick promise to Apollo, and shoots. The bird, hit on the wing, flaps wildly out of the sky and falls dead. So Meriones gets the double-bladed axes, and Teucer has to settle for the single-bladed ones.

Last event is the javelin throw. This one is tricky, the only event that Agamemnon has a chance of winning. He's been sulking through the events so far. If he competes and loses, he might make more trouble.

So Akilles hands him the prizes immediately, with some outrageous flattery: "King Agamemnon, we all know you outstrip the rest of us in throwing the javelin! So please, spare us the trouble of sitting through an event whose outcome we all know and take first prize from me now."

Agamemnon is pleased. The day ends well.

24

PITY

EVERYONE SLEEPS WELL except Akilles. He lies on his back, side, face, but he knows sleep will never come to him again. He lies awake, waiting for dawn.

When it comes at last he pushes the leather thongs through Hektor's feet, and drags the corpse after his chariot around Patroklas' burial mound. But there's no comfort in it.

Some of the men see Akilles defiling Hektor's body again and fear what will come of it. You don't treat the dead like this. Someone will have to pay. But no one feels like scolding Akilles to his face.

Apollo has been shielding the corpse, lifting Hektor's face from the tussocks and jagged rocks so that when Akilles gives up and un-yokes the chariot, the face is unbruised.

But Apollo is weary of this work. It's beneath him. And it's all Hera's fault! She and her daughter, persecuting the Trojans just because the fool Paris said out loud what any man can see—that Afroditi is prettier than the two of them. Holding a grudge over a trifle like that! "How to Hold a Grudge"; that's the first maternal lesson Hera taught little Athena when the girl gnawed her way out of her father's aching head.

Apollo is in a mood for a showdown. He finds the gods at table, drinking as usual, and says, "You say you love the humans, but you let Akilles defile Hektor's body like this. You should be ashamed! Hektor burned as many thigh-bones, spilled as much wine, in your honor as any Greek ever did, but you let Akilles drag his corpse over the tussocks!"

Hera sips her nectar, nudging her daughter.

Athena's eyes begin to burn. She loves these face-offs with her male kin.

Apollo goes on, making the walls shake with that great gong of a voice, "What has Akilles lost, anyway? These mortals wade through death all their lives! Don't we watch them weeping over their little babies? Just yesterday I floated over a plague-hit village by the Black Sea. I watched those humans sob till they choked as they laid their children in a row!"

Hera purrs, "And did you weep for the little dead humans, Lord Apollo?"

He seethes, his face melting to metal in his anger. "A stupid question! I don't pretend to love these creatures as you do. My point, stepmother, is that Akilles has only lost a vassal. Patroklas wasn't even kin to him! Every animal that runs across the face of the Earth, whether on four legs or two, loses more than that. Every day, floating across the sky, I see people bury fathers, mothers, sons, and daughters—but even when they've lost their dearest kin, those people obey our rules. They don't violate corpses like Akilles is doing!"

Hera says, "You seem to forget, stepson, that Akilles is more than half god. Hektor is just a human. He has only the vaguest fourth-generation sniff of god about him, whereas Akilles is like one of us, except—"

Ares yells from the end of the table, "Except he's gonna die, hah!"

Hera ignores him and goes on, "Hektor is just another animal who sucked milk at its mother's teat. But Akilles is a member of our circle. I attended his father's wedding. Do you remember, daughter?"

Athena nods smugly.

Hera points around the table: "You were all at that wedding! Even you, Apollo, though as I recall you snuck off to drink and play the lyre with the local riffraff."

She takes another sip of nectar, drawling, "And so, stepson, it comes down to this: Akilles can do whatever he wants, because he's family."

Ares, already drunk, shouts again, "Except he's gonna die, an' us gods don't die!"

Ares laughs at his own joke, belches, and mutters, "Yup, Akilles is gonna die like a dog! Go down to Hades' place! Thank gods I'm a god! Wouldn't go down there for anything, not even a wedding feast!"

Zeus is disgusted, and leans over the table to growl, "Hera, why do you have to be so bitter? You're a snob, that's what it is!"

She shrugs, and Athena glares at her father. But Zeus has had enough. He holds up his hands, signaling he's made his decision: "No one is saying that Hektor deserves equal honor with a half-god like Akilles. But I say now that he does deserve a little, as a decent human who never shortchanged us on the sacrifices."

There's nodding and muttering from the lower end of the table. Hektor was well-liked among the gods.

Zeus feels the support and uses it to lay down the law: "So we're going to do this right. Iris—" He snaps his fingers.

And the messenger is there at his side, as if she'd always been there.

"Girl, you go down in the sea and tell Thetis we're going to have Hermes steal Hektor's body and give it to Priam."

Hermes, the god of theft, retail, and people who can't sit still, insinuates his long, slim, plausible self at Zeus' side. Hermes is smiling, as he always is. He loves his job. He says, "I can steal you the body easily enough, sir, but I do fear Akilles would try to recover it. And he's got those god-horses, so he'd catch up. There'd be a fight. Noise, trouble, no end of fuss."

Zeus groans, "Yes, you're right. We'd never hear the end of it! Akilles is nothing but trouble!"

Athena suggests, "If the Trojans want Hektor's body, they should pay for it. A compromise: Priam can ransom the body, but he'll pay a big price for it."

Hera is angry: "Athena! How dare you weaken like this! We agreed to ruin the Trojans utterly; why let them have Hektor's body?"

Athena gestures to her mother that this is a matter of policy, peace within the family.

Zeus nods to Athena, "Good girl! You're smarter than your mother. So that's settled. Now, Iris—"

And the messenger, who vanished when Hermes appeared, is standing again by Zeus' side.

"Iris, go tell Thetis that Akilles must let Priam ransom Hektor's corpse. He can set his own terms—"

Ares mutters from the other end of the table, "'Cuz he'll be dead soon too! Die like flies, those humans!"

Zeus sighs—working with these people! It's simpler just to do things himself. So he tells Iris, "Just tell Thetis to come here. I'll explain it myself."

Iris bows, glows brighter, and falls through the sky, hitting the ocean like a hissing comet. She sizzles like phosphorus through the cold sea, coming to a stop at old man Ocean's house on the sea bed.

She finds Thetis already mourning for her son. To the gods, what will happen has already happened. She has already tasted her son's death; her heart is already broken. She rocks back and forth, moaning, weeping.

But Iris has no pity. She orders, "Rise, Thetis, wife of Peleus, mother of Akilles. You are summoned to father Zeus immediately."

Thetis moans, "I'm in mourning, woman, don't you see? I don't want to wrangle with the gods!" But Iris won't listen to any excuses, so Thetis wraps herself in her darkest shawl and swims up, in Iris' burning wake, to Olympos.

Hera and her daughter treat Thetis with great courtesy. After all, she's the mother of their champion Akilles. Athena gives Thetis her seat, and Hera herself offers Thetis a goblet of nectar.

As soon as Thetis takes a polite sip, Zeus gets down to business: "Listen, my lady, I know you're mourning your son in advance, but we're very unhappy with what he's doing to Hektor's body. In fact, we agreed to let Hermes—"

he gestures to the dimly-seen god behind him, who bows pleasantly—

"steal the corpse from your son's camp. But in the interests of peace—"

And here he gestures toward Hera and her daughter.

"I've decided to give Akilles a chance to do the right thing, instead of just taking the body from him. Go to him, tell him we're angry at him, dragging Hektor behind his chariot like a dead dog!"

The lesser gods nod and mutter angrily.

"And tell him that I'm the angriest of all! And then give him an out: tell him he has one chance to redeem himself by selling the corpse to Priam. We'll send Iris to Priam to arrange the ransom; your son will give back the body, take the ransom; everything'll be settled nicely. Now, go talk some sense into your son."

She bows, draws the black shawl over her, and runs down the sky to Akilles' tent.

He's mourning as hard as ever. There's something improper about such mourning, so long—and for a mere vassal! She says, "Son, instead of grieving, you should think of drinking good wine and caressing women. You don't have long, you know."

He says, "I know, mother. How could I forget when everyone reminds me?

You have some news?"

"The gods are angry with you for dragging Hektor's body in the dirt. It's not proper. They want you to give the corpse to Priam. He'll give you a fine ransom for it."

He shrugs, "Fine, the old man can have his dead son if he brings the ransom. It doesn't help, dragging that corpse around. It won't even rot and the dogs won't touch it."

Iris goes to Troy, burning through the air to land in Priam's courtyard. He and his surviving sons are sitting in the afternoon heat, mourning for Hektor. Priam is covered with horse-dung. He's been rolling in the stable-filth.

The daughters and wives are wailing through the halls, while the sons and sons-in-law sit on their haunches around Priam, weeping.

Iris stands before the old man and says, gently enough: "Don't be afraid, Priam Dardanus-son! I come from Lord Zeus. He's sorry for your trouble and wants to help. You must get a fine ransom together, put it on a wagon, and bring it to the Greek camp. No one must go with the wagon except you and a driver. Don't be afraid of robbers, because Zeus is sending Hermes himself to protect you. Akilles has been warned to treat you properly."

Priam bows to the luminous messenger; she vanishes.

He tells his sons, "You trash—good for nothing, all of you—d'you think you could manage to get a mule-wagon ready for me? I'm going to ransom the corpse of your brother, who was worth more than the lot of you put together. I wish you'd all died instead of him!"

Hekuba comes hobbling out shrieking, "What? Have you gone dotard at last, husband?"

Priam smiles bleakly, "So you're not so deaf when you don't want to be, eh?"

She hobbles toward him, ranting, "You'll go to that monster Akilles on your own? At your age?"

He gestures to the sky, "Iris herself gave me a promise—"

She screams, "What promise? Akilles doesn't respect the gods or anyone! I wish I had his liver between my teeth!"

She shuffles up to him. He holds her while she finishes her rant, "You can mourn Hektor right here, where I fed him with these breasts! Mourn him here, and live a little longer at least!"

He sighs, "Now, now, Iris gave me Zeus' word I'd be safe! Besides, even if Akilles kills me, I'll get to put my arms around the boy one last time. Now let me go, wife, don't make a coward of me in my last days."

He goes to the store room and has the slaves take twelve of the best from the cedar caskets. Twelve of everything: cloaks, carpets, shirts, capes. Then the coins: ten gold, ten silver. Then metalware: four cauldrons, two burners, and a cup the Thracians gave him in the good old days. There's no cup like this in all the world. After all, the Greeks will get everything in Troy soon enough; he's giving them what will soon be theirs anyway, and in return he can have his beloved son's body, to hold and honor one more time.

A crowd has gathered. They've heard stories about the treasures in there, and they skulk around trying to get a peek as Priam leads his slaves out with the ransom. He flails at the gawkers with his stick, shouting, "Don't you have any sons of your own to mourn? You'll have grief enough, don't worry! Without Hektor to protect us, we'll all have grief enough!" The crowd scatters. He calls, "You, my worthless sons! Since you're not brave enough to die like your brother Hektor, make yourselves useful and get the wagon ready! It's good practice for you, cowards! You'll all be Greek slaves soon enough!"

As he's inspecting the wagon, Hekuba comes back with a goblet of wine, saying, "Here, husband, make a drink-offering to Zeus for your journey. And one last favor, I beg you—ask Zeus for a sign! A black eagle on your right as you travel. If he won't give you that sign, come back."

He nods, "I'll do it. I can ask him for that, at least."

The slaves pour clean water over his hands and he offers the wine, calling, "Zeus, father of gods, I'm going on this journey as a father; give me a sign, a black eagle on my right side as I go."

Instantly the eagle comes, swooping low over the city on Priam's right. His wings are as wide as the door of a rich man's house. The whole city sees the eagle gliding slowly over the roofs.

Priam is ready, standing in his chariot. He signals to Idaeus, the old servant driving the treasure-wagon. They trot through the gates just as the sun is going down, followed by a huge crowd. But as soon as the wagon and chariot are out on the plain, the crowd scurries back in, afraid of Greek raiding parties.

Now Priam and his old steward are alone on the plain, two weak old men. Zeus looks down and says, "Hermes, you see old Priam down there?"

Hermes bows, "I keep a close eye on all travelers."

Zeus smiles wryly, "I know all about the eye you keep! Well, this time you're going to watch over these two old men, as faithful as a sheepdog."

Hermes bows suavely, "It will be my pleasure! May I ... discourage ... any Greek interference?"

"Well, no rough stuff; Hera wouldn't stand for it. Just hide the chariot and wagon. I want them unseen and unheard until they're inside Akilles' compound."

Hermes laughs, "Two clumsy old men and a creaking wagon? Ah well, I enjoy a challenge."

He takes up his stick, which gives sight and takes it away, as he pleases. Then he slides down to Earth, like a man floating down a fast stream. He comes to Earth on the riverbank in Priam's path, taking the form of a young, handsome fellow with a beard just beginning to sprout, and waits.

Soon the wagon and chariot plod into sight. Hermes chuckles at the two old men, squinting with their weak eyes to try to see the road ahead. Poor mortals! What a nightmare it must be to grow old! They get so slow and weak when their little lives are almost done. These two are easy prey for any party of Greek irregulars, and there are plenty of two-legged jackal packs prowling these plains. Over nine years of war, many soldiers have deserted; robbing and killing travelers is easier, safer, more profitable than battle.

Priam and his servant are terrified of meeting some of these brigands. So when old Idaeus, squinting ahead, cries out, "Lord Priam, there's a man standing by the bank! Should we try to flee?" Priam feels his old heart pound like it's about to come up out of his throat.

He can't even answer, let alone slap the reins to run.

Hermes can barely hide his laughter as he watches the old men shiver and shake. He runs to them, asking in a well-bred young man's voice, "O uncle, why are you driving a wagon full of loot through this wilderness prowled by brigands?"

Priam stands there in the darkness, holding back the horses. They want to get to the water, and they're pulling the feeble old man toward the stream in spite of himself. His mouth is wide open with fear. Idaeus hides behind him like a shy toddler.

Hermes stifles his laughter and goes on in a self-righteous tone, "Poor uncle, I see you are well stricken in years—yes, very well stricken indeed! Do you not fear marauding Greeks? They may take your goods and abuse your, er, daughter standing there behind you—though I perceive that she too is, ah, well stricken in years!"

Priam can only groan in terror. Hermes pats the old king on the back, then puts one hand on his sword and striking a grand, heroic pose: "Have no fear, aged sir! I shall be your savior, for you remind me of my own dear father!"

That line was for Zeus, Hermes' father. The god of trickery knows very well that papa is listening, and Zeus won't like being compared to this poor old mortal slithering along on his last legs.

Priam finally realizes this fine young fellow only wants to help. He hugs Hermes, crying, "My boy, you must be part-god, so noble is your bearing!"

Hermes nods solemnly, "My ancestry has been the subject of speculation many times, sir, on Olympos and elsewhere."

Priam says, "Oh, I am sure your lineage is of the noblest!"

Hermes cocks his pretty head and murmurs, "We are indeed a well-established family, on both sides of the bed."

Priam dries his old eyes and takes a breath, reassured. Hermes can't resist one more surprise for the old man, so he says innocently, "It must be hard for you now that your bravest son Hektor is dead."

Priam jumps as high as his old legs can manage. Idaeus, still hiding behind him, gasps aloud. Priam stammers, "Young man, who are you, that you know so much about my family? Who are your parents?"

Hermes blushes modestly, and answers, "Oh, uncle, I have watched noble Hektor cutting down Greeks many a time! For I am the squire of great Akilles, you see. He would not let us enter the fight, for he was wroth with King Agamemnon, as you may have heard."

Priam stammers, "You ... you're Akilles' squire?"

Hermes bows politely, "At your service, aged sir!"

Priam sobs, "Then ... may I ask you, have the dogs eaten my son's body?"

Hermes suddenly pities the old man. Dropping his theatrical manner, he says in his true voice, "King Priam, I promise you that the dogs have not touched your son, nor has his corpse rotted. Instead, his wounds have all closed. Your son is beloved by the gods."

Priam grips the young man's wrist, saying, "Oh, my boy, you see how wise it is to offer sacrifice! The gods have paid me back for all the meat I burned in their honor!"

Hermes nods, "Yes, sir. The gods are helping you even now."

Priam calls to his old slave, "That cup! Bring it!"

The servant rummages and trots up with the fine Thracian goblet. Priam pushes it at Hermes, begging him, "Young man, please take this!"

Hermes says haughtily, "Sir! You are taking advantage of my youth and callowness to bribe me!"

Then he says cheerily, "Still, I'll take it—just to make you feel better, of course. And in return, I'll get you to Akilles' compound as easily as if you were a puff of wind."

He jumps into the chariot, lifting Priam in beside him with one hand. Idaeus clambers up onto the wagon and they trot toward the Greek camp.

There are sentries posted at the gate, but Hermes waves at them, whispering, "Sleep," and they start snoring with their eyes open. There's a heavy wooden bar across the gates, but Hermes waves his hand again and the huge log draws back on its own. The chariot and wagon pass through, unseen and unheard.

They move undetected through the maze of tents and huts, coming at last to the log hall Akilles' men built for him, roofed with tussock-grass, surrounded by a wooden wall. The gate is closed with a tree-trunk bar that three men can barely lift (though Akilles can lift it on his own). Hermes waves the bar open; with many a crunch it pulls back, and the little party rides in. He unloads the wagon with a single gesture, then turns to Priam, who's staring at him in amazement.

Hermes assumes something of his true form—not too much; he doesn't want to scare the old man any more than necessary—and says, "King Priam, I am Hermes, god of journey and chance, tasked by Zeus to escort you here. I wish you well in your interview with Akilles. Clasp his knees, remind him of his father and mother; he's a moody one, and younger than he realizes. And so, sir, I bid you goodbye."

Hermes disappears. Priam blinks, absorbing all that's happened, then turns and walks into Akilles' hall.

Akilles' soldiers are sitting near the door, as far away as they can get from their lord. He's down at the head of the hall, where two men are serving him dinner.

Priam goes up to him, kneels and grabs the Greek's huge knees. Akilles stares at him, astonished. Priam begs, "Akilles, think of your father! Imagine how happy he would be to know you're alive! Maybe the next town is making war on him, or his people are mutinous—, when he hears his dear son Akilles is alive, he's happy in spite of everything! As I was happy in my sons! Fifty sons I used to have! Most of them are dead, many by your spear—but it was Hektor I loved best! You killed him—"

Priam breaks down for a moment, catches his breath and goes on,

"And I've come to buy his corpse from you."

Akilles can only stare at the old man kneeling at his feet. It's been so long since he felt anything but bitterness.

Priam takes his silence for refusal. He falls to the floor crying and calls, "You should fear the gods, Akilles! If you won't pity me, then fear them! They see what I'm doing now!"

Before he can pull his hand away, Priam takes Akilles' hand and pulls it to his old, dry lips, kissing it. "There! I, a king, have kissed the hand of the man who killed my son!"

Akilles is stunned. He can't move or speak for a moment. Then he lifts Priam up and embraces him. They're both weeping now, Akilles' huge groans overwhelming the old man's dry sobs.

He picks Priam up and sits him down, saying, "Old man, it's you who are the bravest of the Trojans. You came here alone? How did you get through the gates? I can't believe it!"

He sits silent, wiping his tears away, patting old Priam on the shoulder, then says, "The gods don't care about either of us, you know. It's a game for them. But for mortal men ... did you really have fifty sons?"

Priam nods.

Akilles shakes his head, "Fifty! My father, Peleus ... you see, he was unlucky. No one saw it but me, me and my mother. Everyone else said, 'That Peleus! What a lucky man! Rich, brave, handsome, and the gods gave him an immortal for a wife!'"

"But Peleus had only one son, not fifty. And I won't live very long. I'll never be able to take care of my father in his old age. He'll be alone, with no one to protect him. My mother ..."

He grimaces: "She's a goddess, you know. These days, she doesn't even like to look at him. He's old and ugly; it disgusts her. She's exactly as she was when they married and she can't see why he's decaying."

He looks at Priam in awe: "But you ... fifty sons! And one of them Hektor! He was a good fighter, I tell you! They say he was a good man too—a good father, a good son."

Priam nods, sniffling.

Akilles takes one huge paw and pats the old man's back, nearly knocking Priam's teeth out of his head: "Mourn as hard as you have to, sir, but don't do it forever. You can't bring back the dead. It's bad luck even trying. I see that now."

Priam tries to stand up, moaning, "King Akilles, please don't make me sit while my son is lying in the dirt. Please, just take the ransom I brought with me, let me see my boy, and then I'll go home."

Akilles stands, looming over the old man, and growls, "Don't provoke me, sir. I'm trying to behave properly."

Priam gapes in terror.

Akilles pushes the old man back into his seat, growling, "I mean to give you Hektor's body. The gods have already ordered me to. I'm not a fool, sir; I know you must have had the gods' help to ride in here unmolested. Just don't make me angry, or you'll ruin everything. We are going to take meat and wine together, as is proper. You are going to sit and eat with me. You are my guest."

Priam nods, terrified.

"And you will spend the night in my home, as is proper."

Priam nods again.

Satisfied, Akilles jumps to the door, roaring to his servants, "Unload the wagon! Unyoke the horses and feed them!"

He stomps out into the courtyard, yelling, "Wash that body, oil it! The finest oil in the house!"

There's the sound of a blow, and Akilles roaring, "Don't bring it inside, fool! I don't want the old man seeing the body till it's cleaned up!" A slave's voice whimpers and Akilles roars through the courtyard, seeing to everything, right down to the clothes to be put on Hektor's corpse.

Just as he's about to go back in, he stops suddenly and groans, "Patroklas, don't be angry! You ghosts love to gossip, I know; they're probably telling you I gave Hektor's body back, even though he killed you. It's true, but his poor old father came to see me, all alone—the bravery of that old man! And I felt sorry for him. Besides, there's a ransom, a good one. I'd share it with you if I could!"

Then he ducks under the doorway to sit with Priam.

He notices that the slaves have arranged their seats improperly. So he picks up Priam, chair and all, putting him at the right hand, the place of honor. Then he sits down and says solemnly, "King Priam, you are my guest. Your son has been laid on his bier, and you can take him away in the morning."

Priam stutters, "May I go now? Please, I'd like to start as soon—"

Akilles pushes him into his chair: "We will dine. Weep for your son on the drive back to Troy. Now we dine."

He takes down a heavy one-bladed sword and goes out, muttering, "One moment; our meat! I'd forgotten." Priam hears a heavy thud, then Akilles shouting, "Skin it, fools, roast it, and quick! We're waiting in there!"

Then he's back, sheep-blood on his forearms. He clears his throat and says stiffly, "Yes, the storytellers say that Niobe herself had to eat at last, even after losing all twelve of her children."

He relaxes a little: "She offended Leto's children, Apollo and Artemis. You know that bunch? Bad enemies to make! Not as bad as Hera, but bad enough. So they slaughtered her children. They say Niobe cried for nine days, but then she had to eat something!"

Priam can only stare. There's a long silence before the stewards bring in the steaming lamb, with rounds of bread. Akilles snarls, "About time! Leave it here, we'll deal with it!" He passes Priam a plate of bread, then begins to eat, tearing huge chunks of meat off the steaming carcass.

Priam gums his bread, mimes a few bites of meat, and finally stands up, saying stiffly, "A fine meal, sir, but now I would enjoy the boon of sleep. I've been lying in dung, you see, for days, mourning my son; now that we are agreed on the return of his body, I think I might be able to sleep."

Akilles, relieved to have this awkward dinner behind him, says, "Of course!" He claps his hands and the slave women bring thick red carpets for Priam to lie on. The old man starts to settle on the floor, but Akilles slaps his forehead and says, "No, what am I thinking? We can't bed you down here; Agamemnon's gold-sniffing nose would start twitching—he's like a hound, that man! He'd nose you out, and you'd be a hostage!"

He leads Priam to a small gatehouse. As the slaves arrange the rugs, he asks, "Now, how long do you want for a truce to bury Hektor properly?"

Priam hems and haws: "Well, you know ... firewood is hard to find, sir, and people are afraid to leave town to get it. For a good pyre, a proper pyre ... nine days, I'd say. Nine to build the pyre, the tenth for his funeral, the eleventh to build a mound over the bones. And on the twelfth day, you can attack."

"You have my word. No fighting for eleven days." And lifting Priam's dry, bony wrist with his left hand, he puts his huge right hand over it, like a tree trunk fallen on a pile of twigs.

Priam and his servant lie down, exhausted. They're soon snoring, while Akilles goes to lie with Briseis—the first time he's touched a woman since Patroklas died.

The two worlds are asleep, are sleeping now. All but Hermes. As old Priam snores, Hermes floats in mid-air above him, then says, "Oh King Priam!"

The old man wakes up, moaning in terror. Hermes, stifling a guffaw, puts one hand over Priam's mouth, whispering, "My apologies, sir, but I think it might be best if we left early. If Agamemnon ever learns you're here ... well, you know those Atreus-sons, gougers to a man! Those rogues will take every copper you've got!"

Priam nods with the god's cold, huge hand over his mouth. He and his old servant dress silently while Hermes yokes the chariot and wagon. Silent, invisible, they trot out of the camp.

By dawn, they reach the ford over the river Yellow. There Hermes takes his leave, vanishing with a bow before Priam can make a long speech of gratitude.

In the light of dawn, Priam can see Hektor's face. He weeps all the way back to Troy, turning back to look at his son's body and weeping harder. His daughter Kassandra is on the walls, looking around for some bad news to disseminate. She sees the chariot and wagon far off across the plain and runs through the town, calling, "Come out, Trojans! Come out and mourn Hektor, who will never defend the city again!"

Everyone in Troy, old and young, rich and poor, swarms the wagon, screaming their grief as Hektor's body moves through the alleys to Priam's palace, looking almost alive in the pink dawn light.

Priam has no patience for this mummery. He knows his people. They're making a show of grief, but not one had the courage to come with him to get the body back. He lashes out with his whip, shouting, "Weep when I've brought him home! Get out of the way!"

They put Hektor's body on a table and arrange musicians around it. Women are brought in to wail.

Andromakhe takes Hektor's head in both hands and sings, "Husband, you left me! You left me a widow, to live on while the Greeks smash our gates. I'll live to see our little son sold to a farmer far away, to be beaten and starved! If he lives at all, if some Greek who lost a brother to your spear doesn't buy the boy for the pleasure of tossing him off the walls, to watch his little body break on the sand!"

The line of women rocks side to side, hair thrashing like a thousand whips.

She sings, "And I'll see it all from the auction block, sold to a Greek who'll look at my teeth before he offers a price for me!"

The women are chittering now, like the grief of swallows at dawn.

She finishes, "You left without embracing me, you died out on the plain with no sweet words to give me to sweeten these tears!"

Two women pull her from the body. It's his mother's turn. Hekuba grips her son's temples and sings in a deeper, slower voice, "Hektor, Hektor, dearest son, dearer than all the rest! Akilles would sell the rest into slavery when he caught them on the plain, but you he killed outright, because you were too brave to leave alive! Alive, the gods loved you; dead, they have preserved you;

you lie as handsome as the day you left. Akilles tried to defile you, but you are as fresh as morning dew under my hands!"

They pull her away, Helen takes his temples, singing, "Beloved brother-in-law, when I came here everyone cursed me in the streets, but you took my side, defending me! When the bodies came home women spat at me, saying I was the cause of their sons' and husbands' deaths; but you never reproached me or gave me those looks I see everywhere I go. You alone protected me, so these tears are for you and my wretched self too."

Priam steps in and calls, "Enough!" He waves the women away and gives orders to his servants, "Go find wood for the pyre. You'll need to go a long way into the hills. I have Akilles' word they'll leave us alone."

For nine days the ox teams bring in heavy tree trunks, scoring deep ruts in the sandy soil. At dawn on the tenth day they light the pyre and Priam keeps his sons pacing around it all day, making sure every branch and bone is well burned. Next morning they come back with huge jars of wine and douse the embers. A smell of burnt wine, wood, and flesh spreads in a fog around the city. Then Hektor's brothers gather up his clean white bones, wrap them in purple from Sidon, and put them in an urn. They put the urn in a tomb lined with huge flat stones and raise a mound over it.

Then they go back inside the walls and hold one last feast in the doomed city.

That was how they buried Hektor, the best of men.